Fear of Animals

Aflame Books
2 The Green
Laverstock
Wiltshire
SP1 1QS
United Kingdom
email: info@aflamebooks.com

ISBN: 9781906300005
First published in 2008 by Aflame Books

First published in Spanish as *El miedo a los animales*
by Joaquín Mortiz, Mexico, in 1995

© Enrique Serna 1995

This edition is published by arrangement with
Literarische Agentur Ray-Güde Mertin Inh. Nicole Witt e. K.,
Frankfurt am Main, Germany

Cover design by Zuluspice www.zuluspice.com

Printed in Poland
www.polskabook.pl

Enrique Serna

Translated by
Georgina Jiménez Reynoso

To Lucinda, my masterpiece of callipaedia

Fear of Animals

Sleeping it off in the office was a habit that Evaristo had mastered to perfection. He could snore his lungs out, feet on the desk, newspaper covering his face to defend himself from the sunlight and mosquitoes, without detaching himself from reality. A self-defence mechanism warned him when someone walked by his cubicle in such a way that he was never completely unconscious, even though he may have been half-dreaming. That morning's dream was pleasurable to the point of drunkenness. In an auditorium, chock-a-block, the cultural elite had gathered to pay him well-deserved homage. Unsure of his real importance, despite his fame and awards, he could not help blushing when listening to the bucketful of praises heaped on him by the most select members of the intellectual universe: "master of combative prose", "incontestable courage that stands out in every genre", "extraordinary writer of everyday fables". When the accolades in his honour had ended, as he was thanking them with a light-hearted comment to ease the emotional weight of the event, reporters from the radio and television and other members of the press cornered him at the platform, fighting among themselves for an interview: Maestro, how did you realise you were born to write? Which writers have mainly influenced your style? Do you think a writer must adopt a political stance? For all the questions he had a clever and fast answer that came with a smile reflecting shyness, goodness and a radical detachment from the spotlight: "I believe political commitment must emerge spontaneously from a writer in response to the horrors and miseries of everyday life. I had my start, like you all, in journalism and from there jumped into literature, which for me is not a pure art form but a means of civil resistance."

A schoolgirl from a poor background, with a satchel and a raw cotton shirt, managed to make her way through the swarm of reporters to ask for his autograph. While giving this to her,

Enrique Serna

Evaristo felt like he was in heaven: there was nothing more encouraging for a writer than the appreciation of a studious, hardworking and respectable youth. Behind the girl came a mob of university students, every one of them holding a copy of his book, pushing away the journalists and cornering him against the top table. Despite the discomfort and lack of oxygen, he enjoyed the situation intensely. It was like having an enormous family, as if he had given birth to a child in every reader. Ignoring the people from the cultural press and the posh ladies who had come all the way from San Francisco to interview him about the abuse of human rights in Mexico, Evaristo devoted all his attention to the youths and did not skimp in his dedications: *For Javier and Marilu, comrades, allies, accomplices, with love and affection from a humble fighter of the word.* The warmth he felt from the youths was worth more than a thousand prizes. They love me because I'm honest, he thought, because against all odds I denounce crimes of power. But suddenly the spell was broken: an admirer tugged him violently by the arm, another pricked his arse, and when Evaristo turned to remonstrate with them – how dare they treat a national treasure in such a way – the auditorium was now completely empty, his glory had evaporated and he understood that at the other side of this dream his guardian angel was calling him to order. It was time to return to the indignity, frustration and hangover: someone approaching his office was just about to open the door.

"That's the life, you bloody lazy intellectual! Look at the huge lumps of sleep stuck in your eyes. I've been working my balls off in the streets since early in the morning and here you are, asleep."

Commander Maytorena suddenly jumped over the desk. He was about 60 but amazingly agile for his age. Evaristo, on the swivel chair, retreated, crashing against the blinds. The commander's vigour seemed to emanate from the vileness drawn across his pock-marked, greenish face, where little brown eyes shone from between swollen cheeks. His nose was curved downwards and he had a mean mouth, almost a slit without lips, that he only opened slightly to talk. Ten years ago the commander exchanged his smart officewear for tracksuits to affect a youthful air, and that very morning he was wearing a bright yellow outfit and a baseball cap.

"I thought you were in Pachuca," Evaristo said in his defence.

Fear of Animals

"Someone told me you were going there to check on the case of the stolen cars."

"I've been and come back," said Maytorena, spitting black phlegm in the rubbish bin next to Evaristo's desk. "One advantage of not being a lazy git is that the day is well spent. Chamula and I left at dawn and, because the motorway was empty, it only took us half an hour from here to Pachuca. The guard at the agency didn't want to open up because we didn't have a search warrant. Poor arsehole, right now he'll be in hospital with two broken ribs. I broke the lock with a shot and we confiscated all the cars he had in the garage: twelve Cutlasses and a latest-model Lincoln. Chamula is going to sell the Cutlasses at the scrapyard but I kept the Lincoln to give to Laurita, my daughter, who's graduating next year. Check out all the work we've done while you were here napping."

"Sorry, commander, it's because I spent the night writing up the final version of that report you asked for."

"You won't make a fucking fool out of me." Maytorena grabbed him by the tie and gave him a yank. "I can smell your drunken breath. You almost certainly got shitfaced at Sherry's." Evaristo did not answer. "Answer me, imbecile! You got really pissed, didn't you?"

"I did go to Sherry's sir, but I left at one in the morning."

"One in the morning, my balls. You only need to drink one and you can't stop. You must have the hangover from hell, it's obvious from your face. Here, to resuscitate you." The commander threw a little bag of cocaine at him. "I need you to be fit because I'm assigning you a very important job."

With a trembling hand, Evaristo spread the cocaine on his desk in two parallel lines which he inhaled with fervour. Colour returned to his face, blood irrigated his lethargic brain again and, momentarily, he saw Maytorena as his benefactor.

"Tell me, chief…"

The commander took a yellowed newspaper cutting out of his briefcase.

"Read what it says here, but very carefully."

On a cursory glance, it was about something innocent: an article about the arts published in the cultural section of the daily *El Matutino*. Its author eulogised the works of a young Oaxacan painter who had exhibited his paintings at a Zona Rosa gallery: *Chacón captures in strong lines, sometimes telluric, the hidden genius of a race that remains loyal to its ancestral mysteries, a precise code of colours and shapes where the innovative will maintains an equilibrium with tradition*...The article kept the same tone until the fourth paragraph where, in a sudden, harsh manner, the natural sequence of the phrases was cut ...*and even when the serene cleanliness of the series "White over Blue" constitutes a success, we prefer the paintings of expressionist style such as* Go Fuck your mother Jiménez del Solar, *where we can notice a greater domain over chromatic textures,* Death to Jiménez, Traitor to Mexico, *and a well assimilated influence of the Flemish school...*

"Crikey, that arsehole is telling Mister President to go fuck his mother."

"He tells him to go fuck his mother and even calls him a queer. Read on." Maytorena pointed to the line that had the insult, next to the author's byline, someone called Roberto Lima.

"And who is this nutter?" asked Evaristo.

"That's what you're going to find out. You have a day to get his address, but beforehand I want to know if he writes under his real name or if he uses a pseudonym. I'm asking you this because you're supposed to be familiar with that environment. You were a reporter, weren't you?"

The comment hurt Evaristo more than the yanking of the tie: Maytorena had mentioned his past, the only clean thing he had.

"And how did you find out about this article? No one reads that newspaper."

"I didn't want to read it either. We were driving by Tula's refinery, suddenly I needed a crap and I told Chamula to stop at the next petrol station. The toilet was filthy, there was even shit smeared on the walls. But I said, 'Never mind, you're not going to find golden toilets in a place like this', and I did it squatting. I'm not as intellectual as you, but I do like reading while I crap, and in that toilet there were no mags or anything, just squares of newspaper hanging from a wire. I picked one to keep myself amused and, because I didn't understand what it said, I almost wiped my arse with it. Luckily I landed on the insults bit, and realised that this piece of paper was a goldmine."

Maytorena's triumphal smile indicated that he intended to exploit his finding, so Evaristo wanted to know how.

"Well, chief, what do you gain by keeping this cutting, if it's not a secret?"

Fear of Animals

"You're still hung over, you bloody moron. This piece of paper is no use to me, but the guy above me is going to jump with joy when he sees it." Maytorena pointed to the ceiling, alluding to Attorney Tapia, whose office was on the top floor of the building. "Where do you think they screen all the newspapers to check that there are no attacks against the President?"

"In the interior ministry?"

"Exactly. It looks as if you're waking up. Just another little sniff and you'll be as good as new...The Minister of the Interior is the attorney's enemy and he hasn't stopped playing politics against him since the presidential term started. Who do you think ordered the campaign against him when Lieutenant Garduño snuffed out that little teacher from the academy? Everything was set up at the interior ministry to knock Tapia down and set up a mate of the minister instead, because that bastard is going for *the big one* and wants to put his own people in important positions. So now do you understand?"

Evaristo nodded, even though he did not understand. "The minister and his people want to discredit the attorney but, with this, everything is going to backfire on them, because now the attorney can approach the President and tell him: 'You see, boss, how the press is controlled by those arseholes at the Ministry of the Interior? Look what is being said about you. And, because Jiménez del Solar is so vain, he'll get the shits, for sure. The interior minister is going to pay for this, and with a bit of luck he'll even be sent to China as an ambassador. Thanks to me, Tapia's going to get an enemy off his back and, even though I'm not one of his cronies, at the very least he'll promote me to junior minister. You'll see the bread raining down when I'm in that position – with the crumbs alone you'll be a rotten millionaire. All thanks to whom? To your Daddy, who's even good at crapping."

Maytorena's cackle boomed around the thin walls of the office. His euphoria degenerated into a convulsive, choking cough that Evaristo calmed by slapping him on the back. When Maytorena regained his breath, he asked Evaristo what he thought about the plot. "Isn't it fucking genius?" Evaristo nodded with a faked enthusiasm. As satisfied as a lion tamer who had managed to get the usual desired response from his toothless beast, the commander warned Evaristo as he said goodbye not to have even one little sip of alcohol before finding Roberto Lima.

"Of course not, commander, I promise I'll stay sober."

When Maytorena was out of sight, Evaristo took a bottle of Old Parr from his desk and drank a fixer that allowed him to order his thoughts. Maytorena's plot was so twisted that, without a doubt, it would be successful. On the subject of bureaucratic intrigues, the commander never took a single step barefoot. And, even when Tapia avoided all contact with the shady underground of the judiciary, like the great majority of the attorneys he had seen parading before him in that position, he would have to mingle with the mob this time and shake hands with Maytorena, even though he would later have to disinfect them with 96 per cent alcohol. The link between the two men would be the body of a journalist, because Maytorena, wanting to show off, would not be satisfied just with a simple beating.

Evaristo was used to covering up his crimes, but until then Maytorena had merely limited himself to executing grasses, traffickers, enforcers or federal police agents of his own kind who were fighting over the loot. This was different. It was about an honest man who may have lost his mind in a moment of rage. Independent journalists and combative writers had a privileged place in Evaristo's affections: he admired them to the point of blindness but, at the same time, any comparison with them hurt him, because they demonstrated that his own destiny could have been different if he had not betrayed the ideals of his youth when, on the police beat in an evening newspaper, he had struggled to reveal in his reports the social background of delinquency.

At 45, weakened by partying, degraded on a daily basis by his dealings with the institutional underworld, Evaristo needed to be reminded that at some point he had been an honest journalist. He needed this so as not to visualise himself detached from his past and confirm, day by day and with renewed astonishment, his gradual collapse into the mire. At least that way he avoided getting used to corruption, which for Maytorena and his people was a habit, a way of life. To a certain extent he had managed to keep his distance from his boss, but that did not exempt him from guilt. As Maytorena's secretary, he only did office jobs and never participated in detentions or shootings. But if he profited from a little slice of Maytorena's business, obviously he received the corresponding splash of blood when there were corpses in the middle. This time he would not only have passing remorse: his hands had now started to sweat as he was envisaging the moral suicide that Lima's assassination would mean to him.

Fear of Animals

Arms crossed, eyes half-closed and head back, he wished for enlightenment to show him the way. If he disobeyed Maytorena he could lose his job, maybe his life. Obeying him meant sending a courageous journalist, for whom he was feeling some affection, to the slaughter. The more he ruminated about the issue, the more difficult it seemed. It was impossible to look good both to God and the Devil. He raised his head and saw his own reflection in the door pane: a shadow, a human smudge. From yesterday to today, new wrinkles had grown on his face. With a brush of his hand he combed back his stiff, brown hair, which at the temples had begun to whiten. The violet stains on his cheeks, a sign of poor circulation, gave him the aspect of a budding wino. He had been advised by some doctors: either you drop the drink or soon you will get cirrhosis. But, while living in total disagreement with himself, he could not face life without a whisky at hand.

He stood up to open the blinds of his cubicle, which was as hot as a sauna. Outside, in Reforma, a demonstration by teachers had stopped the traffic. Their "Death to Jiménez del Solar" made his own blood boil: "Dwarf, thief, you'll face the firing squad". Bravo, that was the way to speak. He would have liked to join them, but when he saw them throwing eggs at the windows of the Attorney General's office, he understood that he was seen as an enemy, so he went back to his chair more depressed than before. He could not blame the fatality of a destiny that no one but he had chosen. He alone was responsible more for eternally postponing his decisions when circumstances put him face-to-face with a difficult choice than for the decisions he eventually reached. He could well have renounced the good life and sought work in a newspaper before being sunk up to the neck in Maytorena's crap. But who would have thanked him for such sacrifice? The news editors, who always dealt with him using the tips of their shoes? In a way he had joined the federal police in order to flee their despotic ways. Enemies of talent and critical reflection, they demanded that he describe the events, only the events, in frozen and concise language, when he felt the need to elucidate the motives of each crime, paint a portrait of the possible author, be the spokesman for the victim's family and frame all this information in the social context in which the crime had been committed. As a journalist he had only wished that the readers of the crime pages, instead of being horrified by the bloody facts, would be horrified by the injustice. The bourgeoisie of Lomas and Pedregal, who humiliated the oppressed mob with their luxurious ostentation and their mansions, should know that in the miserable shanty towns there was warfare over a few chickens, a purse, or a bloody quartz watch. But the news editors wanted brief information and, when they received his extensive articles, they boiled with anger: "I asked you for something short and you delivered me a mini-novel! This is journalism, not literature. Just put everything on one page, without wanky adjectives. You won't be winning any Nobels here, arsehole."

In his reporting years he could never write an article the way he wanted. Without the motivation of leaving his personal stamp on his work, it was unbearable to spend the night in police stations, hospitals and morgues waiting for news that he should dryly transcribe, without comments or personal opinions, like a vile stenographer at the Public Prosecutor's Office. Looking for a boss who would allow him to express himself more freely, he stumbled from newspaper to newspaper – *Novedades, La Prensa, Últimas Noticias, El Sol de México* – gathering frustration that he now carried in his heart like a dead weight. At the beginning of the Seventies he got his longtime girlfriend Gladys pregnant and, under duress, had to marry her. She was a primary school teacher and with both their wages they could only afford to rent an egg-sized flat in Ramos Millán, two blocks away from Calzada de Tlalpan, where his one and only daughter, Chabela, was born. Until then, because of his own temperament and conviction, he had despised bourgeois consumerism and the accumulation of wealth. When he had first held the baby in his arms, he started to see life pragmatically and to worry about money.

But he could not blame Chabela for the turn his life had taken. Really. And his perspective at that moment allowed him to see clearly and stopped him deluding himself with mirages. He had allowed himself to be pushed into corruption by choice, without anyone pressing him. He could have sorted his economic problems out by setting up a *tamale* stall in Ciudad Universitaria, as Gladys had advised him. In fact, he was excited by the project, but when he started to request permission from trading standards, the newspaper that changed his life fell into his hands: The Federal Attorney General (PGR) invites all young males with a vocation to serve to join the Federal Judicial Police. Requirements: aged between 22-35 years old, minimum height 1.70m, high-school studies and a certificate of no criminal record. DO NOT LEAVE IT

Fear of Animals

UNTIL TOMORROW: THE COUNTRY NEEDS YOU TODAY. It was a golden opportunity to get to know the heart of the judicial police, the Feds, and write a book from this world that, at the same time, could bring him fame and fortune: the adventures of an intrepid reporter who takes the training course like any other aspirant and, when he has obtained the agent's ID shield, filters into the monster's entrails inch by inch. He would risk his skin for two or three years in raids and shootings, taking a secret diary in which he would write his impressions, and when he had gathered evidence against the high government officials who pulled the strings of corruption, he would resign from the Feds to write the book – a reportage in the style of Truman Capote that would turn the Mexican political system upside down. Gladys tried to dissuade him with sensible warnings – it was not certain the book would end up as a bestseller and those individuals he denounced could kill him – but he ignored the advice because his own vocation was at stake. Writing that book was, in a way, a paternal duty, he explained, as he wanted to gain Chabela's future admiration, so when she grew old she would still look up at him as a giant.

"Are you still there sitting on your arse?" Maytorena's shout brought him back to the present. "Start working on what I asked you to do or I'll kick you out of there."

"I was just going, commander."

Evaristo stood up and left the cubicle, evading Maytorena's spiteful gaze. He walked between two rows of desks occupied by bureaucrats reading a sports tabloid, *Esto* or *Ovaciones,* until he got to the other end of the building, where there was a filing cabinet from which he took the Yellow Pages. He looked for the telephone number of *El Matutino*, scribbled it in a notebook and went back to his cubicle with it, under pressure from Maytorena, who had not taken his eyes off him. He called the newspaper's switchboard and the lady who answered put him through to the cultural section, where nobody was picking up.

"Looks as if nobody is working today at *El Matutino*," Evaristo told his boss.

"I don't care how you do it, you have to get me that bastard's address. I've needed it since yesterday."

"I'll have to go to the newspaper." Evaristo stood up and took his jacket. "I'll call you on your mobile tonight to give you all the information."

When he entered the lift he dropped his shoulders and sighed.

Maytorena's virtue was to make him feel tense. They met every day, but there was always the same vibe of hostility. And Evaristo put up with it all like a maize-lugging mule with a scar on its back from being thrashed. The street was hotter than the building. Rolling up his sleeves he walked through Violeta until he reached the exclusive parking for PGR employees where he had parked his car, the latest-model green Spirit. He had not yet made a decision about Lima and, when he turned the engine on, he felt a weight upon his chest. His mistake had been to take the damn training course to get into the Feds. Who had told him to get between the horse's legs?

He had passed, with honours, the final exam, where his greatest problem had been the shooting tests in which he had gained the lowest mark, leaving journalism from one day to the next without confiding in any of his colleagues about his intentions so that they would not steal his idea. He worked for a couple of months under his shiny new title of auxiliary agent in ballistics and fingerprinting, where he had very few opportunities to nose about: the laboratory technicians were lazy and negligent, but were miles away from where the big money moved. Nonetheless, the post allowed him to rub shoulders with some commanders and team leaders who visited the department from time to time to collect the results of specialist reports. He used a primitive diplomacy with them that consisted of breaking the ice from the first hello, as if he had known them from childhood. Turned into a professional charmer, he discussed football or got heavily involved in double-edged jokes with his new-found friends, whom he treated as mates or bros and with an effusive and brutal camaraderie – a punch on the shoulder, fraternal wrestling locks, slaps on the head, a kick in the arse. He looked for a sign that could reveal who was protecting them, how favours were done to gain a pay rise and where they were getting the big money that was revealed by their solid gold Rolex watches or Grand Marquis cars with leopard skin seats and their pharaonic train of parties. To reach the point at which they confessed was not easy at all. Evasive and misleading when talking about themselves, these Judases abruptly changed the subject when Evaristo tried to get information, despite his tact when introducing the muddy subject after long-winded chats and efforts to play down the issue's importance.

He began to believe that his long public relations campaign was a failure when he met Chamula, who was not yet into the dance of the banknotes but knew where to find them. Disproving the legend of the ancestral muteness of the indigenous people, Chamula loosened his tongue after three drinks and, even on the great majority of occasions that, in long stuttering monologues, he lamented God not making him white and bearded, he also used to boast of his prowess as a Fed, especially when a dancer was sitting on his lap. From Chamula, Evaristo learned of Maytorena's importance. Chamula had a veneration for Maytorena that bordered on idolatry because, thanks to him, he had been freed from a brick factory in Santa Fe where he had charred his hands for a miserable wage. As if the commander were a king or Pope, he avoided calling him by name when paying tribute to him: "The *Señor* is a bastard, he takes crap from nobody. I have seen him cut some swine's throat just because he raised his voice in the cantina. But one thing is certain, the *Señor* is very straight, very generous with his money. He takes care of me because I watched his back in a shoot out. He even gave my wife a fridge on Mother's Day. This is why I appreciate the *Señor*, because he has been very kind to me."

Chamula's tales about "the *Señor*", anxiously trying to share even a pale beam of "the *Señor's*" glory, could well have launched the criminal current of magic realism. At the start of the Seventies, accompanied by three of his men – all in balaclavas – Maytorena had robbed a bank in Constituyentes avenue. Half an hour later, with the booty hidden in the back of his car, he had returned to the scene of the crime to start the investigation about that same robbery, which was later attributed to the Liga 23 de Septiembre terrorist organisation. As he was a protector of drug barons, he had had armed encounters with the Federal Security Agency, even with the army itself, but Maytorena always came out without a scratch because, according to Chamula, he carried a lucky charm in the shape of an iguana that made him immune to bullets.

Maytorena's corruption and excesses made Evaristo's daily secret even richer, although he needed to know the character in the flesh in order to describe him. After insisting for a long time, he finally got Chamula to introduce him. The encounter happened in La Mundial, a cantina in Colonia Doctores whose regulars were Feds and drug traffickers. The commander was playing dominoes with some other gunmen and Evaristo did not have the nerve to say hello until after he had finished the game. "So you want to join my team?" Maytorena examined him from head to toe. "I'm going to give you the chance just because you have been recommended by this dickhead, who is like a brother to me. Sit down and ask for something to drink. Tonight we'll see if you really are game."

As Evaristo did not want to appear different he asked for the same as everyone else was drinking – Napoleon cognac with cola. The rest of the afternoon he silently observed the domino games and noticed that everybody was purposefully letting Maytorena win. They came out of the cantina at night, now very drunk but still alert. Maytorena ordered two of his men to pick up his lover, someone called Anaís, and take her to the Fiesta Palace Hotel's piano bar while he was doing a little "job" to test "the new entrant".

"I'll see you guys at ten. Tell the manager of the bar that I sent you."

Evaristo got into a white VW van with tinted windows with Maytorena and Chamula, not knowing where he was going. When the van started, Maytorena passed him a bottle of Napoleon. "Guzzle it, so you don't sober up." They took Insurgentes heading north, crossed Reforma ignoring the red traffic light, and Chamula turned left at Villalongín. Sitting in the passenger's seat, Maytorena sweetly whistled 'Dove or Hawk': "That's Anaís's favourite tune," he told Chamula. "We fell in love while dancing in a Zona Rosa whorehouse that I had closed up that night just for the two of us. She's 18 and real tasty." Evaristo was drinking compulsively, writing in his mind the super chapter he'd get out of his creepy adventure. When they arrived at a dark and deserted street in Colonia Anzures, Chamula parked opposite a liquor store that was about to close and the commander handed Evaristo a Magnum .357 that weighed half a ton.

"Be on your toes. We're robbing that shop's owner. Today is the day he takes the dosh to the bank. You're coming with me and, when you see me gripping the old fellow, you thwack him like a rabbit with the Magnum."

They waited five minutes until the owner had finished closing the metal door. Undecided about whether to see it through or flee, Evaristo shook while he gripped the Magnum, but when he saw the old fellow leaving with a briefcase and the commander gave the agreed cue he carried out the instructions Maytorena had given him without flinching, as if in a hypnotic trance. He regained his composure when they were running away with the briefcase and was shocked to see that the end of the Magnum was bloodstained. For a long time he could not rid himself of the image of the old man lying on the floor in the middle of the road, the back of his neck bleeding and his eyes blank. When they arrived at the Fiesta Palace, Maytorena gave him a wad of banknotes and a tap on the shoulder.

"You're in, son. What a great whack."

Because he was a sheep, Evaristo agreed to drink "a last one" at the hotel piano bar where Anaís was sitting in a dark and distant corner waiting for Maytorena. She was not a little whore, but a young copper-skinned, platinum blonde transvestite wearing a very provocative blue lamé dress. He looked as if he was on drugs because of the stillness of his pupils. Maytorena introduced the boy as "his fiancée" and Evaristo preferred not to look when they kissed on the lips. Neither Chamula nor the two other agents who had brought Anaís seemed to notice what was going on, or maybe they were just accustomed to Maytorena's whims. To them, Anaís was "the Mistress" and they made every effort to treat her as such, lighting her cigarettes and refilling her champagne glass with feigned politeness.

Afraid that someone might decide to invite him to dance too, Evaristo made his getaway with the excuse that his missus was waiting for him with dinner, evading with a little smile Maytorena's mockery, which branded him "henpecked" and an arsehole.

He walked towards the monument to the Revolution and boarded the train for Taxqueña, his left hand in his pocket, clutching the bank notes. His clothes were impregnated with Anaís' perfume and he thought all the other passengers were looking at him remorselessly. When Evaristo came out of Chabacano station the drizzle and wind sobered him up. It was ten o'clock, but he had just lived several extra hours and to his conscience it was dawn. Because of the Christmas season the shops in Tlalpan were still open and, with an urge to cleanse the money, he went into a toy shop and bought a bunch of dolls for his beloved Chabela, who had just learned to walk and who greeted him walking a few little steps on her own when Evaristo arrived at the flat. When he held Chabela in his arms he felt absolved, disinfected, innocent. He locked the Magnum inside a desk drawer then entered the bedroom, where Gladys was watching a music programme, so he huddled with her in bed. He was beginning to relax when on the screen appeared José José singing 'Dove or Hawk'. He rushed to the toilet and vomited violently, kneeling by the bowl, like a sinner begging forgiveness before the Altar of Pardon.

I should have resigned then, thought Evaristo, trapped between the crossing of Hidalgo and Reforma, where the striking teachers had stopped, defying the riot police watching over the demonstration. Yes, at that moment, he could have left without consequences, because he was not yet in Maytorena's noose. But such a premature desertion would also have been cowardice. After all, he had joined the Feds to descend into hell and could not start crying now because Maytorena happened to be a queer. The next day, having recovered from the shock, he tried to narrate in his diary the robbery at the liquor store, but could not even string two words together. A censor within his own emotions prevented him from confessing that, deep down, he had felt euphoric, relieved, and wild when he had knocked down the elderly man. Evaristo now understood the animal feeling of wellbeing and the happy butchery by the Feds, but he was also terrified to discover his own predatory instinct. What right did he have to condemn a behaviour that he had imitated with such gusto, even if it were just once in his life? As a matter of mental hygiene, a week after the robbery, Evaristo went back to the shop in Colonia Anzures and, when he saw the old man behind the counter, with a bandaged head and serving some customers, he congratulated himself for not having crossed the line that made him different from Maytorena and his people. This test gave back Evaristo his tranquillity, but not his egalitarian spirit, the one he needed for writing. Voluntarily, he left the notebook within Chabela's reach, so she could fill it up with scribbles. And while the creative block lasted ever longer, with the prospect of turning into an incurable disease, life confronted Evaristo with a brick wall, as if by leaving that notebook lying around he himself was turning into the character of another novel, written by his worst enemy.

Warned about the seductive effects of violence, he intended to play his part without involving himself directly in bloodshed, but the commander could not stand any of his men fooling about when someone was having the shit beaten out of them. They had their first clash during a raid at the Cordiale, when Evaristo refused to kick some call girls lying on the floor who had previously run to the

Fear of Animals

toilets to dispose of the little envelopes containing cocaine which they used to put down their cleavages. In the holding cells, when they had finished the raid, Maytorena threatened to have Evaristo arrested if he disobeyed during the next operation, and from then onwards he excluded him from the group playing dominoes at the Mundial. Chamula told Evaristo he had fallen into disgrace: "You screwed up, bro. The commander can't stick people who don't participate." He thought his career as a Fed was over, but because Gladys insisted, as she scolded him for not bringing enough money home, he began to take the idea of selling *tamales* seriously again.

But the novelist now commanding him from above had prepared an activity for Evaristo more suited to his literary vocation. In the ballistics department, some employees who could hardly even read the Kalimán comic had asked his help in writing letters to their relatives in the provinces. They were so happy with his epistolary style that his fame as a good writer spread throughout the whole of the Attorney General's office. When Maytorena got to know that Evaristo's pen was good, he decided to give him a second chance: Evaristo was a coward and had no balls, but he could be very useful as a secretary. One of the bureaucratic chores that Maytorena detested most was having to write his weekly reports detailing his investigations. He delegated the chore to Evaristo and, even when he never bothered to hide how much he despised him, he rewarded Evaristo with the same monthly allowance at Sherry's bar, one of the dives with a clandestine coke trade to which Maytorena sold his protection.

Believing he had finally found a place from which to see hell without the risk of being burned, Evaristo rapidly learned the legalistic language of police reports and freed up Maytorena from a fiddly task. In his writing, the capacity to invent was as important as style, because he had to replace the commander's criminal acts with the fictitious itinerary of a model cop. If Maytorena and his gang had dedicated themselves to extorting drivers at Insurgentes Avenue, planting drugs in their cars, the report spoke of a successful anti-drug operation. The robbery of a security van at Gustavo Baz road could be presented as the decommissioning of fake bank notes, the death of a suspected illegal car trader under torture was camouflaged as a suicide by the excessive consumption of psychotropic drugs and, when Maytorena spent two weeks partying at Acapulco's red light district – until his very own wife went to get him back – Evaristo assigned him the delicate mission of searching the port for a Palestinian terrorist who was found in Interpol's registers. He had the room to let his imagination run free, because the reports were directed to those functionaries who were Maytorena's accomplices, and who would also accept every fact without a second glance or never even bother to read them.

It looked like the demonstration was there to stay for a long time. The riot police had formed a line to divert the traffic towards Balderas, but Evaristo had to cross Reforma and he could not proceed in the opposite direction. Why did he decide to use his car, if *El Matutino* was so close anyway? He left the car in a parking space at the corner of the Orreo restaurant, got his Magnum out of the glove compartment – the same gun Maytorena had given him on his debut as a Fed – and went on foot, his jacket buttoned to hide the gun. He was an idiot when it came to driving, the kind of arsehole who uses his car for a journey of five blocks in order not to lose his status by being a pedestrian. Maybe he should blame that ridiculous attachment to property as the origin of his own misfortune, which had degraded him to ignominy. He did not need to seek the obvious: he was a sell-out who had begun to prostitute himself from the very moment he had taken his first monthly share at Sherry's – an amount equivalent to the salary of any successful professional. Gladys, who had pressured him so often to give up the Feds, changed her tune when she received her first present, a golden choker valued at fifteen thousand pesos. Neither of them had really known prosperity and, when they began to enjoy it for the first time, they thought it was their natural state, a prerogative they could never part with. The new washing machine, the sound system, the television with a mega-screen and the fridge that made ice cubes were not only electrical appliances, they were also the attributes of their new personality, a triumphant personality that elevated and raised them to nobility in the eyes of others. Within a short time they had saved enough to pay the deposit on a house in Prado Churubusco – three bedrooms, two bathrooms, back yard, fitted kitchen with dining area – and Gladys, who despised their egg-sized flat in Ramos Millán, saw her dream come true when she finally stepped on to her own piece of land. In debt up to his eyeballs, but satisfied with what he had achieved, Evaristo even had the nerve to buy himself a Le Baron car on instalments and take a shopping trip to San Antonio, with

Fear of Animals

his credit card tottering on the edge of a precipice. Economic worries replaced moral conflicts but, if at any time he felt remorse at the shady origins of his income, he shielded himself behind his parental duty. Everything he earned came from a pigsty, yes, but with that money he paid Chabela's medical insurance, her swimming lessons and the monthly payments of her 'green' nursery school where she planted little trees and looked so gorgeous in her little gardener's apron.

He could not moan about his lack of spare time either. He used to write the activity reports in a jiffy and had many free hours to lock himself up reading undisturbed. In his first year as Maytorena's secretary he had read the complete works of Martín Luis Guzmán, Borges, José Emilio Pacheco and Mario Benedetti. Every morning he arrived at work with a book under his arm, an extravagance soon noted by his colleagues. Mockingly, the cleaners started to call him "the Intellectual" and, when Maytorena heard the nickname, he spread it across heaven, sea and earth, obsessed with making Evaristo pay for his saintly airs. Since that incident at the Cordiale, Maytorena had disliked him and used the nickname as a whip with which to humiliate him, to stamp on him every day that he shat on his cultured air and good conscience: "Stop it, you are going to go blind reading so much. Even worse, it's no use to you: the more you read, the more you become an arsehole. Let's see your book. Is it poetry? Hey, I believe you are becoming a minstrel. Have you seen this, Chamula? Your friend, the Intellectual, has a very delicate heart. Look at the wanky things he reads. Recite us something, won't ya? Recite something or I'll throw your book out of the window."

Evaristo endured the humiliation with a stupid smile, as if he took it as a joke, fearful of losing his monthly allowance in a proud rage. Later, when he did not have any pride left for rage and when he had begun to realise the risk he was taking by being Maytorena's accomplice, he no longer began to see his Sherry's cut as a gift. If any Attorney General ever had the intention of really cleaning up the Federal Judicial Police and all of his boss's scams were made public, he could well end up in jail, even though he was not paid a tenth of what a gunman such as Chamula earned. That inconsistency, added to the accumulated rancour at Maytorena's bad treatment, led Evaristo to consider, at various times, the possibility of writing his book, but the moment he sat in front of the typewriter he always desisted, knowing that if he denounced Maytorena he would be a dead man.

"We are not one, we are not a hundred: sell-out press, count us well!"

"This fist can be seen, this fist can be seen!"

"We totally reject corrupted unions!"

Evaristo went along the rows of those angry demonstrators, with his arm stuck to his side, fearing his pistol could be spotted. On the Reforma slip road, opposite *La Prensa*'s building, he stopped to browse a newspaper stall.

"Give me *Proceso*," he asked the vendor.

He also bought a pocket version of *Slowness* by Milan Kundera and *Paula*, Isabel Allende's latest novel, with the intention of reading it that weekend, hangover permitting. He was disgustingly cultured, his library included over a thousand books, but they had not given him the intelligence to live. On the contrary: they were his refuge, because he knew his life was a collapse being filmed in slow-motion. Divorced from Gladys, who had understood neither his inner life nor the moral sacrifice he was making to give her an easy life, he had spent ten years, dedicated to the brothel bohemia without seeing his own daughter. After the separation, he had bought himself a flat in Río Nazas, overlooking one of the Circuito Interior highway's black walls, where he used to bring Sherry's dancers and call girls when the shows were over. They would do anything in bed just for a few grams of coke which he never had any problems getting, so he never came out of the nightclub, where he had perpetually reserved a table near the dance floor, alone. He spent more of his time there than at the office, drinking whisky by the gallon on the house until he fell asleep at the table. He lived in a bubble of stagnant water, immersed in his own pain, a witness to a self-destructive process that he would not delay concluding when his liver finally exploded into pieces. He almost never saw the few friends he had left, because he had turned his self-loathing outwards, extending it to the whole of the human race. But the errand of finding the *El Matutino* journalist had touched a sentimental nerve. For the first time since joining the Feds, he had flinched before carrying out one of Maytorena's orders. The idea of rebelling tempted him when he passed Sebastián's sculpture of a horse towards Puente de Alvarado. Maybe destiny wanted to test him, maybe there was even a mysterious link between the journalist's fate and his own, a link that sometimes joins the fearless with traitors, the heroes with evildoers. An act of generosity in the dusk of a selfish and cowardly life would not open the doors of heaven for him, but at least it would give him the satisfaction of swimming against the tide, of affirming himself as an individual against the cogs that had reduced him to servitude, anonymity, non-existence. He did not really care about Roberto Lima, but he had to save his life to demonstrate to himself that he still had self-respect.

Fear of Animals

El Matutino's building was right next to the San Fernando graveyard, close to the main square – a few blocks where most of the prestigious newspapers' offices can be found. Evaristo read a bronze plaque above its vaguely art deco façade, overly ornate marble folds of elephantine weight and darkened by the car fumes, with the inscription: *El Matutino, seventy years in the service of truth.* When he got in, he discovered that the building had not been maintained since it was founded: the foyer had sunk more than half a metre from the sidewalk, undoubtedly due to dampness in the subsoil, and the floor mosaic had cracks snaking from the door to the reception desk and a venerable seventy-something woman, as deaf as a tree trunk, to whom Evaristo repeated his name and that of Roberto Lima three times. The granny did not know who Lima was, but she directed Evaristo to the cultural section, third floor, left-hand side. He took the lift with a sliding grille and open cables and felt like he had sunk into a film from the Thirties. The anachronisms continued in the third-floor newsroom, where fifteen or twenty tired-looking youngsters whacked at huge Olivetti typewriters on ancient, grey-surfaced desks. Their faces full of boredom, the thick layer of dust on the filing cabinets, the great pots with plants dead from thirst and the cloakroom's collapsing armchair all engendered an atmosphere of abandonment and professional corrosion that was almost certainly reflected in the daily's pages. At the end of a half-lit corridor, Evaristo found the cubicle of the cultural section and knocked twice with his knuckles.

"Door's open, come in," answered a manly voice.

Inside was a bearded young man wearing glasses, his face peppered with acne, whose desk was brimming with papers and photographs.

"Are you Roberto Lima?" Evaristo asked directly.

"No, I'm Mario Casillas, head of international," he responded without taking his eyes off the papers.

"I thought this was Lima's office."

"Yes, it is, but he only comes to work on Tuesdays and Thursdays. I use his office when he's not around."

"I need to talk to him, it's something very urgent. Could you give me his telephone number?"

"I don't think he has one."

"His address, then?"

"We are forbidden from giving out colleagues' addresses for security reasons." Casillas finally lifted his head, annoyed at Evaristo's insistence. "Why don't you come on Tuesday and speak to him directly?"

Evaristo pushed his metal ID shield in Casillas' face while discreetly unbuttoning his jacket so he could see the Magnum. With his lips blue and a nervous tremor in his voice, Casillas acceded by calling the editor's secretary, who had all the contributors in the paper's database.

"Irmita, would you be so kind as to give me Roberto Lima's address? It is for a friend of his who came asking for him…"

The terrorist who had insulted the President in print lived in Hermenegildo Galeana street, Colonia Peñón de los Baños, just behind the airport. Going there at a time of intense traffic was a terrifying thought, but Evaristo could not afford to dawdle. Under the ruthless sun, his eyes irritated and his heart bloodless because the effect of the coke by now had passed, the trip was a long torture that almost made him abandon his plan. When he reached the crossroads at Río Churubusco and Eje 3, near Palacio de los Deportes, he stopped at a street stall to eat a few pork sausage tacos, which he washed down with a litre of soft drink. Resuscitated by the blast of calories, he continued his excursion without caring about the traffic, trying to guess Lima's motives. He was probably a radical left-winger pissed off with electoral fraud, taking revenge on the government of the Institutional Revolutionary Party (PRI) by throwing bombs of ink and paper at it. It had been really childish of him to insult Jiménez del Solar like that without a reason, risking his life just because of a tantrum, but it was Lima's tempestuous and visceral attack that was the main reason Evaristo sympathised with him. How many times had Evaristo wished to send everything to hell, jump above the ranks and shout to those in power: "I also exist!"? Because of

Fear of Animals

this, when he turned into Peñón de los Baños searching for Lima's residence, Evaristo felt that he was not only going to meet an incredible loony, but the madman he himself had inside, his anarchist alter ego.

After a long trip around the dusty streets of a poor and anodyne *barrio*, he found the compound where Lima had his flat. The door in building C faced a square with slides and see-saws where a boy was pummelling a plastic ball. The door was open and, as there was no intercom, Evaristo went up the stairs to the third floor, avoiding potplants and bird cages. In flat 301, 'Lucinda', the Joe Cocker blues song, was blaring out at full volume. Evaristo remembered his years as a pothead when he used to go to the Chapultepec Audiorama to smoke weed. He knocked three times with an open palm to make himself heard over the racket.

"I'm coming, just a minute!" A man of average height, with thick lips, was peeking through a crack by the door. "What do you want?"

"Are you Roberto Lima?"

The guy nodded without taking the chain off the door.

"I am Evaristo Reyes. I've come to see you to discuss a very delicate matter. There are some very powerful people who are annoyed about what you wrote in the paper."

Lima's face went pale and he opened the door immediately, his voice breaking, inviting Evaristo in. He was a forty-something with thick brows, badly shaven, with bags under his grey eyes and the intense stare of a biblical prophet. He was wearing sandals made out of tyres, a checked flannel shirt and corduroy trousers with patches on the knees. His flat, as tiny as a tomb, was lined with books from floor to ceiling, reminding Evaristo of Dostoevsky's underground man. From all the dishes piled up in the kitchen and the dust on the shelves, one could infer that Lima was single and did not clean up very often. The smoke of the eighty cigarettes he had had in the space of half a day created a black mass in the centre of the room, and the open bottle of tequila Sauza on the dining table revealed the sad loner's drunkenness.

"So an article by me has had a reaction." Lima was trying to calm his nerves and appear in control, although his trembling hands gave him away. "Are you from the interior ministry?"

"I'm with the Federal Judicial Police, but I've come of my own accord." When he sat down on a dining-table chair, Evaristo showed the Magnum, and Lima lost his colour. "Don't be afraid, I have never killed anyone. I was given your address at *El Matutino* and came here to warn you that you have got yourself into a very nasty problem."

"What problem? I'm a reporter in the cultural section and never write about politics."

Evaristo showed him the cutting which told the President to fuck his mother. Lima read it with a face of enjoyment.

"So they were offended by this nonsense?"

"You could die for that nonsense." Evaristo began to get impatient with Lima's childishness. "My boss, Commander Jesús Maytorena, found this piece of paper at a gas station and do you know what he asked me to do? To find out your address so he could come and give you a thrashing. But I know my boss and I know that he has a heavy hand, especially when he wants to show off to those above him. If I call him now and give him your address, tomorrow morning you'll be dead."

"So now I know. What you want is some dough, don't you? How much for not calling your boss?" Lima took his wallet out and started to count the notes.

"I'm going to make you swallow your money, arsehole." Furious, Evaristo grabbed him by the collar. "Who do you think I am? A bloody traffic cop? With all the money you earn in a year you couldn't pay me for what your life is worth."

Evaristo controlled his desire to smash Lima's face against the wall when he realised that Lima, prejudiced by the reputation of the Feds, had good reason not to trust him. He let Lima fall over the chair and straightened his hair, hurt at Lima's reaction. "There was a Fed who tried to be a good person," thought Evaristo, "and the man he tried to help stabbed him in the back." But Lima had already realised he was not dealing with any old police officer.

"I'm sorry," he said. "Nobody has ever done me a favour for free and I thought you were trying to extort money from me. Do you fancy a tequila?"

Evaristo accepted the drink and the tension eased, allowing both men to continue talking in a more amiable tone.

"Are you a militant of any party?"

Lima shook his head.

"But you are against the regime..."

"You're not going to believe this, but I'm rather apolitical."

"So, why did you put yourself at risk saying that about the President?"

Fear of Animals

"Put myself at risk?" Lima cackled. "I've spent the last three years telling him to fuck his mother in all of my articles and nobody has noticed before now. That's the good thing about writing for *El Matutino*. You have absolute freedom because nobody reads you."

"And the editor, is he blind or what? *El Matutino* is considered an official newspaper. How come he has allowed you to write that?"

"Because he never reads it either!" Lima scrunched up his lips in a wry grimace. "The cultural page of the paper is the one he cares about least. He only reads the political pieces and the celebrities section, where he gives free publicity to his favourite whores."

"I don't understand. So why does he publish the cultural page?"

"Just to keep up appearances. Culture looks good. A newspaper that does not dedicate some room to culture loses prestige. In this country everyone promotes culture, haven't you realised? Even the Sinaloan drug traffickers give grants to young writers. The more the rate of illiteracy grows, the more literary workshops there are, but very few people have a real hunger for culture, and those who do don't read *El Matutino*."

"It must feel really crap to write for the warehouse rats, musn't it?" Evaristo poured himself another tequila without waiting for Lima to top him up.

"I have to say at first I did feel very indignant. I would write wonders about a novel, a week later I would meet the author and ask him what he thought of my review. 'I'm sorry, I didn't buy that paper,' he'd say, and the same happened with all the artists, rockers, theatre directors. When I realised that I was an invisible man, I suffered terrible depression, but soon I discovered that anonymity was an enormous advantage. 'What are you moaning about?' I would say to myself. In the final analysis, one always writes for oneself, and you even get paid for doing what you like doing best. So, from that moment, on the cultural page turned into my secret diary. In the middle of reviews and stories I write whatever I fancy: tongue twisters, swear words, confessions of a drunkard, calumnies against others in the business. What I wrote against Jiménez del Solar came right from my balls. One day I said: 'I'm fucking sick of seeing this baldy in the news, on all the first pages of the papers, in government offices, on buses and even public toilets. I'm going to take revenge on behalf of the people'."

"Well, I'm afraid you're going to lose your living," interrupted Evaristo. "My boss wants to denounce you to Attorney General Tapia, and he'll almost certainly call the editor of your paper. He may even close it."

"I'll be so happy. He deserves that for being such an arse licker and an arsehole. If I'm sacked, I don't lose anything, I can find another job anywhere, but that wanker would lose his little goldmine."

"The paper can't earn him much money if nobody reads it."

"Of course it does, and a fuck of a lot." Lima got up to change the Joe Cocker CD for another one by the trumpeter Wynton Marsalis and went on with his explanation, adopting a didactic tone. "Not one newspaper survives just on its sales, the real business is advertising. *El Matutino* has a ridiculous print run, three or four thousand copies, but he charges per advert as if the print run were ninety thousand, because the government repays those who lick their arse very well. The editor is the best mate of all the press chiefs in every ministry, he invites them for lunch at Fouquets in the Camino Real hotel and, when they offer him a line of coke, he obeys them like a footman. This is the way he's made his fortune, gaining the favour of all those ministers who can throw paid supplements at him or contracts to print other jobs, taking his cut from all this, of course. And because he doesn't give a shit if the paper sells or not, because the paper is only the excuse for his dirty business, he pays us starvation wages that force reporters to make a living from little brown envelopes."

Forced to stop because of the noise of an aeroplane approaching the airport, Lima took advantage of the pause to go to the toilet. Evaristo knew the miseries of journalism as well as Lima, but he did not want to talk to him about his past because he was ashamed of explaining how he had ended up as a Fed.

"I'm amazed at your library," Evaristo commented when Lima came back from the toilet. "I think you must be a literary man, as well as being a journalist."

"I am just a writer," corrected Lima. "I have published a couple of books of poetry and one of short stories. Very little for my age, but this is because journalism does not allow me to write my own stuff."

"I was told in *El Matutino* that you go there twice a week."

"But that's only one of my jobs. With what I earn at the paper I couldn't even afford the rent on this shithole. I also work as a proofreader for the university's cultural programme and head a narrative workshop at the Institute of Arts and Literature, but I'd like to throw everything to hell: I've had it up to here with the culture bureaucrats."

It looked as if this subject excited Lima because, after he had topped his glass up with another tequila he continued spewing insults against the public cultural officials who, according to him, behaved as a divine caste. He had seen them creep around and plot intrigues with the sole aim of keeping their privileges during the four six-year presidential terms that he had worked for the state's cultural apparatus. It wasn't hard getting on in an environment where adulation and servility opened every door, but he had never played by the rules of that game. He did not have a gift for public relations, which he considered a form of prostitution, he could only make friends with those he really appreciated, without scrutinising their position within the bureaucratic pyramid. While those arrivistes gained luxurious sinecures or placements as cultural attachés in the foreign service, he had remained on the dark side of the budget, with a low wage battered every year by rising inflation. He was a slogging peon, the long-suffering proofreader who checked the copies with tired eyes and a broken back, while those yuppies with a chauffeur waiting at the door attended cocktail parties and ceremonies for beautiful people, where the intellectual courtesans breathed in what Octavio Paz exhaled.

Lima had not envied them at all for having managed to enter that world, because perennial faking and circumstantial smiles were not part of his temperament. What really made him sick was the arrogance of those public officials infatuated with the ostentation of their posts and their tendency to confuse the bureaucratic ladder with the intellectual hierarchy. Mediocre writers who were nobody in the world of literature turned from one day to the next into national glories just by the simple fact of managing a budget. In exchange for a job or a handout, starving culture reporters would create a fake prestige for them that faded like froth when people who were completely unaware actually bought one of their books.

"But beware of pushing them off the cloud they sit on, because you create enemies for life." Lima paused to get into the music for a moment. "I'm one of the few who has dared to reveal them in all their frightening mediocrity. When I worked for the Fund for the

Promotion of Reading, I had to review a book of essays by Claudio Vilchis, the Fund's editorial second in command, in the *Sábado* supplement. It was some erudite shit, you know, lots of quotes in Greek and German but not one spark of intelligence, and in my report I said that it had given me indigestion. Vilchis did not show that he was offended but, at the first opportunity he had, he threw me on to the streets with the excuse that I had arrived late three times in less than a month. From there I went into the publications department of the Simón Bolívar University, where I was also sacked at the first opportunity. My boss was Perla Tinoco, the poet, a sow who doggedly wrote exuberance with an "h" in the middle. Once I corrected her, dictionary in hand, and she went mad. 'What are you doing trying to teach me', she shouted, 'if you are nothing but a bloody pleb and I have a doctorate from the Colegio de México'."

Evaristo looked at his watch impatiently. It was half past six and night was descending outside. Sooner or later Maytorena would call on his mobile and Lima had still not shown any sign of realising the danger he was in.

"Look, Roberto, I'm calling you by your Christian name because we are talking in confidence. Your office problems can be bloody awful, but at this very moment, if I were you, I would be thinking of where I was going to go so I didn't get pumped full of lead."

"Do you really think this is so fucking bad?" Lima went pale.

"Do you think it's trivial to be sentenced to death? Later on I have to give my boss your address and tomorrow he'll come after you. Listen to me: smash your piggy bank and take the first plane to Los Angeles." When he tapped the ash off his cigarette, Evaristo missed the ashtray and it fell on the cover of a thick dictionary of synonyms and antonyms.

"I don't have a visa to get into the United States." Lima hurried to clean the cover of the dictionary with his sleeve. "Last year I went to get one and they asked me for a bank account to show I was solvent. Bloody gringo sons of bitches, they treat you as if you were a wetback. But they'll see: when I'm a Nobel prize winner they're going to beg on their knees for me go to their bloody country, and then I'll give them the finger."

"If you can't leave Mexico, go and hide in a little village in the arse of the world – just don't stay here. Now you are pissed and it doesn't feel like it's in your best interests to go anywhere, but early tomorrow pack your bags and beat it." Evaristo unsheathed his

Fear of Animals

gun and put it on the table. "Take this, in case they find you. It's a little old, but it can get you out of trouble. Do you need some dough?"

Lima took a while to answer, sad. Noticing that he was disturbed, Evaristo took a sheaf of notes from his wallet and stuffed them in Lima's shirt pocket. Moved, Lima asked him why he was being so generous, as he didn't even know him.

"I don't know you, but I admire people who write a lot. You may find it odd, but I like reading very much."

"If you want, I can give you my book of short stories."

Evaristo accepted and Lima went to his room, where he took a couple of minutes writing a dedication. *For my friend Evaristo Reyes, the only human Fed I have ever met.* When Evaristo read it, he shuddered with guilt. Lima may have been resentful, but he fought against the winds and tides to push forward his vocation. What a painful lesson for a clown like himself, who had traded his dreams for crumbs of comfort! They exchanged goodbyes at the door with a hug, promising to meet again to talk about literature when Lima was out of trouble. The stairs were very dark and, when he came out of the apartment, on the first landing, Evaristo bumped against a man with the strong smell of a cigar.

Outside, the October wind messed up his hair and turned his bitterness into joy. At last he had disobeyed one of Maytorena's orders. On the way home he tuned into Radio Capital and sang along to 'You've really got me' with the happiness of a freshly washed baby. Doing what he bloody well liked was a more powerful drug than cocaine. In the flat at Nazas he had a hot bath, served himself an Old Parr on the rocks, dressed in a new suede jacket that gave him the air of a film producer, and went out to celebrate his re-encounter with himself.

At Sherry's, Efrén, the head waiter who had made friends with Evaristo escorting him to his car so often when he was paralytic, received him with a smile.

"You took your time, boss, I thought you weren't coming today."

"You know I never fail. How's your hernia?"

"Better, they will remove the bandages in two weeks' time."

Evaristo sneaked a fifty peso note into Efrén's tuxedo, and he led him to his usual table next to the stage where the *vedettes* did the striptease. The house sent a bottle of Chivas Regal to Evaristo's table, and Juanito, the waiter who brought it to him, entertained him by talking about football until the show started.

That night it was the debut of a new stripper, Dora Elsa, who danced to a rap song and was wearing a minuscule G-string. While the clients of Sherry's admired her gazelle-like body and abundant pubic hair stretching up to her belly button, Evaristo looked at her face, mesmerised by the opal-like light that came from her eyes. She did something stronger than just arouse him, evoking his desire to possess her body and soul and for her to respond with deadly passion. What was he thinking of? Did his little rebellion bring back his youth? When the show was over Evaristo called her over to share the bottle of Chivas and they talked like two lovers on a first date. Dora Elsa was a divorcée. She had a six-year old daughter whom she left at her mother's house when she went out to work. She loved romantic comics, especially *Susy, Secrets of the Heart*, and she had started to exercise her groin muscles in order to learn how to smoke with her cunt at the request of Sherry's owner, who had asked her for a more audacious routine.

Evaristo was amazed that, despite her trade, she had not yet become bitter, like most of the strippers he had befriended. She was fresh, innocent and a bit dumb, like Evaristo's first girlfriend in high school. Instinctively, he knew he could trust her and told her he had just rebelled against his boss, someone called Maytorena, and was celebrating his regained freedom. They danced cheek-to-cheek to the 'Summer of 42' theme and, when he felt her breathe on his neck, he shuddered and had an erection.

"I want you," he said. "Come home with me."

"I can't, we're not allowed to leave until 4am."

After much begging by Evaristo, who paid for her time, Efrén had no problem about letting Dora Elsa go before her contracted hour. While Evaristo waited for her at the dressing room door, he stuffed a five-hundred peso note in her silver handbag, before any request for payment could spoil the situation. He wanted to love her and treat her like a lady, give her his hidden tenderness and prolong the illusion until he could not distinguish fantasy from reality. Dora Elsa came out of her dressing room wearing a black dress closed up to the neck and the same coloured tights. Assuming his role, Evaristo took her by the hand and, inside the car, declared his love for her using the phrases of an old-fashioned *bolero*.

"Come closer, my love. I want you to be mine and no one else's. Today is the day that was marked for our souls to meet."

Dora Elsa let out an incredulous laugh, but Evaristo realised that his refinement did not displease her. Or was she just faking it, not to contradict him? Maybe she had been told he was a Fed and was just playing along out of fear. When they got into the flat they kissed on the lips. Normally they would have just gone straight to bed, but Evaristo wanted to get to know her better, so he invited her for a drink in the sitting room. When he was preparing highballs, while she looked at his book shelves, he remembered that he had not yet called Maytorena. Would he be angry? Fuck him: Evaristo was not going to spoil this beautiful moment by carrying out a repugnant errand. He played a Juan Luis Guerra record, huddled next to Dora Elsa on the sofa, and asked her why she was dressed in black.

"I am grieving. The day before yesterday my brother was killed."

"I'm sorry, I didn't wish to hurt you." Evaristo sunk his eyes in the glass. "Why was he killed?"

"He belonged to a gang and used to steal car batteries which he then used to sell in Colonia Buenos Aires. The owner of a car found him opening the bonnet, so he shot him in the back. We buried him yesterday in a horrible graveyard by Lago de Guadalupe. He doesn't even have a stone, just a bloody square in the middle of a dusty plot." Dora Elsa burst into tears. "Worst of all was that at the police station they did not want to give us back the body. I had to bribe half the world."

Evaristo held her in his arms, telling her soothing words until she stopped sobbing and blew her nose with a Kleenex.

"Thanks for getting me out of Sherry's and for paying for me to come. I feel so bad that I really did not want to dance naked."

They kissed again, first gently, then furiously. Forgetting about himself, in a state of grace that he had not experienced since he was twenty, Evaristo made love to her, giving himself totally, without skimping on caresses. Dora Elsa seemed to enjoy it. Or was she moaning to please him? Concentrating on her hair, which smelt of aloe vera, he felt he was wearing his skin, heart and testicles for the first time, that he had been reborn after a long hibernation at the North Pole. When he explored her clitoris with his tongue, he went back again to being a careless and happy child, alien to the miseries of conscious life. But the best came later, when she took the initiative and rode astride him, commanding his penetration with her educated groin muscles that opened and closed to imprison and release his penis. It was a vagina with a life of its own, a perverse and intelligent animal, capable of driving anyone wild. The slow friction started to speed up until it became a frantic gallop. On the edge of ecstasy, Evaristo closed his eyes and held back from coming several times until Dora Elsa reached him on the ascending curve of orgasm and they poured out screaming in tune, like two fireworks fused to burst at the same height.

    Half an hour's pause followed, in which they did not think about anything. Then they made love again, a bit more calmly, stretching out the pleasure to the point at which their bodies were about to melt. With the second orgasm came a sweet fatigue. Evaristo put his head on the pillow and fell asleep. When he woke, Dora Elsa had made herself scarce. It would be normal for her to do so, after earning her pay, but he had fooled himself and felt even more lonely than ever. How much he would have liked to have had breakfast with her, to take her to eat in a good restaurant, to the cinema or the race track. He put on his slippers and walked to the kitchen to reheat a white coffee. Best to erase that night from his memory, to pretend that he had never met her. But he could not forget her so easily because, when he came back from the kitchen, he found a note on the bedside table with Dora Elsa's telephone number and address: *I really liked you. Call me.* Underneath the note there was a five hundred peso note.

Fear of Animals

With the windows wide open, clean carpet, sparkling mirror-like kitchen and a bathroom smelling of pine disinfectant, the sordid den in Nazas street had turned into a living place, almost welcoming. Lying on his bed, amazed, Evaristo admired his cleaning work. For the first time in many years he had held the mop, the broom and the duster without waiting for the maid, who came to tidy up once a week. In love and jubilant, he had brushed the carpet like someone who writes a poem, to project his happiness outwards. Dora Elsa was the prize that God had granted him for saving Lima's life. His rebellion had returned to him the ability to be in love, maybe because he now respected himself more. Wearing only his briefs, he walked towards the window across the impeccable sitting room where the serape from Saltillo acted as a rug and the wine velvet sofa shone as if it had been bought only yesterday. The morning was luminous and cheerful, with the unusual sound of the sparrows on the scrawny sidewalk trees. Even the depressing wall of the Circuito Interior highway, with graffiti scribbled on it by gangs of youths, sparkled anew, as if the sun was shining on it for the first time. He filled his lungs with the dirty air of Colonia Cuauhtémoc that seemed as clean as the air on a snowy mountain, and closed the window as he whistled 'Love Bubbles', the song that he had repeated all night as he frolicked in bed with Dora Elsa. He had just turned on the cooker to make himself some poached eggs when he heard a loud thump on the door, followed by an angry yell.

"It's me, Intellectual! Open or I'll smash the door down!"

He did not even have enough time to run to the bedroom to put on a pair of trousers. While he was getting them out of the cupboard, Maytorena kicked the door off its hinges and came into the flat, knocking over chairs and ornaments. He was wearing a raspberry coloured Fila tracksuit, dark shades and a black cap.

With him came Chamula and The Sheep, another one of his gunmen, so named because of his curly blond locks. Before Evaristo could ask for an explanation, Maytorena shut his mouth with a brutal blow of his hand, something between a smack and karate chop, that landed him on the floor, spitting blood.

"Who asked you to finish him? Answer, arsehole! Who told you to kill him?" Maytorena lifted Evaristo's face by grabbing him by the hair while crouching to the level of the floor, waiting for an answer.

"I don't understand. Who was killed?"

"Who else, you bastard? Roberto Lima!"

The news fell upon Evaristo like a second blow to the face.

"I didn't do it. I never killed anyone." He stood up, confused. "You know that I don't do that."

"Don't try to be fucking smart with me. Last night Lima was killed, the news appeared this morning in *El Universal*," Maytorena clicked his fingers like a sultan and The Sheep handed him a newspaper folded up in the middle. "It says here that the witnesses saw a guy of your height leaving the flat."

"I swear I didn't do it, chief. I only asked for his address at the newspaper, like you asked me to."

"And why didn't you give it to me, bastard? I was calling you last night and your mobile was switched off."

"I was thinking of calling you this morning."

"You don't fool me. You were scared of calling me because you were coming back from killing that idiot."

"I swear to God I didn't do anything," sobbed Evaristo.

"So then, who killed him? A ghost?"

Evaristo stayed silent, his eyes fixed on the floor.

"Look you fucking intellectual, I don't care if you killed him, I couldn't give a shit about it. What pisses me off is that it was done so clumsily. When you're drunk you talk a lot of nonsense. You're capable of telling all the whores at Sherry's."

"Yesterday I didn't talk to anyone. I spent the whole night with Dora Elsa, a showgirl."

"I'm not interested in your flabby bottomed old bags. What I want to know is why they are lumbering us with this little corpse. That bloody reporter says some Feds killed Lima because they wanted to shut him up for his attacks on the President."

"Maybe some other colleagues took advantage," speculated Evaristo.

Fear of Animals

"Who, if I was the only one who knew about Lima? Yesterday afternoon I saw the attorney and showed him the cutting telling Jiménez to go fuck his mother. He did not praise me because you know how arrogant he is, but I noticed that he was flushed with pleasure. This must be made known to the President, he said, so that he doesn't trust those incompetents who supposedly cover his back. He ordered his secretary to send the article by fax to the presidential residence, Los Pinos, and told me not to punish Lima for whatever reason. 'With journalists one has to tread carefully, commander. A little scratch and they start to cry like professional mourners. Let's proceed by the legal route against that wretch, even though he deserves a good beating.' Yes, of course, *Señor* attorney, I said, we won't touch him, and this morning bloody Lima shows up dead. When the fuck did you decide to do as you wanted? Do you know who's going to be blamed for all this? Do you know who?"

Maytorena shook him by the shoulders, his jaw clenched and his arteries sticking out. He was going to smash his head against the floor, but stopped, held back by a question.

"Do you really swear that you didn't kill him?"

Evaristo nodded yes, his cheeks drenched in tears.

"I pity you if you are lying to me," Maytorena wiped the sweat off his brow with the sleeve of his tracksuit. "Let's suppose you didn't do it. That means the real killer is still on the loose. I need to get him so Tapia doesn't lumber me with the problem."

"If you want me to, I can help you," Evaristo suggested timidly.

"Of course you'll help me. This problem is not only mine, it's also yours and these bastards," he pointed at Chamula and The Sheep. "Because if Tapia slashes my neck, you all go to fucking hell with me."

"I think this is a dispute between queers," Chamula interjected. "I think this journalist was a swordsman and had a fight with his lover. Let me interrogate the stiff's friends, chief, and in two days I'll get you the guilty one, I promise."

Even after Chamula kissed his crucifix to give his oath more authority, Maytorena discarded the hypothesis with a peevish click of his tongue.

"No. Chamula, this can't be fixed like that. Lima's friends are journalists, writers, people that kick up a stink about anything. If we detain them for interrogation, they aren't going to stay silent and the thing will be to stop the scandal."

"We must find out if Lima had enemies within his profession,"

Evaristo proposed. "I can start to investigate by myself, without telling anyone I'm a Fed, so as not to scare people."

Maytorena remained thinking for a moment, weighing up the idea, resting his chin on his hands. Used to fabricating guilt and to resolving crimes through torture, he was disgusted by the prospect of conducting an investigation by the rules. Suddenly his mobile phone rang, and when he answered the call he went livid.

"Yes, attorney, Commander Maytorena at your service... Yes sir, I read the news, but let me explain... No sir, I can assure you that I followed your orders as you requested... I can't explain that either, sir. There must be some misunderstanding... Yes, of course, right now, I'm going there." He switched off the phone and turned towards Evaristo, his greying moustache revealing pearly drops of sweat. "Tapia is fucking nuts and wants me to see him in his office. Your plan sounds good, but you have to start working a-fucking-sap. Go and see Fat Zepeda. He's taking the case with the capital's own judicial police, but he owes me a lot of favours and we have agreed that he's going to let me carry out the investigation. He was the first to arrive at the flat. Ask him if he found something we can use as a clue. Then go by the funeral parlour where there's a vigil for Lima and prick up your ears. The Sheep and Chamula are at your command, to help you with whatever you may need."

Before leaving with his two gunmen, Maytorena stopped in the doorway.

"I'm only warning you of one thing: if you are cheating me, you've earned yourself the golden ticket."

When he finally left, Evaristo unfolded *El Universal* and hurriedly read the news about the homicide by reporter Ignacio Carmona. According to the Public Prosecutor's Office, the police had collected the corpse at ten o'clock at night after a call by a neighbour who, when passing Lima's flat, saw the door open and found the journalist lying face down in the living room in a pool of blood. There was a disconcerting fact: Lima had not died by a gunshot, he had died by a blow to the back of the neck with a dictionary of synonyms and antonyms. Why hadn't he used Evaristo's Magnum to defend himself? *Up to this moment the motive for this murder remains unknown, but an anonymous source, in a telephone call to our newsdesk, assured us that it was a government punishment because of insults to the President written by the deceased and published in* El Matutino *newspaper, where he was in charge of the cultural section. According to this version, the Federal Judicial Police and the interior ministry themselves could be involved in the crime...* Shaking, Evaristo remembered the cigar smoker he had bumped into while going down the stairs of the building. What was he doing in the darkness, crouching like a rat? Without doubt he was waiting for him to leave in order to murder Lima.

He left the paper on the bed and washed his mouth in the bathroom. His upper lip was swollen, still bleeding a bit, but what hurt most was to have remained a wimp in front of Maytorena. At the end of the day, the renaissance of his self-respect had been as ephemeral as the blink of an eye. He did not even have the consolation of having helped Lima, because now he was dead and on his epitaph there would be the inscription 'Don't defend me, mate'. That was what Mexico was like: a country where any good deed was punished immediately with the full force of the law. Miraculously, the *El Universal* article did not mention Evaristo's Magnum, but if Maytorena happened to find out that his gun was at the crime scene, he would find out that Evaristo had disobeyed him and that would be his death sentence.

Dressed in the first thing he found in the closet, he went like greased lightning to the District Attorney's office. It was a Saturday, but the traffic was as bad as on any weekday. When he got to the building in Niños Héroes avenue, a postmodern horror with a mirrored glass façade, Evaristo had already decided to leave the country if Fat Zepeda did not help him. Zepeda's office was in the Department of Preliminary Inquiries, the only department that did not close for the weekend. He found Zepeda wearing a short-sleeved shirt, having a *tamale* sandwich. His love handles were overflowing from the chair, his eyes bulging out of their sockets, his nose red, and he was beginning to lose his hair. He was one of the most feared licensed assassins in the country. He had been expelled from the PGR because of his links with the Gulf cartel, but his face, like that of a good pig, gave him a harmless air. They had got drunk together several times when Fat had been working for Maytorena, so Evaristo felt sufficiently at ease to ask for a favour.

"Hiya, Fat." Evaristo patted him on the back. "And I find you stuffing carbohydrates just for a change. Weren't you on a diet?"

"I'm still on a diet: I'm drinking my coffee without sugar."

"You're going to drop the belly that way, but down to your knees."

"What's the miracle? With so much to read, you don't even come to say hello to your mates. Why the honour of a visit?"

"I need to talk to you about the journalist killed last night."

Zepeda stopped chewing his sandwich, gave Evaristo a knowing look and proposed that they take a trip in his car to talk without ears surrounding them. Zepeda's car was a beaten-up and dirty Topaz with bits of crisps all over the floor and seats. He took one of the few streets where there was not an open market, turned left into Doctor Jiménez, went a few blocks more at a very low speed, and stopped at a park with young trees and paved paths in a place formerly occupied by the commerce ministry, before it had been razed by the 1985 earthquake. While Fat finished gobbling up his enormous *tamale* sandwich, Evaristo told him in general terms everything that had happened the previous day, from the cutting found by Maytorena on the road to Pachuca to his tequila chat with Lima. Finally, his voice breaking with anxiety, he asked Fat if he had found the Magnum at the journalist's house. Zepeda made a theatrical pause while he devoured the last bite of his sandwich. After wiping his fingers on his trousers, Fat opened the glove compartment and took out the weapon inside a polythene bag.

"Here's your little gun. You really fucked up, Intellectual. How could you leave it there, fingerprints and all? Did Maytorena order you to kill him? Give me the naked truth. You don't need to be mysterious with me."

"I swear I didn't do it, but I know you're not going to believe me. Maytorena didn't believe me either. And if any journalist gets to know that I was with Lima last night, they can take that as an excuse to blame me. This is why I want to ask you a favour: don't tell anyone that you found my gun in his flat."

"How could I? I never want any grovelling when it comes to giving a mate a hand." Zepeda gave him back the Magnum, smiling like one of Rubens' angels. "I also have Lima's phone book, but it is in the Public Prosecutor's Office. If you want me to, I'll photocopy it for you."

"Thanks, bro, I'll come for it later."

Back at the District Attorney's office, Evaristo asked him who had claimed Lima's body and which funeral parlour he was being kept at.

"This very morning his mother went to the police station to collect the body, accompanied by some long-haired bloke. I think he was taken to Sullivan's Gayosso funeral parlour."

Fear of Animals

They said goodbye, shaking hands in the car park but, when Evaristo opened the car door, Zepeda held him by the arm.

"Wait a minute, a favour is repaid with a favour. You're going to laugh at me, but I have changed a lot lately: for some time now I have had the itch to write poetry." His chubby face was ablaze with blushes. "It was a magical revelation: suddenly I felt that I needed to let out all the emotions I had inside, so I grabbed a pencil and paper and let myself be carried by inspiration. It was as if I was being born again, as if wings had sprouted on me. I have been writing poetry for six months and the drawers of my desk are full of verses. I think I'm not too bad, but I would like to know the opinion of an intellectual, such as you."

Zepeda took from his briefcase a folder stained with *mole* sauce and oil, containing his complete works of poetry gathered together under the title *Autumn's Harvest*.

"I hope you like them. I had sent them off to a bunch of contests and I never win anything, but I don't trust the juries because they only award their friends. The people in the literary world are quite corrupt."

Evaristo promised to read the poetry collection that same night and to give him his opinion very soon, although he could foresee that Fat's harvest was already rotten. On the way to Gayosso, free from anxieties and fears after recovering the Magnum, Evaristo coldly analysed the intentions of that "anonymous source". In the first instance, it was evident that Lima had at least one reader, because the mysterious informant who had called *El Universal* knew about the insults to the President. It was without doubt the assassin himself, who had sought to divert the inquiry with that false lead and mask his own motive for the crime – maybe a personal feud with Lima. Could it be one of his literary enemies whom he detested so much? If that were the case, he would have the cheek to attend the wake, to be free from all suspicion, and maybe he would even make the mistake of smoking a cigar.

In the antechamber of the funeral chapel a small group of literary people or aspirants, the majority bearded and with satchels hanging from their shoulders, had gathered, talking in low voices in animated groups. It appeared as if they were not that perturbed by Lima's death or hid their sorrow well. From their looks, Evaristo supposed that they belonged on the fringes of the literary republic. A reporter with yellow skin and alcoholic bags under his eyes circulated here and there, collecting impressions with a tape recorder. When he brushed past him, Evaristo overheard the guy introduce himself as *El Universal*'s reporter. Evaristo watched him attentively as he interviewed a guy with the looks of a rocker, dark and thin, wearing a U2 T-shirt, his hair gathered in a pony tail. When the interview ended, Evaristo stopped him by the arm.

"Are you Ignacio Carmona?"

"At your service."

"Come with me to the cafeteria. I need to talk to you." Carmona resisted the invitation, so Evaristo had to show him his metal Fed's shield to convince him. In the cafeteria, illuminated by harsh neon lightbulbs, they sat at the bar and asked for two americano coffees.

"Who were you interviewing just now?"

"A writer called Rubén Estrella. He was a friend of the deceased. He negotiated to get the Institute of Arts and Literature to pay for the funeral and the burial."

"Did he say anything about Lima's articles in *El Matutino*? Had he ever read them?"

"No. He says he never used to buy the paper."

"Nor did anyone else. Only your contact read that fucking crap. Who is he? Did he gave you his name?"

"When I was about to ask him, he hung up."

"Are you really an arsehole or you are trying to be smart with me?" Evaristo stared spitefully into the reporter's eyes. "How dare you publish stuff coming from an unidentified bastard?"

"I thought he was well informed."

"Of course he was well informed," Evaristo smiled. "Have you never thought that your informant could be the murderer?"

Carmona choked on his coffee.

"Look sir, I have a family and don't want trouble. If you want, I'll publish a correction. The bad news is that the snowball is already rolling. Up there, signatures and money for a paid insertion calling for the murder to be investigated in the name of freedom of expression are being requested."

"Now they are going to turn him into a martyr. Can you see what you've done with your bloody story?"

"I'm sorry, I never thought it was going to lead to that."

"Although you really deserve to be beaten to a pulp, you're in luck: my boss doesn't want to hurt anyone. I'm warning you about just one thing." Evaristo lowered his voice. "When you know something new about Lima or your informant calls you again, let me know before anyone else or I'll accuse you of concealing evidence."

Evaristo gave him a card with his home telephone number and paid for the coffees. They went back together to the room where the vigil was being kept over the body, and the marginal contingent had increased with the arrival of some long-haired youths wearing ripped jeans. Evaristo observed them slowly. None smoked a cigar. In an attempt to blend in, he slipped with his head lowered towards a corner of the funeral chapel. At the end, on a settee just next to the coffin, an elderly lady wearing a shawl, her white hair gathered under a scarf, with smooth and shiny skin despite her age, was crying on the shoulder of a dark teenager with braces and a checked school skirt.

"Who are they?" Evaristo asked Carmona.

"They are Lima's mother and sister. They were the only relatives he had in Mexico City."

Opposite the ladies, an attractive woman with an absent air, about thirty or thirty five, with tanned skin and wearing a turtleneck jumper that emphasised the splendour of her chest, sat on a maroon leather sofa, gazing intensely at the floral crowns. In his chat with Lima, Evaristo had not even thought of asking him if he was single, married, divorced or a queen but, because of the special place this woman had at the wake, Evaristo deduced that she was his widow.

"And that gorgeous woman?"

"She's called Fabiola Nava. She was Lima's student at his literary workshop. It seems they were lovers, but recently they had split up."

For a moment he observed her with the eyes of a man, forgetting his role as Sherlock Holmes. She had wavy chestnut hair, a small and sensual heart-shaped mouth and almond-coloured eyes, slightly reddened. Under her black tights there was a hint of a delicious dancer or gymnast's thighs. It looked as if Lima had tasted happiness before abandoning this world. In an outburst of funereal gallantry, Evaristo introduced himself to her as "a friend of Roberto", took her by the hand and, whispering, advised her to be strong. The circumstances obliged him to give his condolences to the mother and sister too. Then he kept watch by the coffin, along with two other blokes wearing suits and ties who had just arrived, and, even though he did not like looking through the coffin's glass panes, he ended up looking out of the corner of his eye at the blue face of the dead man. *That* was not Lima any longer, yet he felt as if at any moment he would get up from the coffin to point at the killer, who could well be one of his companions in the vigil, even though none smoked a cigar.

When the vigil had finished he devoted himself to circulating among the small groups of people, catching snippets of conversation that had nothing to do with Lima's death. They talked about books, cinema, *canto nuevo*, politics and sex. The only thing missing for this wake to turn into a public relations cocktail party was someone opening a bottle. In the little room at the end, where there was a telephone and a reclining chair, he bumped into Rubén Estrella, who was coming out of the bathroom.

"I am Luciano Contreras, of *Macrópolis* magazine," lied Evaristo as he introduced himself. "I have been told that you were a friend of Lima's and I wanted to ask you for a brief biographical sketch of his life and work."

"Roberto was the greatest fucking writer of my generation," Estrella sighed sadly. "It's a shame he died so young. He was going to be our next Carlos Fuentes. He was writing a really good novel. Last week he read one of the chapters to me: it was about a lady from Las Lomas who goes into a hippie commune in Oaxaca. It would be worth publishing it, even though it's not finished."

"I'd like to read it. Do you know who is going to keep his manuscripts?"

"I'm going to ask his mum to let me keep them but, at this moment, I don't want to bother her with those things. Poor woman: she was very proud of Roberto's writing, even though she could not understand his book. She is a street vendor and can hardly read."

They were interrupted by a blond man with Jamaican rasta-style dreadlocks who was collecting signatures for the open letter. Evaristo gave his bogus journalist's name and scrawled an incomprehensible signature among the extensive list of signatories while he continued his chat with Rubén.

"I want to write a report about Lima's death, but I need to know more about his life."

"If you want, I can help you. We'd been friends for donkey's years, so I knew him really well. Come round to my office one of these days and we'll have some coffee. I work at the arts and literature institute."

Fear of Animals

"And, apart from you, who were Lima's best friends?" Evaristo asked after taking note of Estrella's telephone number.

"Daniel Nieto and Pablito Segura, who, by the way, are also around here. Daniel is that very tall guy talking to that chick wearing a blue dress. Did you see him? The one with a hoop earring. Pablito? God knows where he could be. Maybe he went outside to have a spliff in honour of the deceased."

Evaristo laughed at the joke spontaneously: he liked Estrella.

"You're also a writer, aren't you?"

"I try."

"And how did you get to know Lima?"

"At the workshop of Silverio Lanza, an Ecuadorian writer with a fantastic sense of humour who lived here in the Seventies. Roberto and I met up there, then Daniel and Pablo came from high school number 6 and stuck with us. Together we launched a magazine called *The Hangover*."

A middle-aged lady wearing a flowery poncho, who had just arrived at the wake, clung on to Rubén's neck, crying buckets.

"Why did such a thing have to happen to Roberto?"

Evaristo moved away respectfully, waiting for an opportunity to talk to Daniel Nieto, who was still very busy with the chick in the blue dress whom he seemed to be pulling. By mental association, he remembered Dora Elsa and an electric shock made his hair stand on end. What barbaric love. He lit a cigarette and sat before a crucifix, thinking about her. He would have wished to pray to her, to invoke her so she would come and get him out of there. He spent ten minutes or more miles away from the wake, his eyes fixed on the wall, in a long, sentimental lethargy. When he returned to reality, Daniel Nieto had disappeared with his catch. Rubén Estrella too. Evaristo assumed both were downstairs at the cafeteria. He got up with the intention of finding them, but at that moment a bearded guy wearing glasses, whose face looked familiar, arrived at the chapel. When he got closer, Evaristo recognised him with a sudden shock: it was Mario Casillas, the chief of international at *El Matutino*, the one he had threatened in order to obtain Lima's address. He would be lost if Casillas identified him because, for sure, he would blame the crime on him. Faking an outburst of religious fervour, Evaristo turned his back and knelt on a red, velvet-covered pew before the coffin until Casillas had passed him by. Outside, in the corridor of the funeral parlour and mixing with the people attending other wakes, he felt safer, but also guilty, as if in a tangential way he had contributed to Lima's death. Evaristo went down the stairs two steps at a time until he reached the car park and, when he got into his car, tired and gasping, loosened his tie. The glove compartment was open, his papers messed up, and there was a message for him on the windscreen: *Consider yourself dead, you fucking shit federal cop. I know where you live and I have no fear of animals.*

Fear of Animals

Time had frozen inside a caramel bubble in Dora Elsa's bedroom. The childlike freshness of its owner was reflected in the pink wallpaper with golden arabesques, the fake fur rug, her chest of clothes loaded with dolls, teddy bears and Hello Kitty toys. Even for a fifteen year-old, this decor would have been quite affected, but it matched beautifully the temperament of Dora Elsa, who kept the innocence of her childhood intact despite making a living in a sordid environment populated by riffraff, incompatible with tenderness. While he shaved in the bathroom, Evaristo was looking at her in the basin's mirror, thanking God for having found her. 'She could be the woman of my life,' he thought, 'if I get out of this crappy thriller novel alive.' On an exercise mat, naked from the waist down, Dora Elsa boldly tightened up her buttocks in her daily exercise session for learning how to smoke with her cunt.

"Do you think I like working out so fucking hard all morning?" she explained to Evaristo, her face contorted by effort. "I do this because I need to do it. Now the competition is really stiff with all the table dancers. Now the clients do not just pay to see a show. They prefer a young chick of seventeen climbing on them. I am thirty two and I can't compete. I need to do something to attract attention. Do you think they will like the cigarette routine?"

Evaristo came out of the bathroom, shaving cream still on his face, and held Dora Elsa by the chin.

"I don't like you doing those circus numbers." He took the cigarette from between her legs. "I want to get you out of your job and marry you."

"Have you forgotten that I have a daughter?"

"So, what's the problem? I will love her as if she were my own."

"Look, skinny, you don't have to promise me anything," Dora Elsa kissed his hand. "Do you think I care about a filthy piece of paper? I left you my number because I fancy you."

"If it was up to me, I'd marry you tomorrow." Evaristo stroked her hair. "It's just that maybe you'll end up a widow."

"Why?" Dora Elsa looked into his eyes, uncomfortable. "Since yesterday I have noticed that you've been weird – you were even talking in your sleep. Do you have problems with your boss, that Maytorena?"

"With him and a lot of other people too, but just now I can't tell you about it. The less you know about it, the less danger you'll be in."

"Things are that ugly, huh? Tell me what it's about, maybe I can be of some help."

"You are already helping me. You are the main reason I have to live. Do you think that is something small?"

Moved, Dora Elsa kissed him on the lips. Evaristo closed his eyes and tried not to think about anything, but fear was thinking for him, like a second conscience. If Lima's assassin had had the intention of scaring him, he had succeeded, because Evaristo had gone to hide under Dora Elsa's skirts for fear of spending the night in his own flat. And now, instead of getting out there to look for him among the friends of the dead who had attended the wake, he just wanted love and protection, like a baby frightened by thunder in a storm. While Dora Elsa was preparing breakfast and he was getting dressed, he remembered the grotesque feeling of empowerment that he had experienced while interrogating the reporter from *El Universal*. The sadistic compulsion to crush the weak, which he detested so much about the Feds' behaviour, was suddenly revealed to him as an attribute of his own temperament. Or could it be a common defect of the human species? The anonymous note on the windscreen had not been an insult, but an accurate diagnosis. In fact, he was an animal because he had taken advantage of his authority to humiliate a defenceless being, just as he had on the day he indiscriminately attacked the old fellow from the liquor store. But he could not blame this instinct for everything: on both occasions his mind had stayed cool, as if at the moment he had released his aggressiveness he had had an out-of-body experience and observed from above the actions of his savage half. Was that cerebral and complacent bestiality what Lima's killer had discovered about him, like when you recognise a twin brother? Or was the killer so inflated with his own cultural vanity that he had branded him an animal just to emphasise that they were not of the same caste? The anonymous note was proof that the killer belonged to the cultural ghetto in which Lima had mingled, but that gave Evaristo no advantage in the war of nerves he was fighting.

Along with the coffee and *chilaquiles,* Dora Elsa brought *La Jornada* to the table. It had gone three o'clock, but the night before they had come out of Sherry's at five in the morning and so breakfast had turned into lunch. Flicking through the paper, Evaristo found the paid insertion in which Lima's friends demanded that the Human Rights Commission bring clarity to his death: *We, cultural workers and members of civil society, cannot remain with our arms folded in the face of the cowardly assassination of the writer and journalist Roberto Lima, perpetrated by members of a police body as yet unidentified, with the clear intention of silencing an independent and critical voice. We are the first to condemn the visceral rants of our former colleague as chief of the cultural page of* El Matutino, *but if Roberto committed the crime of defamation, the authorities should have proceeded against him legally, and not executed him unawares, with methods that remind us of the Gestapo. With our colleague and friend's death a climate of intolerance and barbarity that we had believed gone has been restored. We demand that those responsible for this outrage against freedom of expression and who seek to intimidate critical journalism as a whole are punished with the full force of the law. Roberto Lima's assassination must be fully investigated for the well-being of the public, for the well-being of the free press and for the well-being of all Mexicans...*

Evaristo had been expecting something along these lines, but was surprised to find Palmira Jackson and the political essayist Wenceslao Medina Chaires, two legendary figures within the democratic and progressive intelligentsia, among the signatories of the paid insert. With their support, the protest could resonate terribly and create a huge problem for Attorney Tapia, who had put his neck in the noose when he had sent Lima's article telling the President to go fuck his mother to Los Pinos. Maybe at that point he had been forced to resign his post. Or would Jiménez del Solar keep him in place?

Anyway, Maytorena and the *Señor* attorney could sort themselves out: Evaristo was not going to risk his life to get them out of trouble. Who was Tapia anyway? An arrogant public official who refused to say hello in the lifts, a doctor of law who did nothing to apply it, a budget scrounger dedicated to embellishing his office with Japanese silk screens and antiques from the vice-royalty while his mob created a state within the state. Fuck Tapia. Evaristo would take the first plane to Los Angeles, and from there he would learn from the newspapers how the case had been solved. For a moment, he forgot about the plate of *chilaquiles* and stayed thinking, recalling the names of some old friends who could give him a job on the other side of the river. He was going to propose to Dora Elsa that she accompany him on this trip when his eyes returned to the newspaper. If the killer was at the wake, camouflaged among the friends of the dead man, surely his signature for the paid insertion had been requested too. It was impossible to distinguish him among the extensive list of names, but Evaristo did not have any doubt that the killer was there, confident of his impunity, spitting up posthumous phlegm over Lima's tomb.

His pride wounded, Evaristo recovered his courage and his vocation of justice: he could not scurry off to Los Angeles and consider the war lost without fighting a little. He needed serenity and valour, to act with a cool head. Dora Elsa had a wireless phone shaped as a red high-heeled shoe. He picked it up and called Rubén Estrella. Evaristo hoped to obtain information about Lima's enemies, but a secretary informed him that Mr Estrella had gone to the convention of writers taking place in Villahermosa and he would not be back until the following Monday. He dialled Chamula's mobile and ordered him to go to the District Attorney's Office to collect the phone book that Fat Zepeda had found in Lima's flat.

"I want you and The Sheep to interrogate all those men listed in the book. Don't beat them or give them a fright. I just want you to look carefully if any of them smoke cigars."

"It will be bloody hard to go to so many places. Why don't we just arrest 'em all and stick them in cold water down in the dungeon?"

"Do you want an even greater fuss? Haven't you seen the paid insert in *La Jornada?*" Chamula remained silent, disconcerted. "Look, Chamula, I don't want to fabricate a culprit, I want to find out the truth. The commander assigned me this task, so we are going to do it, and that's how it's going to be."

"All right, but explain to me: why the fuck do we have to find out who smokes a cigar?"

"Right now I can't explain. Go to Sherry's tonight and bring The Sheep with you, and we three will have a meeting."

Fear of Animals

Evaristo went back to the breakfast table, where the *chilaquiles* had gone cold. He drank the orange juice. He had not yet decided whether to call Fat Zepeda to find out Fabiola Nava's telephone number – with her in the middle, he could not dismiss the possibility of a crime of passion, if there was a third person in the relationship – or whether to go back to Lima's flat looking for clues. He had not yet checked Lima's correspondence and did not even know if he kept a diary, but he would have to examine his papers, with the permission of Lima's family or not. A third possibility, the easiest, was to fester in Dora Elsa's bed and to read Lima's book of short stories in case it had autobiographical clues. Overwhelmed by having to make a decision, he fell into inaction and started to flick through *La Jornada*. In the cultural section he found an advert that jumped from the page: *Prisma Editorial invites you to the launch of the book* The Gifts of Daybreak, *an anthology of poems by Perla Tinoco. The event take place today at 5pm at Casa de la Cultura Reyes Heroles, Francisco Sosa 97.* Within the mist of his mind, as if it had happened many years ago, Evaristo remembered that Lima had slagged her off while drunk, branding her a "mental dwarf" and a "cultural bureaucrat". It looked as if Tinoco had sacked him from his job arbitrarily, the excuse being a dispute he could not remember the cause of. A few lines down he discovered something even more intriguing: her book would be launched by the poets Pablo Segura and Daniel Nieto, two of Lima's best friends that he could not interrogate at Gayosso's. It seemed that among literary people, there was no loyalty. How could they talk so happily with Tinoco if she had been such a bitch with their friend? Curious, he checked the signatures of the open letter to the Human Rights Commission: Perla Tinoco's was in the first row of names, among Palmira Jackson's and the illustrious Medina Chaires's. What cynicism? Evaristo put her first on his list of suspects, but immediately changed his mind: just because she was a hypocrite who begged notoriety was no reason to blame her for the crime. The launch was a fortuitous opportunity to contact her, and also get some information out of Segura and Nieto, who did not inspire trust in him either. He looked at his watch: it was half-four. He took his jacket and went back to the bedroom to say goodbye to Dora Elsa, who had just had a shower and wrapped herself in a towel.

"Goodbye, my beauty, I have to run to Coyoacán. I am going into the enemy's den."

Alarmed, Dora Elsa pulled him against her body and begged him to be careful.

"Don't worry, my love. I'm just going to a book launch. I'll see you tonight at Sherry's."

Dora Elsa lived in Iztacalco on a modest housing estate surrounded by green areas that neighbourhood carelessness had turned into rubbish heaps. He came out of the building in high spirits and felt that he had finally conquered his fear, but when he touched the wheel his hands were sweating, and during the whole trip he did not stop looking in the rearview mirror, thinking he was being followed.

Because of the traffic, he arrived at the launch ten minutes late. The small hall, located on the ground floor of an old colonial mansion, had room enough for 80 people and was almost empty. Grouped in the first row, the sparse attendance seemed to form a closed rank, a proud-to-be-exclusive minority. On first impressions, Evaristo noted the difference with those who had attended Lima's wake. Here the men were wearing denim or corduroy trousers too, but matched them with cashmere jumpers and the most fashionable Italian mackintoshes. What in those attending the wake had been a necessity imposed by their pockets, in this crowd was merely showing off. The women, now freed from any populist temptation, showed up in their best cocktail clothes: short, silken dresses, their best otter fur coats, matching jackets and trouser suits with attractive scarves. Evaristo had not been to a book launch since the Seventies, when the folklorism of the Left imposed an equalising trend across the cultural family, so he felt nostalgic for the raw cotton shirts, the ponchos, the sandals and the bandannas, because at least they blurred class differences. Was this now what you call post-modernity? Fucking great. On the stage, at the centre of a rectangular table covered by a green tablecloth, was Perla Tinoco, her fist under her chin in the pose of a thinking woman that at the same time helped to mask her double chin. He calculated that she was about fifty years old and weighed ninety kilos. The fine features of her bloated face proved that in the old days she had been beautiful. She wore her hair in a coiffed style that was a bit elaborate, played with her pearl necklace nervously, and blushed about the excessive praise she was getting from Daniel Nieto.

"Delicate bird with a refined image that travels from dream to dream, lonely and haughty in its freedom, Perla Tinoco knows that a poet's search consists in forever flying higher, until the shores of the great silence, the darkened mirror of the unnameable, are reached. In her poetic flight, Perla at moments describes risky turnings, at others gently glides like a seagull and delivers verses of the most enchanting simplicity, as in her magnificent series of haikus entitled *Portico*, where the conjunction between lightness and brevity produces a fan of fulgurations. But it is in the lengthy poems that Perla finds her own voice, a renovating and highly personal voice that has no precedent in the Mexican poetry of our century..."

Shrinking into his seat, Evaristo felt that he was being watched and then rejected as a cultural yuppie. A smell of financial stability that clashed with his romanticised idea of literature was in the air. For him, any writer worthy of the name, even more so if a poet, had to be a non conformist and desperate to change the world. The guys he had in front of him seemed to have been fashioned out of different clay: they did not wish to change a thing but to dress up the rot with their precious rhetoric, as if they lived in a cultured country, developed and free, where combative literature would be superfluous. Reluctant clapping for Nieto followed the end of his intervention. Just to fit into the surroundings, Evaristo clapped too, with a bit more enthusiasm than the stiffened toffs in the audience. Pablo Segura, a forty-something blond man with sunken cheeks and John Lennon-style glasses whose hair was beginning to thin, took the microphone. A second round of praise for Perla, now in language inflated with conceptual depth, closer to nuclear physics than to literary criticism.

"Constellation of signs, oxymoronic adventure of high centrifugal power, *The Gifts of Daybreak* sets up a landmark in contemporary Mexican poetry. Explorer of parallellisms as yet unpublished, forever at the edge of semantic-discursive anarchy, Perla Tinoco through this book reaches the plenitude of her style, a style that at the same time is a metalanguage, a radical inquisition of the paradigms of writing in fashion..." The men coughed impatiently, women crossed and uncrossed their legs, and even Perla Tinoco kept drinking glass after glass of water, unshielding her double chin when she swallowed. Undaunted, only Evaristo listened to Pablo Segura's extensive theoretical tripe, fearful that his boredom would denounce him as an intruder. He had taken a notebook to pretend he was a journalist and was pretending to take notes. "If this is culture," he thought, "I'd rather keep reading *The Cowboy's Handbook*." Just when he thought the torment had ended, Segura handed the microphone to Perla.

"Good afternoon, friends. Thank you very much for joining me. Also, thanks to Pablo and Daniel for their interest in my work, which gives me more of a commitment to write better. You are the immense minority who keep poetry alive in a world that has lost its ability to dream. I owe myself to you and it is for you all that I write. When I was a little girl I was told that words were blown away by the wind. I grew up among books and when I reached adolescence I discovered that I was made of words. Then, fearing being blown away by a gust, I wrote my first ever poems, which I titled 'Songs to stop the wind'. Now I know that every poem is a line in the water, a vain artifice of careful work, as Sor Juana said. Nonetheless, by habit, tenacity or vice, I have remained loyal to a vocation that for me is as indispensable as bread or salt..."

Following that, Tinoco read a selection of her poetic works, starting with the haikus in *Portico*. Every one of them had six or seven epigraphs by many other poets (Elliot, Rimbaud, Kavafis, Ungaretti, Novalis) Perla quoted in their original languages with impeccable pronunciation, as the prelude to her own evanescent spark of inspiration:

Under the loquat's shade
My soul is a bird
rocked by the foliage.

"So much farting for such runny crap," thought Evaristo, who by now had filled up the notebook with scribbles and was drawing a sow with Perla's face. "Chamula is right: it would be best to put all these bastards in solitary confinement so they can read this fucking shit there in the cells." Still, the most emotional part of the recital was yet to come, when Perla read in a crumbling voice an 'Elegy for my mother's death' which, by her own admission, was "written with blood and tears". Evaristo was happy to learn that it incorporated only four epigraphs, two of which were written in Old Bulgarian. The elegy lasted almost ten minutes, and there was a moment at which Tinoco almost burst into tears. When the reading ended, Evaristo gave her a standing ovation to start ingratiating himself.

Fear of Animals

"Once more I would like to thank you for your company and now I would like to invite you to the end of the hall, where Prisma editorial will offer you cocktails and some nibbles."

Anxious because he did not know anyone there and had to drink on his own while everyone else was talking in groups, Evaristo felt that his solitude was a stigma, a brightly coloured carnival costume. To engage himself in something, he bought a copy of *The Gifts of Daybreak* from a stall that had been improvised at the entrance of the hall. The book gave him a pretext for infiltrating the ring of people surrounding the writer.

"Professor Tinoco, would you be so kind as to give me your autograph?" Evaristo handed her the book with a gaze of veneration. "My name is Luciano Contreras, I am a literary critic, and I deeply admire your poetry. I never imagined that you could be so young."

"Thank you, you are so kind." Tinoco granted him a brief dedication while smiling at him condescendingly. "Your name sounds familiar. Do you write for *Novedades weekly*?"

"No, for *El Matutino*."

"The newspaper for which that boy who was killed used to write?"

"His name was Roberto Lima. Did you know him?"

"Of course I did. We worked together at the Simón Bolívar University. We didn't become friends, but I appreciated him quite a bit, as a person and as a writer."

"He also used to speak highly of you," Evaristo said ironically. "Before he died, he asked me to interview you."

"Really?" Perla arched her eyebrows suspiciously. "Well, right now I can't, because I have to attend to my guests, but call my office and we can arrange something. I am going to give you my number..."

From her business card, Evaristo learned that Perla had the position of sub-director of the National Committee for the Promotion of Culture, Conafoc, Mexico's most fashionable cultural institution that co-ordinated all the other state cultural organisations, with a multi-million peso budget. Alone again, but with the psychological support of a highball, he started flicking through Tinoco's book and, on page 34, discovered an exuberance with "h" in the middle that reminded him of Lima's anger about her. Bloody cow. So much Old Bulgarian but she couldn't even write in Spanish. His regard for Lima was reaffirmed as he considered him a victim of that little *snobbish* world, inhabited only by arrivistes of the likes of Daniel Nieto and Pablo Segura, who chatted animatedly with a very tall and distinguished-looking young man wearing a silken scarf and a tweed jacket (surely a banker and a poet, he inferred) without abandoning the table where the drinks were being served. Their friendship with Tinoco was an affront to Lima's memory, but Evaristo was there for biographical information, not to give them a homily about loyalty. When Mr Million Moneybanks with the silken scarf went into mute mode and left the room, Daniel and Pablo remained nibbling next to the table. Evaristo gulped down his highball to approach them.

"Good evening. Excuse me if I'm disturbing you, but I would like to speak to you. My name is Luciano Contreras and I'm writing an article about Roberto Lima's death."

"Good for you." Segura shook Evaristo's hand. "Someone has to investigate this crime, to press the police."

"Yesterday I had a word with Rubén Estrella, who told me you were really good friends with Lima."

"Friends, we weren't just friends, we were as close as muck to the nail," Nieto corrected him. "Tell him, Pablo, about that time when we went to Acapulco without a penny and ended up sleeping on Caleta beach with a pack of dogs on top of us."

"Roberto was a hell of a guy, a free spirit who was not afraid of anything." Segura stared into space in consternation. "He lived at the sharp end because he never compromised with the moral misery of this world, neither as a writer nor as a person. I cared for him a lot. The news of his death was a really hard blow for me. Why did he have to have such a fate, for fuck's sake?"

At the start, his comments had the rehearsed air of those condolences that you spell out on the telephone to reporters, but as the drink trays went by, they became overcome by emotion and sincerity. Nieto remembered with amazement the intellectual discipline of Lima who, at the age of 21, had read the whole of Tolstoy, Borges, Flaubert, the Mexican poets of the *Contemporáneos* group, the entire Latin American *boom* and even the whole of Casiodoro de Reina's version of the Bible. Segura interrupted to evoke the passion which Lima had in defending his literary choices, the way he did not sit on the fence: there was only black or white, genius or trash. His radicalism and integrity had prematurely marginalised him from the literary establishment, where any intemperance was viewed with disapproving eyes. Because he struggled so much against the faked values of the circle, he became a wolf of the steppes, loathed but respected, whom nobody invited to a cocktail party because at the first opportunity he would tell the host the naked truth, putting him on the spot in front of the whole world.

Hearing them speak with such warmth about their absent friend, without the rigid expression which the literary authorities wore on stage, Evaristo grew more confident and interrogated them about Lima's life over the past few months. Did they know of anyone who wished to kill him? Did he have problems with any family members or with his lover? Did he owe any money? Which places did he frequent? Neither thought that Lima's enemies had anything to do with the literary circle.

"We literary people could hate each other to death," said Nieto, "but we never kill each other because we would lose our main means of entertainment. You'd better go and investigate the Federal Judicial Police, which is where the order came from. They are the ones who did it, but no one will ever get to know the truth."

Segura expressed the opinion that, deep down, Lima had had a death wish. In fact, Lima had already confessed that to him a few weeks before the crime, when they had ended up at Garibaldi square after having initiated a long drinking session hours before at a cantina. "Poor me," he had sung to the mariachi band, "it is best for this life to end", and because of his pride as a man he did not say what the reason for his sorrow was Segura attributed this to cheating by Fabiola Nava, the last of Lima's lovers, who ended up being a really bad card to bet on.

"What did she do to him?" asked Evaristo. "Did she dump him for another bloke?"

"Why don't you ask her that yourself, if she grants you an interview? I don't know who killed Roberto physically, but she really crushed his soul. And on top of that she even had the nerve to go to the wake. My wife wanted to drag her out by the hair."

Segura was interrupted by a couple saying goodbye, and Nieto took the opportunity to call the waiter who, from a distance pointed at an empty tray.

"How come there's no more whisky?" The waiter shrugged his shoulders. "It's always the same with this bloody publisher. They only tease us."

The cocktail party had ended before it had even started. Very few remained in the hall, the waiters were beginning to pick up the glasses and even Perla Tinoco was leaving, escorted by a group of friends. Evaristo pricked his ears and managed to hear some of their chatter. They wanted Perla to choose where they would be going for dinner. Was *Tajín* okay or would she prefer the new *nouvelle cuisine* restaurant that had just opened in Polanco?

Daniel and Pablo looked sadly at the bottom of their glasses. Intrigued by the betrayal of Fabiola, who could have been the key to solving the crime, Evaristo proposed they go for a drink elsewhere. Their quick and enthusiastic acceptance dissipated his suspicions: it was evident that they did not belong to Tinoco's clique of the crème de la crème, but to the democratic circle of bohemia where class differences and intellectual rank disappeared with a bottle. In Plaza Santa Catarina each got their cars and Nieto suggested they went to the Trocadero, a bar in San Angel whose "regular clientele were some of the best pieces of arse in Mexico".

As Evaristo feared, the place ended up being a warehouse of dissatisfied vanities where *chic* people went to be seen, not to drink. In an old house adapted as a luxury cantina, with hand-cut crystal chandeliers, dwarf marble tables and original artworks for sale, there congregated a marginal, but well-heeled clientele of theatre actresses, set designers, writers of easy inspiration who poured their genius out on serviettes, film critics, creators of performance and well-off chicks who went there to rub shoulders with famous people, despite the fact that famous people, according to what Nieto had told him as they waited for a table, never showed up in that place, but only a few of Octavio Paz's 'aristocats', who landed there from time to time. They all dressed with knowledgeable informality, as if they had spent a few hours choosing their kits. They asked for a round of highballs and Evaristo told them straight.

"You guys left me curious about Fabiola. What did she do to Lima?"

"Let's talk about something else," stopped Nieto. "I don't want to catch herpes on my tongue."

"But I really need to know..."

"Daniel is right. There are some things which it's better not to talk about in a place like this, where anyone could be listening. Just be happy in the knowledge that she betrayed him, and not with any old guy, but with his worst enemy."

"Who's that?"

Fear of Animals

"His name is not going to mean anything to you and, if we tell you who it is, we'll get into terrible trouble. What if you decide to print our names in your report? We don't even know who you are."

"But this is confidential. I swear I'm not going to print anything you tell me."

"Please don't insist." Nieto took his interest as a joke. "We're gonna think you're a detective."

"I have to be one if I want to write an article worth appearing in print."

"Then go investigate the Feds." Segura lost his patience. "They were the ones who killed him."

"I have my doubts. I don't think Lima's rants in *El Matutino* posed any danger to the system. Lima did not have a readership, and his voice did not have any weight in public opinion. Did any of you ever read the articles he published in the cultural section?"

"We loved him, but not that much," admitted Nieto.

"You see those big shits in government may be corrupt, but they are not stupid. Why kill a helpless loony? Manuel Buendía wrote the political column with the largest readership in the whole of Mexico, and with proof in his hands he denounced people at the very top. *He* was really a threat to power. Lima just lashed out wildly, without really afftecting anyone's interests."

"But if the government didn't kill him, who did?" asked Segura.

"I don't really know, but among writers there are very strong rivalries. I have not yet discarded as suspects some in the literary circle..."

"You think one of us whacked him with the book, don't you?" joked Segura.

"You were his friends, but many people didn't like him. I have been investigating and I know he had some enemies, Perla Tinoco among them."

"Man, are you suspicious of her? Perla Tinoco is incapable of killing a fly," Nieto assured him. "Her only crime is writing bad poetry."

"'Tubboco' did have an argument with Roberto about ten years ago, but the row didn't go any further," recalled Segura. "I think he called her ignorant and she sacked him from a job. That's how the sow behaves. She can't stand being told the truth."

"And I thought you admired her."

"I do admire her," interjected Nieto. "I admire her because, being the corniest, coarsest and most illiterate of poets in Mexico, she has crept up with an incredible ability to get where she is."

"But a while ago at the launch you said she was wonderful," Evaristo pointed out.

"And what did you want me to say? Yes, Miss Piggy is the vice-queen of Conafuck. Everything goes through her office: she gives grants, prices, editions, trips abroad, and she has a lot of bad blood when she feels offended. Watch it if you are on her blacklist, because you're fucked for the rest of the six-year term. I'm not a hero like Roberto, I love the money and, if she believes she is Sor Juana reborn with a few extra kilos, what do I lose playing along?"

"Sometimes you must be a liar for the sake of diplomacy," explained Segura. "Tubboco did invite us to the launch of her book. What did you want? That we shredded it before her mates? That would have been fucking awful. She knows that we did her a favour and sooner or later she'll have to pay us back. This is the way it works: I scratch your back today, you scratch mine tomorrow."

"Well, I lapped it all up," Evaristo lied. "I thought she really was a pro."

"This is because you don't know how critics work in Mexico," intervened Nieto, lecturing. "What is said in public doesn't count. They are only rules of etiquette. It is in chats over coffee or friends' parties where we tell the naked truth, but only when whoever is being criticised is absent. This is what Roberto never understood. He wanted to tell the truth in newspapers or to shout it to their faces, so this is why writers and others in the circle dreaded him."

"Poor bastard," continued Segura. "His life became bitter because he was stubborn. I can't count the number of times I told him: Roberto, come on, understand. What do you get by throwing blows left, right and centre? Take advantage of those idiots instead of fighting them. But he considered our little literary world a tragedy, which really is enough to make you die with laughter. He was a character out of Tolstoy, obsessed with the truth and righteousness, in a picaresque novel full of crooks, liars, arselickers and whores."

Evaristo took a look at the clock, worried. He had an appointment with Chamula at Sherry's and this conversation was moving down a path that could lead to many places, but not to that of Fabiola Nava's betrayal. He had fallen out of Nieto and Segura's grace again and he feared that, when he turned round to go to the toilet, they were going to give him Perla Tinoco's treatment. And even though neither smoked cigars, he wrote them down on his list of suspects, under the hypocrites label. To say the least, the ambience of the bar exacerbated his complexes no end. The vulgarity of his jacket did not match the sophistication of everyone else around him. The greatest failure of his life had been not to be a writer, and his clothes exposed him to the four corners of the earth, to the joy of the clientele, whom without a doubt were laughing at him under their breath. How dare you come here, they seemed to tell him with their gazes, if you are a nobody in the cultural world?"

"Gosh, what a pity." Evaristo stood up suddenly. "I have to write a story for my newspaper. You must forgive me, but if I don't hand it in before 12, my boss is gonna kill me…"

"That's not allowed," protested Nieto, dragging his "s". "First you bring us here, and then you cut us off here."

"Please forgive me, I completely forgot I had to work."

"Gee, you're evil. Just drink a last one, man, and if your boss gets cross I'll get you a job in some supplement," proposed Segura. "What do you want to do? Interviews, reviews, columns?"

Evaristo promised to consider his offer, but he did not want to stay for "the last one", despite their objections. They exchanged telephone numbers and arranged to meet again to continue their talk about Lima when the first part of the reportage was published. He was going to pay their bill but, when he got his wallet out, he remembered that he was assuming a false identity and limited himself to paying in cash for what he had drunk: Luciano Contreras was a penniless journalist and could not afford to waste his money inviting people as if he were a millionaire. Outside, freed from the psychological pressure imposed by the place, he took a big swig from his bottle of Old Parr, looked at himself in the rearview mirror and examined his feelings, thinking aloud: "I have not written anything, you bastards, but I'm the boss man."

When he arrived at Sherry's, his second home, he enjoyed the confident treatment of Efrén, the waiters' jokes and the smile of Rosita the cigar seller as never before. Pleased, he shook hands with the little old whores sitting at the darkest tables where they could disguise their flabby flesh better and, from a distance, he blew a kiss at Dora Elsa, who was sipping champagne as she sat on some Texan-jacketed fat bloke, who looked like a rural tyrant. As Evaristo had guessed,

Chamula and The Sheep were waiting for him at the table nearest the "bottydrome" – the aisle where the table dancers circulated naked – with the usual bottle of Napoleon cognac. Bottled up in a drunken argument, they didn't even notice when Evaristo arrived.

"You're not going to say that in front of me, you bastard. The commander is my friend and you have to respect him," Chamula shouted furiously.

"I say what I fucking well like," insisted The Sheep. "Maytorena is a son of a bitch and you are a poof who bows down before him."

"You're the queer, because you say this behind his back," Chamula stood up, pushing the table away. "Go shout in his face what you are saying to me, and then we'll see if you're such a macho man."

"Will you bastards stop!?" intervened Evaristo, splitting them up. "With all this shouting you're going to scare the people here. What's buggin' you?"

"This big mouth, who feels so fucking great, is slandering the commander," Chamula said.

"Let's get Evaristo to say who's right here." The Sheep turned towards him, appealing to him as to a judge. "Yesterday we were going to raid a warehouse in Agricola Oriental, where supposedly some Hondurans were hiding coke. When they saw us they came from inside carrying their machine guns, and bloody Maytorena shouted: 'Go on, you idiots, hit them hard'. But instead of joining in the shooting, the cunt stayed hiding behind the Suburban. And this bastard is even angry with me because I speak badly about his bloody boss."

"Maytorena rescued you from poverty," shouted Chamula. "If it wasn't for him, you'd be selling chewing gum at traffic lights."

"I'm as exploited as you are. Don't be such a fucking idiot, Chamula. How much has he earned since you started working for him?"

"For me, *Señor* is like a father, you bastard, and if you don't shut up, I'll shut you up with lead."

"Do you really have such loyalty to that queer? Just because he gave you a house with a leaking roof and a wheelchair for your mum? You're worth very little, bro. What about the mistreatment? And the daily humiliation?"

"Enough!" Evaristo shut them up. "Later you can go and smash in each other's faces outside, but while you are here you have to stay calm."

Fear of Animals

"I'm calm." Chamula went back to his chair. "The one who's provoking me is him, with his lies."

"Lies? Are you going to deny that Maytorena hid during the shooting? Gee, he sends you to your death and you still defend him. So much love stinks. I think you also give it to him, like all of his girlfriends."

"That's it!" exploded Chamula, throwing a glass at The Sheep, who leaned backwards to duck and fell to the ground, chair and all.

The Sheep went to pull the gun out of his holster, but Chamula pulled his own out first and shot him point blank. Everything happened in a matter of seconds. By the time Evaristo had tried to intervene, The Sheep was lying in agony on the floor, with two bullets in his stomach and one in his forehead. When the orchestra heard the shots they stopped playing, the table dancers jumped behind the "bottydrome" and the clients went under the tables. Efrén tried to shut the door on Chamula, but he hit him on the forehead with the butt of his gun and ran into the street. Even though The Sheep was by now stiff and blue, Evaristo called the ambulance and removed his Fed's shield to avoid a possible news story. Along with the ambulance came two uniformed policemen. They wanted to detain all the waiters, the clients, the call-girls with the best bodies and even a blind man who worked in the bathroom and asked to be tipped. Evaristo had to threaten calling the attorney to free those detained. At Cuauhtémoc police station, where statements were taken, Evaristo arranged a bribe under the table to the public prosecutor, an old acquaintance of his and an accomplice of Maytorena in a thousand deals, to present the incident as an argument between drunkards that had taken place outside Sherry's and ignore that the victim was a Fed. In that way, he avoided the possibility of the den of iniquity being closed, paying back at the very least all the favours he had enjoyed over the last 15 years.

At four o'clock, exhausted, Evaristo arrived at his flat without Dora Elsa, who had left for a hotel with the fat bloke in the Texan jacket. He had started to get used to her body heat and, when he turned off the lights, his bed seemed enormous.

An unstoppable flood of reflections kept him awake until daybreak. The Sheep's incredulous gaze when Evaristo removed his ID from his jacket had created a terrible impression. He had looked surprised that Chamula could have taken a joke so seriously. Nonetheless, he found the betrayal and murder that he had witnessed minutes before at the Trocadero bar, when Segura and Nieto had stabbed their friend Perla Tinoco in the back after having praised her in public, even more repugnant. As a killer, Chamula was indefensible, but he could give those two literati living in a world of words who had degraded the language until they had stripped it of any moral integrity a lesson in loyalty. How many writers had been the victims of their fraudulent rhetoric? The Sheep was dead because he said what he thought and Chamula had killed him because he dared to say it, following a code of honour incomprehensible to Nieto and Segura, who in matters of nobility and manliness were far below any gunman. To a certain extent, their conduct explained the anonymous note on the windscreen: if Lima's assassin was a writer, Evaristo could not expect him to open his cape and play a clean game.

Fear of Animals

"How's it going Evaristo? This is Fat Zepeda, just to ask you if you have read my book. Forgive me for insisting, but your opinion matters a lot to me. I'm going to be here at the office the whole day. Please call me to see if we can have lunch together."

"Good morning, I have a message for Luciano Contreras on behalf of Professor Rubén Estrella, from the Institute of Arts and Literature. The professor says that he is now back from Villahermosa and will be in his office this morning, in case you wish to see him. The address is Avenida Revolución 1137, fifth floor, close to Museo del Carmen."

"Good morning, Evaristo, sorry... Luciano, I forgot that you have two names. Someone told me that yesterday you were at the Trocadero bar, sticking your nose where you should not. Who do you think you are? An ape like you cannot and should not attend such places reserved only for cultured people. Or are you going to tell me that Jünger is read by the Feds? If I were you I would tread carefully in case something bad happens to your Sherry's sweetheart if you keep asking questions."

With his stomach turned inside out, Evaristo pressed the *Save* button and listened again to the threat from the hunted hunter, whose horse always seemed to have an advantage over his own. Was it one of the blokes sitting at the bar? Nieto or Segura? If it wasn't any of them, how could he have been followed so closely?

He rewound the tape twice to study the message. The nasal voice, surely distorted with a handkerchief, did not give him any clues. Nor did the background noises, the typical motor vroooming in the background could be heard from any public telephone. His lowering blood pressure forced him to take a seat. He wasn't the only one in danger now. Dora Elsa was too and, if something bad happened to her, he would never forgive himself. What did he care about Lima anyway? He had let himself be dragged in by a sentimental outburst, naively believing that both were joined by a common cause, a supposed affinity between twinned souls. From this error derived all the difficulties and risks that he now had to sort out with his fading, alcoholic nerves.

He was a failure as a detective and he did not need to be shot in the temple to confirm that. Why was he waiting to run away to Los Angeles?

Fearing that his spy may have been watching with a telescope from the building opposite, he got up to shut the window facing Rio Mississippi. Dressing himself with the first things he found in the closet, he went to have breakfast at the Sanborns in the María Isabel Hotel. He bought *Proceso* at the book section, which was heaving with queens on the prowl dressed in shorts, with the excuse of being interested in reading. He started flicking through the pages while on the toilet, as he evacuated a nervous colic. As he feared, the magazine gave ample space to the murder: JOURNALIST ROBERTO LIMA'S DEATH ATTRIBUTED TO A FED, said the headline above the report, which was illustrated with an artist's impression of the suspected murderer, *according to the description of Mario Casillas, who hours before the crime had been intimidated by a subject who introduced himself as a federal agent and abusively demanded from him Lima's address while at his office in* El Matutino. Fortunately, the pencil sketch was so rough that a million Mexicans could well be in danger of being arrested. The report included fragments of various articles in which Lima had insulted President Jiménez del Solar and highlighted the existence of a mysterious informant who had called *El Universal*'s newsdesk the night before the crime: *Presumably this could be a witness present during the homicide, who was concealing his identity for fear of reprisals.* Palmira Jackson's declaration, highlighted in a box at the side, attributed the crime to the President: "*Adding this to the tally, 36 journalists have now been murdered so far during the term of the current presidential administration. How many more should fall before the government puts a stop to this impunity? Every year, the President toasts the press to celebrate the Freedom of Expression Day, but in Mexico censorship exists and is exercised with gunshots. It is terrible to write while there is the threat, hidden in the shadows, somewhere, that you are being watched by a murderer, the holder of a police shield.*" More than being a writer, Jackson was a figure with moral authority. Since her serial reports about the repression

Fear of Animals

of the railway workers, she had turned into Mexico's conscience. All the rebels, all victims of political abuse or natural disasters counted on her unconditional support. She was the defender of the poor, to whom she gave her pen and trust against the powerful. Evaristo had read her since his teens, professed an unlimited admiration for her and could not take her accusations lightly. He had no blood on his hands and had even wanted to save Lima but, to the public jury, convened by the magazine, where Casillas played the role of prosecutor, Evaristo personified the sinister "murderer, holder of a police shield" who threatened independent journalists. Guilty on paper, Evaristo felt embarrassed and hurt, almost guilty in reality, because, to a venerable institution such as Palmira Jackson, he was now a suspect.

The report acted as a moral purge making him abort his idea of leaving for Los Angeles. Back home, he decided to clear his name, looked for Fabiola Nava's number in Lima's phone book and called her. After several rings, the maid answered.

"She has just gone out, who is calling?"

He suspected that Fabiola was pretending not to be there. Evaristo gave his false name and his mobile number, without any hope of obtaining an appointment. Something was clear, though: beautiful Fabiola had left a trail behind her – there was a reason why she did not want to see him. With his head full of novelistic guesswork, he listened again to Rubén Estrella's message and noted down his office address. For his mental health, he did not want to listen to the enemy's message again. It was evident that whoever it was, they had wanted to demoralise him, make him lose his head, although his animosity suggested he was also feeling threatened, which was a good sign, because it meant that the killer was nervous. This time Evaristo did not fear going into the streets but, on the way towards the Institute of Arts and Literature, he took the precaution of calling Dora Elsa on his mobile to warn her to get out of the house if necessary and to carry her tiny .22 in her handbag.

"Why so many precautions? Is anything bad happening, love?"

"I'll tell you later, but for the moment just do as I say. And something else, my doll: watch out for Sherry's clients. Don't go to a room with any of them who talk to you about books or if they look like a writer."

When he got into the institute's building – a 28-storey tower with four lifts and a palatial mezzanine where you had to show an ID to enter – Evaristo was surprised that a country as poor as Mexico could have such cultural elephants. He calculated that two thousand people worked there. Doing what? When he got out of the lift on the fifth floor he was surprised by the secretaries' tasty rumps, unusually luxurious for a public office, which gave him the impression of budget frivolity and largesse. What did not surprise him, for the working environment was similar to that of the Attorney General's office, was the lack of haste among the employees, who were gathered in happy circles where they drank coffee and ate biscuits. The only difference, really, was that the bureaucrats in his office read sports papers and those of the institute, more leisurely in their politicisation, devoured *La Jornada* or *Proceso* with grave and concentrated expressions, stealing the time of that oppressive state which paid them for warming their seats. Rubén Estrella waved at him, calling from his cubicle. He was the only employee in the surrounding hundred metres actually working.

"Please, sit down. I'll just finish correcting these proofs and we'll chat."

He was wearing a flowery waistcoat, the latest Pink Floyd tour T-shirt and very dirty white trainers. On his right arm, close to the shoulder, a turquoise mandala tattoo gave away Estrella's orientalist readings. The sunlight shining on his face made him appear older and, as a result, his youthful attire seemed even more anachronistic. Evaristo respected Estrella from their encounter at Gayosso and felt he could trust him. It was evident that he had come from below and had managed to integrate, with difficulty, within a very elitist circle. They belonged to the same generation, their humble origins making them almost brothers, but between both existed an insurmountable moral barrier that discouraged Evaristo from revealing his real identity: if Estrella thought the same way as he dressed, if he kept his Sixties-generation ideals, he would never trust an agent from the Fed.

"Now I'm done. Forgive me, but on Mondays I have to put the edition to bed. Do you know the institute's magazine?" Estrella showed him some proof copies. "I don't know why they want to print this fucking shit, if nobody reads it. We print forty thousand copies, but 90 per cent of the editions stay in the warehouse."

Evaristo wanted to break the ice before getting to the point.

"How was the writers' congress in Villahermosa?"

"Fucking awful. You don't know how hard it is to co-exist for

Fear of Animals

three days with so many big-headed people. Your liver ends up being turned into a puree. You either turn into a hypocrite and get right into the exchange of false praises or end up being seen as an annoyance. I just got there, read my paper and the following day went to Palenque. I was lucky there weren't many tourists, so I had a little spliff at the Templo de las Inscripciones with the whole of the jungle stretched out before me. When I came down I thwacked myself on the stairs, but the trip was fucking marvellous."

"Well I wanted to talk to you about Roberto…"

"How is your report going? The Feds are stonewalling this investigation. They want time to fly and for everyone to forget the subject, but this time they're fucked. Have you seen *Proceso*? They published an artist's impression of the guy who murdered him."

"I don't think he killed him."

"So then, who? Do you suspect someone?"

"Not yet, but I'm on the trail. Last Friday I had some drinks with Daniel Nieto and Pablo Segura. They told me that Fabiola Nava, the last of Lima's lovers, left him for his worst enemy."

"You are fucking me! Do you think it was her?"

"I don't know, but I want to end my doubts. This is why I came to see you. How did they break up?"

Estrella nodded.

"Roberto was very reserved when it came to his women. He would never confide in anyone, not even when he was pissed. I saw Fabiola only a couple of times, at book launches. I know she is a actress in children's theatre and Roberto met her during his short story workshop, but I hardly exchanged a word with her. When they broke up Roberto was really depressed. He looked so bad that I never asked him about it."

"Do you know who the guy was who stole her? Segura and Nieto said it was a very powerful public official."

"His name is Claudio Vilchis and he is second in command at the Fund for the Promotion of Reading. I don't know what Fabiola saw in him – his wallet probably – because he's a really ugly bastard."

Evaristo remembered what Lima had told him in his rant.

"Did Lima have a fight with him because of Fabiola?"

"Yes, there was a bad argument, but I don't know if I should tell you about it." Estrella, apprehensive and doubtful, spun his pencil on the table.

"You can talk in all confidence. In my report I will not mention any sources."

"Okay, but I'm warning you that if you mention my name I'll deny everything. I don't want any trouble with Vilchis. He is a very vengeful guy and he could have me sacked tomorrow if he wanted to... The argument was at a cocktail party at the Manuel M. Ponce hall, when Bioy Casares came to Mexico. When the conference was over, Vilchis and Roberto bumped into each other in the toilets at Bellas Artes palace. God knows what they said to each other but, the thing is, they punched each other. If we hadn't come and separated them I'm sure Roberto would have killed him. He broke Vilchis' nose and, when I got to the toilets, he was drowning him in the bowl. Fabiola almost fainted from fright. She walked the corridors feeling very sorry for herself, asking if there was a doctor to cure her latest dick. I felt like grabbing her and telling her: have you seen what you are provoking, fucking whore?"

"How long ago was this?"

"About two months."

"And don't you think Vilchis could have avenged this beating by killing Lima?"

"I don't think so. To kill you need certain greatness of spirit, which Vilchis has never had, neither as a writer nor as a person. Rats like him don't kill face to face: they kill you from a distance, by just signing a memo."

"I understand that Lima had already had an argument with him, when he worked at the Fund..."

"I can see that you are well informed." Estrella looked at him suspiciously and Evaristo asked himself if he had put his foot in it by showing his cards too soon.

"Vilchis sacked him because Roberto had hit him heavily in a review. With his sacred air he could not stand someone putting him in his place."

"And is he really feared?"

"In his little mafia he is. Beyond that, nobody listens to him. He is the typical exquisite Mexican literate, really highbrow, regarding himself as a classic in his own lifetime, his prose so considered that it gave him airs, and he just writes about authors who are unknown in Mexico, to dazzle the rabble. In his essays you will never find an original idea, even if you look at them with a magnifying glass."

Fear of Animals

"If he is so crap, how come he is where he is?"

"Because of his friends. Politicians do not know who's who in the world of culture and let themselves be guided by appearances. Vilchis has made them believe that he is a prestigious intellectual because he always hangs from the arms of international figures when they visit Mexico. Without the sparkle of others, he simply does not exist. At our magazine's newsdesk we have gathered a huge archive of photos of writers and artists. The other day I was looking for one of Vilchis and I could not find one where he was on his own. Instead we have several where he appears with Harold Pinter, García Márquez, Vaclav Havel, straining his neck to be in the picture. That will give you an idea of who he is."

"What I cannot understand is how Fabiola could be with Lima and then with Vilchis, who are like oil and water."

"That is also what I'd like to know. Why don't you ask her? At the wake she looked terribly sad. They say she is now repentant for having left Roberto. If you can catch her at a good moment, she may tell you."

Evaristo was going to answer that Fabiola was hiding from him when his mobile rang, and he even imagined he saw a mocking grimace on Estrella's lips. Second consecutive mistake: Luciano Contreras earned a pittance, so he could not afford a mobile phone. Why hadn't he left it in the car? To make matters worse, the call was Maytorena's.

"What's going on with you, bloody intellectual? You've spent four days being stupid, doing nothing."

"Of course I haven't, boss. I'm making a lot of progress." Evaristo made a "wait a moment" sign to Rubén Estrella. "I have some information that you may find useful…"

"I don't want information, I want Lima's assassin. Have you seen *Proceso*? They are blaming you, imbecile. This morning the attorney asked me to look for the pratt in the artist's impression."

"I just need a couple of days to finish the investigation. I have discovered things that are really going to interest you."

"You better have, because the noose is round our necks. Both of us can pay a very high price for this. Tonight I'll wait for you at La Concordia to find out how you are progressing."

"Of course, boss, I'll be there."

"Don't hang up yet. Chamula wants to send you a message: thank you very much for the favour you did him at Sherry's."

"It's nothing really, that's what friends are for." Evaristo turned off his mobile and faced Estrella with an apologetic smile. "It was my boss. He saw the article in *Proceso* and is now pressing me to deliver the report. That's the bad thing about carrying this thing, you get pestered everywhere."

"You must pay a lot for the rental, do you?" Evaristo perceived a twinkle of envy in Estrella's eyes.

"I don't know, the paper pays for it." He cleared his throat. "What were we talking about?"

Estrella returned to the issue of Claudio Vilchis, but limited himself to insulting him with greater bravery but without giving new information about his enmities with Lima. Evaristo had been rattled by the call and felt he was wasting time.

"I think it's time for me to go," he interrupted. "I have to dash to a press conference at the anthropological museum. Thanks for the Vilchis tip."

"If you want, I'll tell you how the arselicker's career started when he was studying at the faculty," offered Estrella, enjoying the slaughter.

"I'd really love you to, but right now I can't, thanks. We'll go for a coffee to talk more calmly another day."

In the street, at the wheel of his overheated Spirit that burnt like a ring of fire, he dialled Chamula's mobile and asked him if Fabiola Nava's address was in Lima's notebook. He was in luck. The enigmatic beauty was at the top of the "N" page: she lived in Atlixco 163, flat 601, Colonia Condesa. To settle his account with Maytorena he needed something more concrete than a simple suspicion and she was his best card for not turning up at the appointment empty-handed. Without yet being clear about how to approach her, he went by the fast route of Patriotismo towards the north. Half an hour later, having proved that Fabiola was not at home, he stood guard at her building, a luxurious condominium with flowerpots on the balconies. He waited for more than an hour listening to Radio Capital broadcasting the Doors hour. It was weird, his taste for rock had been rekindled since he had become a man of his own. He was listening to 'L.A. Woman', remembering his glorious times as "funky guy", when he saw her in the rearview mirror, lean and golden like a model from the adverts, getting out of a Volkswagen driven by a female friend who had given her a lift. She was the Angelian Venus from the Doors' song, transplanted to Tenochtitlán. Rejuvenated by her arrival, he got out of the car with the impetus of someone on the prowl.

Fear of Animals

"Good afternoon. We met at Roberto Lima's wake. Do you remember me?"

"Mexico City Woman" removed her black shades and examined him from tip to toe without enthusiasm.

"I don't recall you. What's your name?"

"Luciano Reyes, at your service."

"Ah, are you the reporter who called this morning?" Fabiola gave a grimace of annoyance. "Well, I don't want to give interviews, even less about Roberto."

"Think about this. It would be a good opportunity to defend yourself against the rumours."

"What rumours?"

"It has been said that Lima's assassination was a crime of passion."

"They can say whatever they want." Fabiola went pale. "I'm not going to waste my time putting gossip right."

"What does it cost to answer a few little questions?"

"I'm very tired, don't insist."

Fabiola took her keys out of her bag and opened the condominium door. Evaristo stuck his foot in to stop her slamming it.

"You loved him quite a lot, didn't you?"

"Don't stick your nose into what is not your business." Fabiola pushed the door, furious.

"I'm investigating who killed him. I thought you would be interested in knowing the truth." Evaristo managed to get his arm between the frame and the door.

"I know the truth. He was killed because of his articles."

"His articles were harmless. Did you read them?" Fabiola denied doing so, shaking her head shyly. "What did the government win by killing a nutter who was not even read by his girlfriend? Lima did not pose a danger to those in power. The real motive for this crime is something else. Help me discover it."

Still disgusted, but with a shade of doubt in her face, Fabiola softened and allowed him to get to the landing.

"All right, but don't ask too many questions. At five I have my bodily expression lesson."

In the lift, Evaristo became nervous about his proximity to Fabiola, who was wearing a very flimsy top and no bra underneath. The amber tone of her skin was an invitation for a vampire's bite on the neck. She had pert breasts, long and shapely legs, defiant lips and a burning gaze that perforated your soul. Evaristo asked himself why she took bodily expression lessons, if her body spoke in fourteen languages and in all of them said the same: "Take me".

"Sorry about the mess," she apologised when they entered the flat. "Help yourself to a drink, please. The bottles are in the glass cabinet. I'll be right back. I'm going to change because I'm being suffocated by the heat."

The small sitting room, carpeted in beige, with modern, elegantly designed furniture and original artworks, suggested that Fabiola, if not rich, was financially comfortable. What would she do with a literary pariah such as Roberto Lima? Literary admiration, neurotic dependency or simple masochism? Because of her varied and chaotic library, he deduced that she had set herself to studying philosophy, the history of religion, political science and English literature all at the same time, without really sinking her teeth into anything. Taking a closer look at the books, he found that many of them had not even been opened: maybe she had bought them by the kilo. A poster of *Notre Dame des Fleurs* in Lindsay Kemp's theatrical version gave a chic touch to the breakfast area: the mystique of sordidness turned into a decorative object. Would Lima have explained to her who Genet was? He did not want to prejudge her, but everything seemed to indicate that culture was not her staple diet, but a simple dressing. Maybe she was one of those well-off chicks bored with their families, yacht and trips to Europe, who adopted a cultural disguise like a second personality, like a volatile perfume they had left on the surface of their souls. Or was he imagining things because he was unable to admit to himself that she was *sooo* hot and, at the same time, also cultured and sensitive? He served himself a Black Label whisky, went to the kitchen to get some ice and, when he came back, found Fabiola in the sitting room in provocative denim shorts, her hair wet.

"Pour one of the same for me, please." She handed Evaristo a glass. "You left me intrigued. What is all this about a crime of passion?"

"It's a rumour circulating among journalists, and maybe it has even filtered to the police. Better that you are warned, in case the Feds come to interrogate you."

"Don't leave me in suspense. Get to the point."

"Months before he died, Lima had a bust up with Claudio

Fear of Animals

Vilchis in the toilets of Bellas Artes and, according to what's being said, you were the reason for this argument."

"That's a half-truth," protested Fabiola. "They hated each other from before."

"But you had broken up with Lima and were going out with Vilchis. That's why they resented each other, isn't it?" Fabiola nodded. "In literary circles, Vilchis has a reputation for being vengeful, and Lima humiliated him in front of many people, so it's not so mad to think about revenge. Do you know where he spent the night of the crime?"

"Sleeping with his holy wife, for sure. Claudio never spent a night away from home."

"But did he ever demonstrate to you that he had the intention of seeking revenge?"

"Don't push me into talking about that reptile." Fabiola scrunched up her lips in repugnance. "He's dead and buried to me."

"I thought you were..."

"Lovers?" Fabiola took a long sip of her whisky. "Don't fear words. Say things as they are. Yes, we were lovers and you don't know how much I regret having been so blind. I fell for him out of admiration. I looked up to him like high school girls look at their teachers. I thought he was a giant, a fucking pro, and I felt proud that he would have fallen in love with me. Then I realised that he only wanted to use me, but we had better change the subject. There are things that are better not talked about."

Fabiola sunk her gaze to the bottom of the glass, struggling to stop herself from crying. Evaristo kept silent while she composed herself.

"Your hypothesis has a flaw," Fabiola continued, sobbing. "If Roberto were ready to kill for me, Claudio would never be."

"Forgive me for intruding into your private life, but there is something I don't understand: why did you break up with Lima?"

"That's another kettle of fish. Roberto was really tender, a wonderful lunatic, but he had a really big defect: machismo. I met him at the literary workshop he conducted at the Carrillo Gil Museum about two years ago, and I fancied him because he was so extreme. He started talking about literature and he was like a volcano spitting fire. He didn't convince you with reasons: he infected you with his enthusiasm for books because, according to him, they had changed his life. Don't read just for reading, he said, live your own novel. I only got into the workshop to see what was up, but he encouraged me to write seriously. You have imagination, he said, you only need to grasp the skill a bit. At that time I was getting a bit sick about my acting career. University theatre is full of faggots who hate women. The directors only gave me the roles of speaking tree in children's plays, and it's not that I was very ambitious, but I was frustrated by not being able to work in something I considered satisfactory. Thanks to Roberto, I discovered my true vocation and who knows how we started to fall in love. Literature was our Cupid. Instead of calling each other 'my dear' or 'my love', we discussed books until we lost our voices. One day it occurred to me to write him a love letter and, when I gave it to him so he could read it, he corrected paragraph by paragraph all of my grammatical mistakes."

She was interrupted by an outburst of tears. Ashamed of having opened in her a wound that was not yet healed, all Evaristo could do was fill her glass with whisky, which she drank like water, and offer her a cigarette, not knowing what to say. The telephone came to the rescue.

"Hello, yes, speaking... What a surprise! I thought you'd forgotten about me... Tonight?"

Fabiola walked towards the balcony with the cordless telephone, giggling joyously. It looked as if this widow was not so hard to console. By the snippets of conversation he heard from a distance, Evaristo deduced that she had soon replaced Lima and Claudio.

"And why don't we go to *Meneo*? They say that a really good Colombian band is playing... We must get there early to get a table... Good, so I'll wait for you at half nine."

Back in the sitting room, as if she was entering a scene after clowning about in the dressing room, Fabiola adopted the hard-done-by expression she had had before the call and carried on with her account in a lower voice, like a sinner in the confessional.

"Roberto was a hermit. He did not like to socialise, but I sank like an idiot into literary circles, struggling to place my first book, a collection of short stories titled *Below the Belt*, with any publisher. Roberto did not like me being here and there. Public relations are for mediocre people, he said when he was drunk, write something good and you'll see how the publishers run after you. Because of so many rejections I felt devalued as a human being. Roberto made me write the book again three times. When he read the fourth version he said that it had got worse instead of getting better. Then I thought that he wanted to clip my wings so as not to appear at a disadvantage if I was a success as a writer, like Salieri with Mozart. I knocked the manuscript out of his hands and threw him out of my house, yelling. Rivalries killed the love. I should never have allowed them to grow between the two of us, but now it's too late to seek forgiveness."

"I'm beginning to understand." Evaristo crossed his legs. "This was when you threw yourself out of spite into the arms of his worst enemy."

"Yes, my head was full of smoke and I convinced myself that I was worth more as a writer than him. It was not just about personal satisfaction, but revenge, do you understand?"

Fabiola lit a cigarette and continued revealing the vicissitudes of her way into the literary circle. For a budding female writer, beauty was more a hindrance than a help. Those editors who tried to corner her at cocktail parties only had eyes for her legs and quickly changed the subject when she mentioned her book of short stories. But finally, when she was about to return defeated to children's theatre, a dazzlingly charming guy appeared who recognised her talent. That dazzlingly charming guy was Claudio Vilchis. She had met him at the San Angel Cultural Centre when Claudio had given a magisterial conference about Pierre Reverdy which she had attended without knowing a word about the subject. She had had with her a copy of *Passwords*, the latest of Claudio's books, and at the end of the conference she had asked him for an autograph, affecting shyness to reflect him in a greater light. He had started to talk to her, drank his wine of honour with her and, when they came out of the auditorium, he had invited her to dinner at the *Petite France*, where they could talk more freely. Animated after the second bottle, she had confessed that she also wrote and, nervously giggling, had given him a story she had written about the extinction of whales, which she casually had in her handbag, to read. A few days later, Claudio had called her to congratulate her (you are a strong writer) and she had thanked him for his kind words in a motel in Cuernavaca, where they had spent the weekend gorged on whisky, sex and literature.

With those toady eyes that gave him a certain look, like that of Diego Rivera, his greasy hair and his flabby forty-something belly, Claudio was not really what you could call a handsome man or even manly, but he compensated for his lack of attractiveness with an aristocratic personality. Educated in foreign schools since the age of seven, he spoke French like a mother tongue, could recognise any opera from the first chords played in the overture, was an expert on colonial art, wines and Egyptian ceramics and, after a few drinks, burst out singing *Provençal* songs from the Middle Ages. Married, with three children, he could not be seen with her in public and limited himself to seeing her on clandestine dates, an inconvenience she did not really mind because of the many things she learned from him. His encyclopaedic cultural knowledge opened a new world for her, but what she enjoyed most was the Olympian contempt he felt for Roberto, whom he called a "lumpen hack" and "professionally resentful". That was the way Fabiola saw him as well, from the exquisite and sophisticated position she shared with her new lover, without any explanation for how she could have fallen in love with a man in whom everything was vulgar, from his soot-coloured urban chronicles to his self-destructive bohemianism. Yet even when she felt as superior as Claudio, she needed to reaffirm it to Roberto and to herself by publishing *Below the Belt*.

From their first meeting in Cuernavaca, she had talked about this issue with Claudio, asking him his sincere opinion about whether the book could be saved or should be thrown into the rubbish, as Roberto had advised. Claudio read it in one go that weekend and, despite correcting a few orthographic and syntactic mistakes, in general terms approved of the book: "For a budding writer, it's not bad at all." Ignited by joy and vengefulness, she called Roberto that same night to inform him in a vengeful tone that Vilchis had praised her short stories – a stupid act that she now regretted because it greatly contributed to the punch-up in Bellas Artes. In the following weeks, Claudio disassociated himself from the book, but Fabiola did not stop pressing, moaning every time about the *Via Crucis* that newcomers had to endure in order to get published, "especially those shy ones, like myself". After much wailing, she made him listen to her and he offered to propose *Below the Belt* to the editorial council of the Fund for the Promotion of Reading. As Claudio was the secretary of the council, she assumed her book would be published and, consequently, that Roberto would be gutted. Publishing with the Fund would mean leaving Roberto far behind, sunk in the catacombs of marginality, while she ascended with honorific fanfares to the Olympus of High

Fear of Animals

Literature. Her illusion almost blinding her, she could not see the black cloud that had gathered over her head until the rain had started to fall on her.

Fabiola's main mistake was pretending not to see Claudio's low ways. She had much evidence that he was a man not to be trusted, but ignored this in order to avoid a clash that could cost her the publication of her book. Vilchis was an arriviste of convenience. He befriended those writers whom he thought at a particular moment would be useful to him, even when he said the worst things about them, and, in order to keep them in his pocket, he did them favours they had not sought to later cash them in with added interest. He spent whole afternoons on the telephone, manoeuvring complex political deals to maintain his net of complicities: I'll include you in my next anthology if you take me to the next convention of intellectuals in Europe; tell me I'm a genius and I will return the praise with two extra adjectives; publish a long interview with me in your paper and I'll stick you in the collection of Modern Classics. To Claudio, everything was a transaction, but with her he had committed fraud because he had cashed in bed, as many times as he wanted, a favour that he did not contemplate fulfilling.

She smelled a rat in his evasion. When she asked him if the editorial council had finally approved her book, he answered irritatedly: "Don't be so anxious, these things take time", or even shut her up with Judas kisses. There were three months of tug-of-war without her tiring of asking and him answering by changing the subject. In her ambition to rise above the crowd, Fabiola had proudly talked of her imminent publication with colleagues at the literary workshop, and now they did not stop asking about the book, with such mocking insistence that it revealed their incredulity. Tired of being ridiculed, she personally went to the Fund for the Promotion of Reading to ask for its verdict, taking advantage of Vilchis being on a trip to the Frankfurt Book Fair. The secretary of the editorial council, a dear old Argentine lady with a scarf and glasses, checked in a filing cabinet slowly, taking folders out, putting them back again and, at last, denying it with her head, assuring Fabiola that neither she nor the members of the council had received a copy of *Below the Belt*. "That can't be," Fabiola protested. "*Señor* Vilchis brought it personally". "Well, it probably ended up lost on his desk," said the old woman. "Why don't you speak to him when he is back?"

Suddenly, as if a bandage had been removed from her eyes, she understood that Claudio had also been doing the business with her, using the publication of her book as bait to keep her at his feet. After a moment of indignation, in which she had thought of telling everything to his wife, Fabiola fell into a state of television-goggling catatonia that lasted for more than fifteen days. Claudio left her a lot of messages on the answering machine – first ones that were happy, then anxious, later furious, scolding her for going back to the "lumpen hack". Sick of his ranting, she told him to see her on a Monday afternoon at the café of the Gandhi bookshop, where she laid a trap for him, asking him how the publication of her book was going. As usual, Claudio responded with one of his evasive answers, but this time she threw a boiling cappuccino over his fine cashmere suit. "Don't lie to me, you son of a bitch! I know you have the book locked up in a drawer. Didn't you say that I'm a strong writer? I'm going to ask Roberto to beat you to a pulp again!"

Unconsciously acting, Fabiola was shouting as if Claudio were in front of her. She then went pensive, her eyes fixed on a point on the wall in one of those theatrical distractions that are only tolerated in a madman or a genius. Evaristo cleared his throat to wake her up.

"So you threatened him with throwing Lima at him...?"

"I said that to remove the thorn," Fabiola reacted, "but later I thought about it more calmly and didn't want to cause another fight. Rancour only lasts a week for me. After the little number at Gandhi's, I completely forgot about Claudio. I did not want to know anything about any other man but, because I was a masochist and a mule, I started to miss Roberto. He was the only person who could relate to me at that moment. Because of pride, I took quite a while to call him, but one day when I was drinking alone I threw my pride to hell and asked him to come and see me. Nobody knows this but, a week before he died, Roberto had come back to me. He slept here some nights, more loving than ever, and left me the diary he had written when we had broken up, as a souvenir. Now I read it and I get goosebumps..."

"Could you provide me with a copy?"

"Of course not." Fabiola was offended. "It has intimate details, secrets about the two of us that nobody else could be interested in."

"But maybe it could give us a clue about the assassin."

Fear of Animals

"Don't insist or I shall get cross. You seem more like a detective than a journalist."

"I'm sorry. I just want to ask you one last question. Did Vilchis know that you had gone back to Lima?"

"And what does it matter?"

"Maybe he had not yet resigned himself to the idea of losing you. Maybe he looked for Lima in his den to settle accounts with him. You are the kind of woman for whom a man is capable of murdering..."

"Thanks for the compliment," smiled Fabiola, "but I have told you that Claudio is not a man, he is a reptile. If he did not take a risk by publishing my book because he did not want to make our relationship obvious to his colleagues at the Fund, do you think he would kill for me? Don't make me laugh, please..."

At that moment, the doorbell rang and Fabiola went to the kitchen to answer the intercom. She came back to the sitting room, different and nervous.

"It's Claudio. I don't know why he's coming to visit me... I have not seen him at all for a month."

"Maybe he was interrogated by the Feds and is coming to ask for your help," Evaristo conjectured, supposing that Chamula had carried out his order.

"Wait." Fabiola stopped him. "You don't have to run away as if Claudio were my husband and you the lover who hides when visiting me. At least let me introduce you both."

Evaristo remained as if screwed to the sofa, uncomfortable about the situation. He suspected that Fabiola had lied to him about Vilchis. He could not trust a cultural prostitute capable of selling her own mother just to get her book published. The real clue could be in Roberto's diary, which without doubt contained something that compromised her. Maybe she was an accomplice or the intellectual author of the crime, how could he know? But what disturbed him most was not Fabiola's possible culpability, but the fear that, when the moment came to treat her with a hard hand, he would fall at her feet at the slightest erotic insinuation. He could not face, with any decisiveness, a woman who just needed to click her fingers to turn him into a slave.

"How do you do, Claudio. I hope you are coming in the name of peace," Fabiola coldly greeted the unexpected visitor. "I would like you to meet Luciano Contreras, a journalist who is investigating Roberto's death. He was leaving as you rang the bell."

Evaristo got up to shake his hand, shuddering with a sudden adrenaline charge. Just as Fabiola had described him, Vilchis was a cold-blooded amphibian with drooping eyelids, a viscous and gentle literate whom he never would have believed capable of killing a fly – if it hadn't been for the cigar in his mouth.

Fear of Animals

Located at Plaza Melchor Ocampo, beneath the underpass of Río Mississippi, La Concordia was a slum with the delusion of being a members' club, whose regulars were drug traffickers, Feds, petty public officials, and well-off kids with sexual conflicts, and where young whores earned in a day what a bank clerk earned in three months. Evaristo was received on the landing by a valet wearing a blue frock coat, then crossed a wide hall with golden tables and red velvet chairs, among bare-breasted teenage call-girls and drunkards rocking them on their laps, simulating copulation. The contrast of their childlike nudity against the fierce appearance of the clients they rode made him nauseous. Absorbed by the giant television screens showing porno movies, the buyers of virtual sex hardly looked out from the corner of their eyes at the hired nymphs rubbing their faces with tits and cunts. When he reached Maytorena's private cubicle, separated from the bar by a mirrored screen, a gunman whom Evaristo did not know searched him.

"I am one of the Commander's people." Evaristo showed him his metal shield.

To make himself heard over the music, the gunman shouted at him, informing him that the commander had been boozing heavily since the day before. Bad news: that meant he would be in a bad mood. Ready to receive a barrowful of insults, Evaristo went behind the screen and found Maytorena calmer and fresher than he expected, fondling a blonde transvestite who, by the look of his smudged make-up and the stubble on his pointy chin, seemed to have spent the whole drinking binge with him. The only traces of drunkenness he noticed on Maytorena were the Coca-Cola stains on his white tracksuit. Next to them, Chamula had curled up like a guard dog on a carpet pricked by cigarette burns, clutching a gun, just in case.

"Sit down, Intellectual, and ask for something strong, to catch up with me. This is Marilú. Isn't she tasty?"

Enrique Serna

Evaristo nodded with a smile. Because of his long experience as Maytorena's lackey, he knew that any joke about Marilú or the slightest hint about the secret weapon she carried under her skirt could land him a shot in the temple, like so many other naive guys who had warned him about his girlfriend's "tricks". To warn Maytorena that he was with a transvestite meant questioning his manhood, and manhood for Maytorena was a matter of life and death. That is why he was never a regular in bars for homosexuals, where he would have sliced up the first faggot to wink an eye at him. His preference was for the dressed-up ones, call-girls in bars with female whores, where he could always blame his mistake on being drunk, even though he had spent the last thirty years intentionally making that mistake. None of his subordinates must spoil the psychological alibi, even when it was unbelievable or repetitive. In those circumstances, the best thing was to pretend not to notice, play his game, and make allowances for the hawk with a dove's vocation.

"Well, as I was telling you, blondie," Maytorena said as he encircled Marilú's waist again, "although I appear to be such a great bastard and womaniser, to me the family is the most important thing in the world. For my children, I break my back every day. They are my reason for living, as the bloody soaps say. And if I am proud of something, it is of how well my children have responded to me. You can't imagine the satisfaction I get from having decent children, clean in their hearts, and with a university degree. When you become a mother you will understand me: you feel it was worth fucking yourself so much to sow a seed and for the seed to give fruit."

With a voice breaking with emotion, Maytorena got his wallet out and showed Marilú the photos of his studious brood.

"This is Genaro, the most dedicated of all. He speaks English and French and has a Corvette that I gave him last year. Isn't he cute? He studied international relations at the Anáhuac University, and he is now trying to get a job in the foreign service. This is Laura, my favourite. She is 22 years old and very soon she'll get her degree in hotel management. I think she's the most fucking clever of the three but, anyway, she may get married soon and will surely leave her diploma to gather dust in a corner. This is Joaquín, the youngest, who is about to finish his law degree. Doesn't he look like me? When some fucking braggart idiot asks me, 'How much money do you have? How many houses have you

Fear of Animals

bought?' I get these photos out and say: 'This is my fortune, they are my treasure.' Because money comes and goes, but a child never abandons you. This is why I am not afraid of death. She can come and get me whenever she wants. I can die tomorrow because I have done my duty in this bloody life..."

Moved by his ode to the family, Maytorena began to cry, putting his head on the shoulder of Marilú, who looked at Evaristo with eyes asking for a way out, but Evaristo shrugged because he knew that interrupting the boss in a moment of emotional catharsis was like pulling the tiger's tail. Resigned, Marilú waited silently for Maytorena to finish crying and, when he finally composed himself, she asked him to pass the snow. Maytorena woke Chamula up with a kick in the back.

"Get up, lazy sod! Give my chick some dust, and also the Intellectual. Let's see if the snow stops him being such a dope."

Half asleep, Chamula spread the coke over the table in two lines. Marilú made herself a straw with a hundred dollar note and sniffed up the two lines like a nuclear reactor. Chamula spread the next two lines, but Evaristo rejected them because he had a little job that night and did not want to continue the party.

"No thank you, my nose is very irritated today."

"So be it, the less the merrier," said the commander, and inhaled the two lines with the note. After a brief facial paralysis in which he looked like the victim of a heart attack, the veins on his neck distended, his face recovered its colour.

Suddenly sober, he ordered Chamula: "Go and get the waiter, and tell him to bring more champagne."

Accustomed to Maytorena's time cycles, Evaristo knew that after the euphoria he got a coke-downer, in which he would tell anyone and anything to go fuck their mothers, starting with his drinking mates. He had to talk to him now that he was in a good mood or else become the subject of a ferocious reprimand.

"I asked to see you because I have good news for you, chief. I couldn't tell you on the telephone, but very soon I will know who killed the journalist."

"You'd better, bastard, because the attorney is steaming with rage." Maytorena finally let go of Marilú and paid attention to him. "All week he's been fucking telling and telling me that he wants to see some detentions to shut the journalists up."

"Well, there is a suspect who gave himself away yesterday. He is an intellectual who made enemies with Lima over some chick."

"What's his name?"

"Claudio Vilchis. He's about forty or forty-five years old and is the sub-director of the Fund for the Promotion of Reading."

"Take notes, Chamula." Maytorena rolled up his sleeves in the proper manner of a gangster. "And you, honey, why don't you go powder your nose?" he told Marilú. "These things are matters for men that don't concern you..."

Marilú stuffed the hundred dollar note down his bra and left the cubicle, swaying his hips obscenely.

"Now explain, Intellectual. How do you know that bastard is the killer?"

"The night Lima was killed the neighbours in the building saw someone smoking a cigar on the stairs." Evaristo lied as he could not reveal himself to Maytorena as a witness. "Of all those who had reason to kill Lima, Vilchis is the only one who smokes cigars. I have just seen him at Fabiola Nava's apartment, the chick who was fucking both of them."

"Well, he's really fucked now!" Maytorena turned towards Chamula. "Tomorrow you go get him at his office, give him a good beating in the car so he softens up and put him in solitary."

"Just a minute, chief," Evaristo said, alarmed. "Vilchis is the main suspect, but we don't have any proof to arrest him."

"Leave the proof to those shyster lawyers. Tomorrow that bastard will confess, because he *will* confess, you'll see. Later we'll take a picture of him with a cigar in his mouth and I'll take it to the attorney so he can call a press conference. Bloody Tapia, he's going to stiffen his collar with this news and probably won't even say thank you to me."

"But it could also be that Vilchis did not really kill him. I just have to investigate if he has an alibi. The thing about the cigar could just be a coincidence."

"Give me a fucking break, Intellectual," interrupted Maytorena. "You've been watching too many gringo police shows. Didn't you say that the bloke with a cigar was fucking Lima's woman and he's the only suspect?" Evaristo nodded affirmatively. "Just with that we have enough to put him in jail. Open the bottle, Chamula. Let's drink a toast to Marilú's rear."

Resigned, Evaristo lifted his glass with a rictus of false joy and tasted the champagne, which was like strychnine. Maytorena was too happy. It was impossible to make him see reason and, if he continued insisting on caution, Evaristo would only manage to exasperate him. Marilú came back from the toilet rejuvenated, with a thick layer of foundation concealing his stubble. Maytorena made a carnivalesque bow to him and made him drink straight from the bottle, pouring champagne down his cleavage. The dark side of his drunken spell began, the total eclipse of conscience in which he did striptease numbers grinning like a bitch on heat, firing his gun in the air and pissing in his pants while invoking his dear holy mother. Evaristo neither wanted to be part of his audience nor to have to drag him out from the club with puke on his trousers.

"Well, chief," he said as he got up from the table, "I'd love to stay for the champagne, but I have an appointment that I can't miss."

"No fucking way, Intellectual. Nobody leaves me drinking by myself," spluttered the commander angrily, and in a more loving tone asked him: "Where could you possibly be going that's better than here?"

"The thing is, tomorrow is my daughter Chabela's fifteenth birthday," he lied, "and I want to arrive in time to dance the first waltz."

"Ah, all right," said Maytorena, moved. "If it's about your family, then so be it. You know that for me children come first, and then the party."

Satisfied at having found a good excuse, Evaristo turned to leave the cubicle, but before he had crossed the screen he was stopped by the commander's resounding voice.

"Wait a minute, Intellectual." Maytorena took from his trouser pocket a thick wad of crumpled dollars. "Take this, buy a good present for your girl. Say hello on my behalf and tell her that I send her a blessing."

Outside, while he was waiting for the valet to bring his car and covering his head with his jacket against the drizzle, Evaristo shivered to think about Vilchis' fate. He wished he was guilty, but guilty in real life, not fabricated by Maytorena, who with torture could make him confess even to Kennedy's assassination. It was too late now to save Vilchis from arrest and being beaten, but at least he had enough time to back up his accusation with proof more tangible than the sweet smell of his cigar. When Evaristo got behind the wheel, he looked at his watch: it was half one. By that time Fabiola Nava should be in full party mode with her new lover. It was the best moment to search her house for some evidence, even though this meant housebreaking. He overtook the double row of cars stopping and starting before the umbrella-wielding whores standing on Melchor Ocampo, and took the Interior Circuit highway towards the south. The good kid in the movie had had enough of asking questions. After all, he was dealing with a bunch of sons-of-bitches – very cultured, yes, but bastards just like Maytorena – and the situation now demanded that he break all the rules.

When he parked in front of the building in Atlixco 163, Evaristo looked at the façade and gleefully observed that none of the flats overlooking the street had their lights on. To make sure that Fabiola was not there, he rang the bell. As expected, there was no answer on the intercom. He took an Italian hair clip from the glove compartment, looking both ways like an old-school detective, and slid towards the entrance of the building, which was providentially dark as the landing light was turned off. He had neither been a locksmith nor a burglar but, having left the car keys in the car so many times, he had learned to open it with hair clips. While poking the inside of the lock with the hook, he thought about Dora Elsa's vagina, soft and moist, that opened so easily with the violence of his tongue. It was a fetishistic invocation, a way of giving himself courage and confidence to open the hermetically-sealed metal vulva. In the middle of the operation, a lorry went past down Atlixco and he rolled to the floor thinking he had been discovered when the lorry's lights swept across him. When the danger had passed, the street went back to being tranquil. There was a rustic and anxious silence in which the little noises of the clip seemed as if they had been amplified by a loudspeaker. After 15 minutes of hard work and a lot of perspiration, the lock finally yielded its virginity. Tiptoeing, Evaristo took the lift, which was impregnated with Fabiola's perfume. He got off at the fourth floor and at the door of flat 601 went back to using the hair clip, with the additional terror of being discovered *in fragrante* by a neighbour peeking into the corridor. Just in case the neighbours kicked up a fuss, he carried the Magnum in his belt, but did not fancy the idea of having to deal with a patrol, despite carrying the ID that would get him out of trouble. The lock gave in very quickly, but Fabiola was cautious and had another huge lock that would not give. Evaristo was struggling to make it open when a big, bloated neighbour in a suit and tie came out of the lift, walking past him, zigzagging. The neighbour was so drunk he said "Good evening" and, not noticing the hair clip, went straight into his flat.

Fear of Animals

"Thank God Fabiola is such a tart, the neighbours are used to seeing men coming in and out of her house," he thought. Recovered from all the heavy pressing that had left him with an annoying itch in the palm of his hand, he tried again with the hook, sticking his ear to the door like professional burglars do with safes. On hearing the long-awaited "click", he pushed the door open gently. Congratulations. There was no latch inside.

Proud of his spotless desecration, Evaristo slumped down on the sitting room sofa, putting his feet on the centre table where Fabiola had piled up the most attractive art books as if by accident: Topor, Mapplethorpe nudes, a catalogue of paintings by Joseph Beuys, Italian Quattrocento frescos. Was this about impressing her visitors or just bedtime reading? As with the *Notre Dame des Fleurs*, they seemed to fulfil an ornamental function, as if Fabiola had the aim of leaving "accidental" footprints of her vast cultural knowledge everywhere. Without doubt, the intellectual window in which she sold herself as a writer was of enormous importance to her. Maybe she would have been capable of killing just to keep her literary image, which for her was not just an ornament but second nature. Evaristo shuddered, thinking that Lima could have died because he had wounded Fabiola's ego. As a woman, she could have tolerated disappointment but, as a writer, she could not bear the slightest scratch. He had noticed that the afternoon when he had heard her account of Claudio Vilchis' betrayal, in which she could not contemplate the slightest possibility that her book was shit. He could expect anything from such an arrogant woman, but what had Claudio's role in the crime been? Was he so fucking obsessed with her that he had killed Lima just to satisfy her whim? His sudden appearance had made it clear that Fabiola and Vilchis were still lovers, even though he had failed to publish her book. He had arrived without notice because he was the master of the house. Fabiola had pretended to be surprised to maintain the act that made them appear guilt-free, not suspecting that Claudio would parade with the cigar in his mouth before the only witness who had sniffed him on the stairs of the building. "You are fucked, honey," thought Evaristo. "You and Vilchis are going to set up a literary workshop in Almoloya de Juárez prison. I just need Lima's diary. That must be hidden somewhere."

Anxious to find it, he stood up to search Fabiola's study. Luckily the studio window did not face the street, so he could turn on the light without the fear of being discovered by Fabiola on her arrival. Poking in the drawers of her dainty *secretaire* he found a notebook with Cioran-like aphorisms, personal documents, dry-cleaner receipts, a little box of Trojan condoms and bound photocopies of the children's theatrical work *Let's Play Dreaming*, an original by Jazmin Bolaños, which he returned to the drawer with the tips of his fingers as if it were radioactive. On the shelves, filled to the brim with books, there were dusty folders and files with notes from the time Fabiola was a drama student. He was wasting his time looking at unimportant papers and did not even know for certain that Lima's diary really existed. Maybe he never made up with Fabiola and, consequently, never went back to living with her before his death. Maybe the diary was another of the lies Fabiola and Vilchis had fabricated as part of their indestructible alibi. And he, an impulsive jerk, was pissing in the wind, with his infallible talent for following false clues.

He abandoned the scientific search for the diary to start looking in Fabiola's bedroom, where he turned to the closet, the chest of drawers and the wardrobe without further ado, lighting his way with a little table lamp that had such a faint glow it could not be seen from the street. When he stumbled upon the lingerie, he could not control the temptation to sniff some panties, stuffing them in his pocket for future masturbation. Next to the bras there was a hardback A4 notebook, with a cover made from a newspaper. Under the lamplight, sitting on Fabiola's bed, he joyously recognised Lima's writing: he was not Philip Marlowe, but he wasn't a complete zero as a detective. It was not a conventional diary, but a notebook with sketches, some literary, some confessional, juxtaposed in a disorderly way as they had come into Lima's head. Evaristo immediately found an untitled erotic poem dated November '94 that explained Fabiola's reluctance to show it:

> *Cave ablaze like burning coal, hospitable hell*
> *tunnel that my tongue travels between emanations of lava*
> *solar perimeter, hidden Helio*
> *under the halo of vapour-like fibres.*
> *Ashes rain at the side of your body,*
> *fusing my hardened weapon and in the fire*
> *where the water crackles I am blurred.*

At least something was clear: Lima had not had such a bad time in his final days. The heated poem dissolved the possibility that

Fear of Animals

Fabiola and Vilchis were accomplices: she could not be involved in the crime unless she had given herself to Lima in order to wrap him in her web. Could she be such a bitch? Without completely discarding that possibility, Evaristo opted for another one, even harder to believe: maybe Claudio had just acted in a fit of jealousy, furious about the reconciliation between Fabiola and his worst enemy, the lumpen hack who had smashed his face in Bellas Artes' toilets. Vilchis could be a big-headed cretin about how cultured he was, but that didn't exempt him from being passionate. Blinded by revenge, he must have believed that Lima had instilled doubts in Fabiola about the publication of *Below the Belt*. After all, he was the person most interested in making them break up and knew how angry she got when she was told she had no talent as a writer. A suspicion like that would certainly be enough to awaken the murderer that we all have inside, according to Evaristo's feverish imagination. He imagined Vilchis going round the beaten streets of Peñon de los Baños, with a bottle of whisky in his jacket to fuel his hatred, and later waiting on the stairs for the departure of the ill-timed visitor, whom he would have bumped into in the darkness before knocking at the door: "Hi Roberto, I'm Claudio Vilchis," he would say. "I've come in the name of peace, just to have a drink. Could you let me in? I want us to talk like friends. Fabiola is a thing of the past." Predisposed to believing in the goodwill of men because of his drunkenness, Lima would have received him without reproach, would probably have apologised for the bust up in Bellas Artes, would have turned his back and, then, eternal blackout. The fact that the dictionary of synonyms and antonyms had been used for this was yet further proof against Claudio, because only a twisted intellectual like him could have converted the act of killing into a gesture of literary humiliation. Feeling just one step away from the truth, Evaristo looked and looked again among the confessional pages for some comment that could implicate Vilchis. But Lima had not mentioned him anywhere. In his soul-searching there was no place for others: *I am going to turn forty and I have seen life behind the barrier. Like the ostriches sinking their heads in the sand when they are in danger, I have buried myself among books since my youth, because I was afraid of existing (...) I am vain even in love. When I go out with Fabiola I enjoy other men looking at her; I hold her by the hand as if she were a prize. I could not stand loving her in secret. Would I be loving her really or am I idealising a projection of my ego?...* The notebook was an invaluable document for getting to know Lima's temperament, but Evaristo needed more concrete information about his last days. Who had he visited before his death? Did he have a previous encounter with Vilchis? He was beginning to feel frustrated at not finding any element of proof when he encountered a brief and disturbing comment that broke the writing's tone of self-reflection:... *Yesterday I met Osiris at the Hijo del Cuervo and he wanted a payback. He was so fucking mad that he threatened to kill me. I calmed him down with the promise of paying him next week, but I don't know where I'm going to get the dough from. At* El Matutino *I won't be paid until the end of the month and I really don't want to ask Fabiola for another loan. I owe her a lot and she's going to think I am a pimp. Fucking Osiris, he has forgotten that I published his first poem when he was a nobody...* Evaristo's reading was interrupted by a shiver when he heard the noise of a key opening the flat. He just had time to turn the light off and hide behind the bedroom door, where he held his breath as he tried to look through the crack between the door and the wall. Fabiola's voice gave him the goosebumps:

"Isn't that Colombian band hot?"

"Yes, my love, but I'll never sit at a table next to the stage again," a slurring woman answered. "They nearly blasted my eardrums."

"Do you fancy a whisky?"

"A very small one, please. Tomorrow I have to give a conference at the university. What a lovely flat you have."

"Do you really like it?"

"Almost as much as I like its owner."

Evaristo managed to see Fabiola serving the drinks, with her girlfriend's arm circling her waist. He would love to know who the other woman was, but a huge flowerpot was covering her face.

"I was sick of those arseholes who didn't stop getting you up to dance at Meneo's, as if I were a painting," grumbled the friend. "Fuck, why are they so stubborn? They saw us dancing together all night."

"They probably thought we were on the prowl."

"On the prowl, my balls. They wanted to fucking annoy us. They didn't even leave us alone on the dancefloor. But one thing's for sure, if you take them to bed, they fall asleep after the first fuck."

"You'll excuse me, but I'm going to take these heels off." Fabiola threw them on the carpet, lay down on the sofa and rested her head between her friend's legs. "Scratch my head, would you? I'm feeling pleasantly tired."

"Next time I'll take you to a gay place to be more comfortable."

"Oh no, bars for chain-wielding lesbians really annoy me," Fabiola protested. "They look at you as if you are an insect if you don't belong to the ghetto."

"Nobody gives you nasty looks anywhere, my love. They just look at you because they fancy you."

Tenderly, Fabiola and her friend kissed on the lips. Evaristo forced himself to focus on the features of the happy sergeantess, whose voice seemed familiar. She was wearing a matching navy suit, suede boots, checked scarf and, on her visible wrist, a shiny gold bracelet. They broke away and Fabiola sighed.

"Tomorrow there's going to be the latest Greenaway movie at the festival. Do you want to come?"

"What's it like?"

"Su-perb, ma-gis-terial, in-cre-di-ble, but it has a postmodernist tone that the Mexican critics are not going to get. It's too subtle for them. When the movie starts, you think it's going to be a tragic farce, then a psychological melodrama and at the end it becomes self-worship. You don't know how I laughed. It's the best thing Greenaway has made since *The Belly of an Architect*."

"Well, I shall definitely see it tomorrow. What I hate about going to the cinema here is the subtitles: when they don't know how to translate something, they just make it up."

"And in the theatre they are much worse. Yesterday I went to see Witkiewicz's *The Madman and the Nun* at the Cultisur and you don't know how gutted I was. They commissioned some imbecile who doesn't know a word of Polish to do the translation. It was a disaster. I had the play very fresh in my mind because I had just read the original."

"Can I borrow it? Don't be mean."

"Of course. Tomorrow I'll send it to you with the chauffeur. But I can tell you I don't understand how they can give such a difficult play to translate to some man who has not even travelled to Europe – even on one of those tours for fifteen-year-old debutantes where you do a city per day. I even felt like sending a letter to the papers."

"But why such a surprise, if in this country anybody believes they can be intellectual? In the literary workshop where I enrolled, all those so-called writers were a bunch of plebs who had not read beyond José Agustín. If you talk to them about Klossowski, Michel Tournier or Thomas Bernhard, they look at you as if they are seeing visions. They don't even know how to ask the time in English. But one thing is certain, even the stupidest of them has won a minor prize in Cuautitlán or Celaya."

"Be grateful that the riffraff remains happily ignorant." The friend cleared her throat as if she had phlegm stuck in it. "In this country the intellectual class has always been very small, fifty people at best, and that's how it should be. Or do you want the circle to fill up with upstarts?"

"If anyone heard you, they would say you were a bourgeois elitist."

"Not elitist, but an aristocrat, and that is different. Disseminating culture is an invention of demagogic politicians. Culture is an inheritance. It is transmitted generation by generation. It's the exclusive patrimony of those with class, something that the mob will never have, even if they are pushed to read. If I directed a literary workshop, I would invite all the students to dine at my place to see if they knew how to use the cutlery. And if there was one that mixed up the knife for meat with the one for fish, I would throw him out without any qualms."

The aristocrat stood up to put some more ice in her drink. When she lifted her head above the flower pot, she came into Evaristo's view. Startled, he now recognised her: it was Perla Tinoco, aka Perla Tubbuco, the flabby fiftysomething poetess with a high-flying job at Conafoc! Without doubt, Fabiola wanted something from her, because it was impossible for her to be sleeping with a woman twice her age and weight just for the pleasure of it. Would she be pimping her for money? Was she disappointed by men because of the setbacks from Lima and Vilchis?

"By the way, you never told me about how your book launch went," Fabiola commented. "I read a story in *Reforma*. How was it?"

"The launch was all right. The only bad thing was those who launched it. I had the blasted idea of inviting two cretins called Daniel Nieto and Pablo Segura. Do you know them?" Fabiola shook her head. "Well, you didn't miss anything. They are the typical supplement larvae who go from here to there looking for someone to fawn over. They kept begging me to allow them to launch one of my books and, in a moment of weakness, I accepted. The poor guys must have thought that my prestige was going to rub off on them just because they were sitting next to me on the stage, but the task was two sizes too big. You don't know how much nonsense they said about me! I was listening and thinking: what do these imbeciles read? But I could not make them look ridiculous in front of the whole world. That would have been rude. I had to grin and bear it and even at the end I thanked them, like the good gentleman I am."

"When you write another book, will you let me launch it?"

"Of course, my love, and it's also going to have a dedication to you." Tinoco slid a playful finger down Fabiola's cleavage.

"Even when I don't know how to use the cutlery?"

"You will be the exception, because I like you so much." From the cleavage she went to the thighs, tracing an imaginary line on Fabiola's body. "Bad girls like you can even eat using their fingers..."

They kissed on the lips, or rather Fabiola let herself be kissed, indolent and rigid, with a reserve that gave her away as a debutante, but consenting enough for Tinoco to lift her skirt and get stuck in between her legs. Evaristo could only see the poetess' hand under the girl's black tights, which was enough to produce in him a combination of anger and arousal. He would have liked to have made his presence obvious, to have separated Tinoco with a slap – get out of here, you fucking dyke, here comes a real man – and take her place to give Fabiola a mighty fuck but, at that moment, crouched behind the door, he was just a witness condemned to seeing and not speaking, a live ghost who couldn't even pass through the walls. Overcoming her shyness, Fabiola sat astride Tinoco's lap, who attacked her nipples like a greedy suckling without stopping as she played with Fabiola's clitoris. Their clothes were getting heavy so Fabiola took off her blouse, exposing her breasts to the air. Heated, Tinoco threw her scarf to the carpet and kept at her dedicated task, while Fabiola, closing her eyes, went from moaning to panting and thumping her feet on the table. From an expression that revealed her intense pleasure, Evaristo deduced that Perla was giving her a high-class hand-job. Impatient maybe to go beyond just prancing, Tinoco picked up Fabiola as if she were a feather, gave her a kiss like a newly wed, and took her in her arms towards the bedroom.

When Evaristo saw them approaching, as if by instinct he got the Magnum out, ready to scare them with a few shots in the air, but Tinoco pushed the bedroom door not noticing there was a man behind, desperate to dive into the bed with her precious load. Now open to being discovered if one of them looked in the direction of his hiding place, Evaristo held his breath, ready with the gun. Tinoco turned on the bedside lamp to see Fabiola's naked body, and the cone of light stabbed behind the door. "They have seen me now," he thought, compressed against the door. It was his lucky day, because Perla and Fabiola kept at it, absent from reality, stuck in a leglock that Evaristo could not see anymore but which he recreated in his imagination, aroused by the whispering. The cold sweat of fear and the hot sweat of lust flowed over his throbbing temples in unison with the gasps of both women. From amid the duo's heavy breathing he heard a kind of long slurping, like a rude child bubbling through a straw. Was it the infamous and long-tongued dyke champion in her cunt-licking phase? The more he thought of such depressive images, the less he could bring down his erection nor remove from his thoughts Fabiola's vulva, which he saw before him, winking at him, open like an orchid. His martyrdom was aggravated by the briny smell that hit his nose from the bed, which was particularly obscene because it came from two intellectuals whom Evaristo, with his superstitious faith in the power of culture, had imagined were scentless and ethereal, absolved of animal secretions. The fishmonger's aroma tortured him as much as the pain in his testicles and worsened his feelings of impotence. It was more hurtful the closer Fabiola got to bloodless and delirious paroxysm, with a sequence of screams, short and acute at first, then long and hoarse, that culminated with a prolonged *cante jondo* lament, the signature of a spectacular orgasm.

Evaristo relaxed as if he himself had enjoyed the glow of pleasure that had warmed the room. He heard the click of a lighter followed by a long sigh and he breathed in the smoke of a cigarette. Happy, they could smoke. Now he was in even greater danger than before because, in the silence of the bedroom, his breath was more audible and either of them could see him behind the door.

"This room has a man smell," said Tinoco, disgusted. "Did the so-called writer you lived with sweat a lot?"

"I can't smell anything. It's your imagination."

"Look girl, I have the sense of smell of a hound and I know that smell very well. It's identical to my husband's when he takes his socks off... my husband!" Tinoco yelled. "Today he comes back from the architect's congress and asked me to collect him from the airport. What's the time?"

"Two o'clock."

Fear of Animals

"Bloody hell! I'll be late because I'm being a womaniser."

With feline agility she jumped out of bed, picking up her clothes as she went. They were promiscuously mixed up with those of Fabiola, who helped her to put on her bra and zip her trousers.

"I can't find my other shoe. Where the hell did I throw it?" She made an angry grimace when she could not find it under the bed and crossed the room on all fours towards the door, where Evaristo awaited her without even blinking, clenching his jaws like someone in agony. He saw Perla's shadow getting bigger, the hand that clutched the doorknob, her messed-up hair by the threshold...

"Here it is! You chucked it underneath the dressing table," shouted Fabiola. Tinoco turned away, not moving the door, put on her high heel and rewarded her lover with a euphoric kiss.

"I'm off now. I'll call you on Tuesday to see if we can go for dinner."

They left the bedroom and Evaristo sighed with relief. But the vaudeville had not yet ended: Fabiola stopped Tinoco by the door as she was running towards the lift.

"Don't go yet Perla, I forgot to tell you something."

"Tell me on Tuesday, right now I don't have time."

"Wait a moment, please, at this hour there's not a soul wandering the city and you'll get to the airport in ten minutes."

"All right. What do you want?"

"I told you before that I write, but I had not told you that I have an unpublished book of short stories. It's called *Below the Belt*. Most of the stories have a social content, but are written in poetic prose. I wanted to ask you to read it and, if you like it, please help me to publish it with Conafoc."

"You were dying to pass me the bill, weren't you?" joked Tinoco. "All right, darling, but take the book to my office. I'll happily read it, but I can't promise you anything, okay? Other people decide whatever is going to be published by the council."

After a last goodbye kiss, Fabiola went back to her bedroom with a look of disgust on her face and Evaristo heard her imitate Tinoco's nasal voice before the dressing table mirror.

"I can't promise you anything, okay? Other people decide whatever is going to be published by the council... bloody ungrateful pig."

With the elegant gesture of a princess, she let her gown fall to the carpet and entered the bathroom naked. Evaristo waited until he heard the noise of the shower before leaving his hiding place.

Clutching Lima's notebook against his chest, he tiptoed towards the door to freedom and opened and closed it with extreme care. The city was deserted and, within a few minutes, he arrived home. After such a busy day, the idea of getting into his pyjamas and reading Lima's notebook while sipping a whisky, looking for more information about Osiris, excited him. Who was this new suspect coming to jumble even further the tangle of hypotheses about the crime? What kind of business did he have with the victim and why had he threatened to kill him? Facing the challenge posed by the new enigma, Fabiola's vile tricks moved down to second place: these were the incidental and ornamental part of the comedy, an interval of cheap pornography that must not divert him from his deductive task.

He went up the stairs with difficulty, pausing for breath on each landing without taking his cigarette out of his mouth, breathing with gusto after having been compelled to abstain at Fabiola's home. On the third floor, when he was feeling for the keyhole, he heard in the background someone clearing his throat and saw in the darkness a silhouette wearing a mackintosh which he thought was his next-door neighbour. When Evaristo turned his head to say good evening, he received a hard knock on the temple that threw him face down into limbo, a uterine abyss, damp, muffled and black, where he saw the light of his cigarette extinguishing in the distance as he drifted, floating like a dead fish.

Fear of Animals

A familiar perfume, a light like a sword tearing the shadows, as if the Archangel Gabriel had lain upon his eyelids, a flutter of thoughts reborn, the coldness of the floor, the smashed body, tickling temples, a soft and maternal hand stroking his forehead and, when he opened his eyes, the sensation of having been through Mictlan or in the depths of Erebus. Dora Elsa smiled at him without being able to conceal her concern, like those nurses who try to bring hope to cancer patients. For a moment Evaristo thought that he was in bed and had woken up in his lover's arms but, when he saw the landing, he remembered angrily the man wearing a mackintosh. As a reflex action he began to feel his body, afraid of having lost a leg or an arm. He was complete, his wallet was not gone nor his car keys but, nonetheless, he felt something was missing.

"The notebook. Where's the notebook?" he asked Dora Elsa, holding her by the shoulders.

"What notebook? What are you talking about?"

"Last night I had a notebook. I found it at Fabiola Nava's and I brought it from the car." Evaristo wanted to get up and suddenly felt a sword-like pain in his head. "It hurts, it hurts so much, I think some bastard broke my skull."

"You have a bump the size of a football. I'm going to get some ice. Don't get up, my love."

Dora Elsa entered the flat using her key, leaving the door open. When he saw the lock intact, Evaristo understood that his attacker had gone there with a purpose: he wanted the notebook and nothing else. Maybe he had been followed from Fabiola's house or even before, since he had left La Concordia, lost between the rain and the traffic, imperceptible for a second-class detective like himself who did not even know how to watch his back. It was his own fault for being so confident, even though he knew someone was watching him. The author of the anonymous notes and the man in the mac were the same person without a doubt, but how could he be identified if he never left a trace? The sting in Evaristo's cranium reminded him with a sharp pain that he was in no condition for mental effort. And perhaps it would be much better not to think: every time he thought, he became even more confused and, with his own clumsiness, he was helping the murderer, who by now must have been considering him his ally. Wasn't it kind of Evaristo to have broken into Fabiola's house to get Lima's notebook for the killer, which without a doubt compromised him?

"Lift your head, my love, and put this bag there to bring down the swelling. Who was the wretched man who hit you?"

"I wish I knew." Burning from the sensation of the ice, Evaristo refrained from moaning. "He attacked me from behind and I never saw his face."

"That happens when you wander the streets alone." Dora Elsa wiped a tear that was melting her mascara. "All Feds work in pairs or groups, but you think you are such a macho. One of these days I'm going to find you dead in the corridor."

"Please don't nag me, I'm a big boy. Better still, help me get up, don't be mean."

Evaristo managed to stand up by clinging on to Dora Elsa's shoulder, and she slowly walked him to his bedroom where she removed his shoes and jacket.

"Now lie down, but don't take off the ice bag. I'm going to bring you a coffee."

The bed was a blessing for his pounded bones that seemed to have crumbled after spending the night on the floor. Thinking was not painful anymore. He relaxed his neck muscles, feeling that his well-being (like the sunlight) emanated from Dora Elsa, the good fairy in every sense – because she was kind and so delicate – who had come to rescue him from his darkness, to demonstrate to him that her love was not a mere adventure. "She does love me," he thought, while looking at her working in the kitchen with her hair in a net and her polyester dress with the high collar concealing her provocative body, giving her the air of a decent lady of the house. It was the morning costume that she wore to take her daughter to school but, on her it had the function of a carnival mask that revealed her true self instead of hiding it. Because Dora Elsa kept inside the honesty and elemental respect for others that Fabiola Nava, Perla Tinoco and other hags of their ilk had lost.

Fear of Animals

What would Fabiola do if she were to find any of her lovers unconscious? Finish him off with a bottle? Spit in his face and take the opportunity to ransack his flat? At least Evaristo had a loyal and straight friend who did not play double games and would not stab him in the back. In her role as mother of a sick child, Dora Elsa put the coffee on his bedside table and picked up the jacket to put it on a hanger, whistling 'The Difference' by Juan Gabriel. Evaristo followed her with his eyes and noticed that, after putting the hanger in the closet, her face scrunched up in a grimace of repugnance.

"Can you tell me who this so-called Fabiola is?" she asked in a despising voice that heralded a storm.

"A writer I'm investigating."

"You must be investigating her well deep because you even kept her knickers." Dora Elsa flung the panties in his face. "You son-of-a-bitch! You get your face smashed because you are fucking that bitch and here comes the jerk to tend your wounds!"

The angel had turned into a dragon and she jumped on the bed to slap Evaristo, who spilt the coffee over the sheets as he tried to avoid her. Her jaw tense and her face distorted, Dora Elsa was throwing blows and scratching the air as he tried to hold her arms.

"Please calm down, I have not had anything to do with that bitch."

"If so, who is the owner of the knickers? Was it a little bird that left them in your jacket?"

Losing to her lover's grip as he held her wrists in self-defence, Dora Elsa started to give in little by little until she broke down sobbing, her head buried under the pillow. Evaristo felt guilty at having betrayed her, albeit only with his thoughts. He had not made love to Fabiola, but he desired her, and that was the beginning of infidelity.

"Don't cry, my love. Let me explain what happened."

"Save your explanations for your grandmother, I don't want to know anything about you anymore. Do you hear me? Anything." She got up from the bed in a huff and picked up her shoes. "This is what I get for being good, for falling in love like an idiot with bastards I don't even know. They all want the same thing, a few lays and then they get bored, because along comes another wretch to heat up their cocks. I am a whore from the waist down, but you win first prize because you have prostituted your soul. And don't think I'm saying this because I'm livid, okay? If I go out into the streets right now, I can have a hundred blokes better than you." She walked to the door with sparks coming from her feet. As she passed through the sitting room, she smashed a picture frame with a picture of Evaristo in it and, when she reached the door, she gave an evil smile. "Don't even think of looking for me at Sherry's because I'm going to ask them not to let you in. See you nevermore, darling. I hope one of your dirty birds gives you Aids."

Evaristo put up with her departure and the slamming of the door without batting an eyelid, with the attitude of a confessed, convicted criminal who accepted the judge's verdict. He even forgot the blow to his head, but he was not completely depressed because, although Dora Elsa's insults were hurtful and had reached his heart, she had acted like a beast because she suspected infidelity. Did he need greater proof of her love? The problem was – and when he thought of this he shivered – that she may never forgive him, out of pride and stubbornness. He went to get some ice from the fridge and served himself a whisky. He had been stupid, tragically stupid, losing the love of his life over a misunderstanding. In his thoughts he cursed Fabiola, opened the window facing the Circuito Interior and threw out the knickers. He enjoyed seeing how the cars printed their tyres on the delicate floral lace when the telephone ringing shook his head like the blow of a gong.

"Hello?"

"Hi, Intellectual. Someone told me that you caught Lima's killer."

"He's only a suspect. Who's calling?"

"Hell, don't you even recognise my voice? This is Fat Zepeda."

"What's up, Fat?"

"Nothing. I just wanted to know if you had cast an eye over my poems."

"Forgive me, but I have not had time. I promise you that, when I finish this thing, I'll read them."

He hung up suddenly to stop Fat chatting. The call had been like a tremor that stirred him from his sentimental loss, planting his feet firmly back on the ground. At any moment Maytorena would arrest Vilchis, if he hadn't done so already, but now Evaristo had another suspect, Osiris, who probably had Lima's notebook, if his guess was correct. But he did not know anything about Osiris. Just that he had threatened to kill Lima and also that he wrote poetry, like Fat Zepeda, Tinoco and other delicate souls he was beginning to fear, as if dealing with muses were a sign of innate perversity, equivalent to prognathism and the cranial deformities found in criminal physiognomy manuals. To get out of the hole, he called Rubén Estrella, his bedside table informant, who knew the intrigues of the literary circle to perfection. Rubén knew who Osiris was, but he was not as accessible as usual.

"I'm sorry, bro. I have a lot of work. We are preparing the anniversary edition and I can't waste time playing detectives. Call me another day and we can arrange something."

"Please, I need to see you today. I think Osiris is Lima's killer. If you call me, we can bang him in jail."

After a doubting pause, Rubén softened.

"All right, bro, I'm going to leave the office so we can talk without ears all around us. Let's meet at 11 at Parnaso's coffee shop, but this must be the last time. You're treating me like your secretary and you don't even pay me for it."

After a quick shower and a strong coffee, Evaristo left in his car for Coyoacán, keeping an eye on all those drivers who looked at him at the traffic lights. He arrived at the appointment before Rubén and ordered some *huevos rancheros*. Even when the square was sunny and the church shone with light good enough for a postcard, under the green gazebo's roof it felt cold. As in the Trocadero bar, the intellectual clientele made him uncomfortable and he felt he was being excluded, despite wearing a denim jacket so as to match Rubén Estrella. Opposite their table was a group of writers or university lecturers, divided in discussing the literary quality of Subcomandante Marcos, and wrapped in a thick cloud of smoke. To the right, a youth with a pale face and bottle-end glasses hid his solitude behind a voluminous book, which may have been about philosophy and which every now and then he underlined in with a pen. Further within the coffee shop, at a table next to the flowerbeds of the plaza, a young and beautiful brown-haired reporter was interviewing a middle-aged lady with distinguished looks, a writer or historian, who wielded a golden cigarette holder and emphasised her statements by moving it like a baton. These people formed an impenetrable and hostile circle against those on the outside, a cultural circle, like a lifestyle, which an upstart like Evaristo would never penetrate, even if he were fanatical about books. The more he got to know the little cultural world and its environs, the more convinced he became that it was not what you read but how you projected this to the outside, turning it into an attribute of your personality, that enabled you to enter. He had read a lot but kept the same personality, the kind of gown that you use at home, mended and full of holes, that disadvantaged him in relation to those cultured folk in the shop window. Nobody was looking at him, but he felt observed, subjected to examination, and, when he was finally brought his breakfast, he ate it without lifting his eyes from the plate, crouched within himself like a caterpillar. When he had nearly finished the eggs that were as hot as his shame, Rubén Estrella arrived at the caféteria, wearing trainers and a tracksuit top and with a satchel full of books. Evaristo perceived a troubled expression on his dark and bony face, like that of a stone idol.

"Sit down, bro. Fancy something to drink?"

"An americano coffee."

When the waitress had left the table, Evaristo wanted to get straight to the point, but Rubén stopped him.

"Wait, Luciano. Before we start, I also want to ask you some questions. I can't trust you if I don't know who you are. You have spoken to many people from the literary circle and nobody knows you. Where did you say you write?"

"In *Macrópolis* magazine."

"That's weird. The head of news there is my friend, you know? Yesterday I asked him about you when we attended a business lunch and, as it happens, he has never heard your name."

"Well, that's because I hand my texts straight to the editor."

"Really, because the editor ate with us and he doesn't know who you are either. Nobody has read you anywhere, Luciano, and really I'm afraid you may be a cop. This is why I didn't want to come here. It's nasty when you are used as a deep throat to fuck other colleagues in the business. Then I changed my mind and thought: hold on, give him the chance to defend himself, the guy seems honest, even though he's got a mobile. Tell me the naked truth, Luciano, if that's what your name really is: are you a Fed or do you work by yourself?"

"I work at the Federal Judicial Police, but I have personal reasons to investigate Lima's death." Evaristo looked into Rubén's eyes. "The night he was killed I was with him..."

"I don't want to be your accomplice or to know any secrets." Rubén got up without even sipping his coffee, so Evaristo held him by one arm.

Fear of Animals

"Wait, please, I'm not who you think I am."

"No? So what are you, then? A holy man who says three Hail Marys before torturing those in detention? Look, old man, I was at the June 10 massacre and know very well how you investigate people, because you took me into solitary. Do you see this scar?" He lifted his fringe and showed Evaristo a cut on his forehead. "It was done by a colleague of yours, Commander Higareda. He wanted to make me confess that I was the leader of the movement. As I denied it to the point of tiring him, he beat me with the butt of his gun. And that was only the beginning. Then he started to play Russian roulette and shot me three times in the temple so that I'd spill the beans. The fourth time I said, c'mon stop it, I'll sign anything, but don't kill me."

"That's not my style. I do clean jobs."

"Do you think it's clean deceiving people behind a journalist's disguise?"

"That was the only way to approach Lima's intellectual friends. If I had introduced myself as a Fed they would have been on their guard. And with you I have proven that I was right: all you need to do is hold a crucifix up to me, as if you'd seen the Devil."

"Man to man, you don't scare me." Rubén raised his voice, attracting the attention of the rest of the clients, who looked towards their table. "We can have a punch-up whenever you want. When you are stripped of your guns, you are all a bunch of queers."

"Well, I have no weapon," Evaristo said as he opened his jacket, "and even if you don't believe me, I have never tortured anyone."

"I've already told you, I don't believe in model cops. If you were as decent as you say, you would have another job. Only the scum of society become Feds, those who couldn't even make it as robbers. And you will forgive me, but I do not want to keep talking to you: I have the right to choose my friends."

Rubén released himself from Evaristo's grip and walked towards the exit amid the whispering of the clients. Evaristo threw a fifty peso note on the table, jumped the barrier and the bushes separating the cafeteria and the plaza and went running behind Rubén, who was speeding up and crossing the square diagonally between the flower pots. In his hurry to catch up, Evaristo stumbled over a stall of earrings laid on a black cloth on the ground, not taking any notice of the seller who shouted insults at him. When Rubén saw that Evaristo was following him, he ran towards the arches and, turning left, entered a paved street, but his old rocker looks attracted the attention of a bank guard who thought he was a criminal trying to flee.

"Stop or I'll shoot," he threatened him, pointing the gun at Rubén's head.

"Don't shoot, sergeant. That hairy guy is coming with me," shouted Evaristo, gasping.

When he got near the policeman, Evaristo showed him his Fed's shield.

The policeman lowered the revolver, took Rubén by his arm and handed him to Evaristo, who had not yet caught his breath but had already lit a cigarette.

"What? Am I detained?" protested Rubén.

"You deserve it for leaving me without a word, but I've told you that's not my style. Let's go to my car. I'll give you a lift to work and we'll talk there."

When they got inside the Spirit, Evaristo felt that Rubén was frozen with fear, perhaps because he had seen the Magnum on the back seat. He could have squeezed some information about Osiris out of him with threats, but he wanted to kill Rubén's suspicions because he appreciated his help and also needed an ally.

"Look, Rubén, I know what you think because I was like you before joining the Feds. To you there's only black or white: on one side, police arseholes and, on the other, cool youths who fuck off to live on Cipolite beach and dream of starting the Revolution. But, in between those two poles, there are many shades of grey. Even the lowest of policemen, when you scratch a bit, have their little corner of goodness, and the most idealistic of university youths hides a mean ambition in the depths of his soul. You yourself may have your own weaknesses, you are not a literary person for no reason. Vanity, for example. Isn't it true that you believe you are the greatest fucking writer in Mexico?"

"That's all I needed," protested Rubén, "a killer from the Feds preaching humility. Where is this going?"

"Just for you to know that moral perfection does not exist. There are no absolutes, neither in good nor evil. If you condemn en masse all those people in the grey area, you are condemning yourself. Everybody in this life, listen well, everyone in this life is capable of doing something fucking evil."

"With that argument you could condone Hitler's crimes, Stalin's purges, the massacre of Tlatelolco and even Roberto's murder. Why are you looking for a guilty person, if he's no better or worse than yourself?"

"Because if I don't find him, I'm fucked." Evaristo turned right at Miguel Angel de Quevedo, where a truck that could not get into a garage had stopped the traffic. "I'm the model of that artist's impression published in *Proceso*. Thank God it's so bad that nobody can recognise me, but I have Casillas against me – that fusspot from *El Matutino* who is blaming me for the stiff. What neither Casillas, *Proceso*, nor you know is that I wanted to save Lima's life, I swear to God. My greatest mistake was to be good to some bastard I didn't even know..."

Even though the midday heat was hitting hard, Evaristo closed the windows to avoid the lorry's fumes, preferring to be roasted than to die of asphyxia. It was a relief to be able to speak sincerely to someone and drain the sewage from his conscience. Trusting in Rubén's good faith, he told him about Maytorena's discovery on the road to Pachuca, his failed attempt to warn Lima, his encounter with the cigar-smoking man on the stairs, the killer's anonymous notes, his reasons for finding him in the literary circle, and the comings and goings of an investigation like snakes and ladders, where one day he advanced and the next he went backwards to the start of the board, and that had taken him from Fabiola to Vilchis and from Vilchis to Osiris..."

"I don't want to lumber you with this trouble, nor am I asking you to erase my name from your blacklist," Evaristo concluded. "You can think whatever you want about me, that I am corrupted, a baby eater and a son-of-a-bitch, but let me tell you something: this son-of-a-bitch, as corrupted as you want to see him, is the only person who can find out who killed your friend. So now you know, either you collaborate with me or you collaborate with the killer."

Rubén looked at the Magnum in the rearview mirror.

"And how can I be sure you're not the murderer?"

Evaristo stopped suddenly at the corner of Altavista and Revolución.

"Because, if I were, you would be dead, imbecile." Exasperated, he rubbed his face with his hands. "You know what, idiot? You'd better get out right now. Get out and go and tell your colleagues at the magazine, those bloody lazy lefties supported by the government, that you were speaking to Satan and flames were coming out of his mouth."

Rubén opened the door, put a foot out of the car and, after a moment of inner conflict reflected in the tension on his face, closed it again.

"Alright, I'm going to tell you what I know, but don't call me to give any statement, uh? I want this to be between us, because there'd be reprisals and I don't want bloody trouble."

"Nobody is going to ask you to declare anything." Evaristo turned the car on. "All this is confidential information that will not appear in any procedure. I just want to know what Osiris' surname is, because Lima owed him."

"His surname is Cantú de la Garza... Osiris Cantú de la Garza. I met him at the Faculty of Philosophy and Literature at a seminar about Góngora by Antonio Alatorre. Even then he was real dandy, you know, silk shirts and English woollen jumpers, mane very well kept, imported lotions, manners of a prince. He came to class in an orange Mustang, sometimes with his dog, a well-trained Alsatian that stayed quietly outside. Logically, all the chicks were nuts about him. They even queued to say hello to him in the corridors. What else would they do if there were so few men at the faculty, and half of them queers? At first, I didn't like him. I came from Colonia Obrera and thought, bloody bourgeois shit. Why doesn't he go study at the private university, but we had something in common: both of us were heavy consumers of dope. I discovered that at the house of Chata Silva, a super-randy chick studying classical languages who lived by herself and organised some fucking great parties. Once Osiris turned up with an extra large spliff of Colombian grass, about twenty centimetres long, and he threw it on the table saying, 'Open it, the Zeppelin is landing'. He knocked out the whole party with just half of it, but only Osiris and I, the hard-core users, stayed puffing until we had smoke coming out of our ears. It was like smoking the Pipe of Peace."

"But what does Osiris do nowadays?" Evaristo asked impatiently. "What had he sold to Lima?"

"I'm getting there, calm down. Since the Zeppelin day, Osiris and I became friends and, as he wrote erotic poems, I introduced him to Roberto, who published his first works at *The Hangover*, the magazine we produced at Silverio Lanza's workshop."

"Lima mentions him in his notebook. He brands Osiris an ingrate because he forgot that Lima was his first editor."

"Yes, with the passing of time, he turned arrogant. The

Fear of Animals

acknowledgments and prizes made him dizzy, and now he looks at you from over his shoulder because he is a fixture of the high ranks. He's been translated into several languages. Every second he is invited to give conferences in other countries, but back then he was cool and, because he had dosh, it was a treat hanging around with him as he would invite you to feast in expensive restaurants and piss-ups with French wines. Once Roberto and I went to Acapulco with him in his Mustang. We pulled these gringas there and he paid for everything: the hotel, the discos, the food. From his surname I suspected he was the son of some millionaire from Monterrey, and once I asked him if his old man sent him dough, but no. As it happens, his family was only middle class and they never gave him a penny. So, I thought, how does he manage to enjoy such a lifestyle? After that I started to observe him and I discovered that the bastard sold grass and pills in the university gardens. He went for a walk with his Alsatian, the clients came to connect, they got into his Mustang, and there he delivered the bricks, wrapped in newspaper. His business was so well organised that he even gave cuts to the security staff, like a professional drug trafficker. I thought that we, the hard-core users, were like a big family and felt bad because he was making a business out of exploiting our brothers. Even more so as he was a poet, no? So much for preaching love, equality, harmony and freedom through the word, and then to fall into the most decadent mercantilism. One day, at a cantina, I told him, 'Hey, I know where you get so much dosh. I don't want to preach, that's your thing, but explain to me what drug trafficking and poetry have in common.' He freaked big time, as if I'd told him to go fuck his mother. 'No,' he says, 'what's happening is that you don't understand. Poetry is one thing, and life is another, life is a bitch. I can't give away the grass to everyone, I'll end up on the streets, I have to pay my rent, buy books, clothes, food, but don't think that I'll dedicate myself to drug trafficking all my life. When I get enough dough to set up a publishing house, I'll throw this away.' Sure. As far as I know he's still doing the business. It's been a long time since I saw him, because I started to avoid him after that, and now he doesn't even say hello to me, but his fame has spread everywhere. In the circle he is known as the Narcopoet."

"I understand," said Evaristo, thinking to himself. "Lima was his client and Osiris threatened him because of the lack of payment."

"Could be. My buddy was as heavy a dopehead as I am, it's just that he mixed it with alcohol and anti-depressants. Maybe Osiris gave him some on credit and penniless old Roberto was hiding from him so as not to pay him back."

"But there's something that doesn't fit." Evaristo stopped in a small, quiet, tree-lined road in San Angel without turning off the engine. "I don't think Osiris needs to sell drugs to make a living if he is such a renowned poet."

"Well, renowned in brackets." A twinkle of malice surfaced in Rubén's eyes. "He has known how to make friends with the right people, he has a resumé that dazzles any idiot, but really he is a pedestrian poet. And, about his business, take into account that he loves the good life. A playboy like him is not happy to have mediocre posts as an assessor and grants to get by on."

"I need to meet him in person. Could you get me his details?"

"Maybe a colleague from the office has them because, apart from trafficking, Osiris is an aviator – he lands on payday every month at the institute and earns twice what I get. Let me call him."

He borrowed the mobile phone from Evaristo, who smiled at him ironically, as if to say, 'Isn't this a useful gadget?' Rubén returned the smile and Evaristo perceived in his face the emotion of a child playing secret agents.

"Julian, could you do me a favour? Could you get me Mr Osiris Cantú de la Garza's telephone number and address?"

Fear of Animals

On guard at Plaza Federico Gamboa, that small island of peace at the heart of Chimalistac, with its 17th-century village chapel and its tiny park carpeted with dead leaves, Evaristo wolfed down a bacon sandwich while sitting at the wheel of the Spirit, on which he had balanced Roberto Lima's book. Osiris' colonial-style, two-storey house with whitewashed walls and flowerpots on the windows, was twenty metres from where Evaristo was parked, and he glanced at the front door every time he turned a page. He had been waiting for more than three hours and soon it would be dark. Every now and then mothers taking their babies for a walk in prams, maids in uniform, policemen on the beat, or high school students messing around would pass by, but Osiris was nowhere to be seen. It was seven o'clock. If he did not turn up within an hour, Evaristo would call Maytorena to send an agent to watch the house. Lima's short stories, with their crude depictions of the misery in shanty towns, their crimes among rival gangs and perverse pleasure in graphically describing all the blood, faeces and vomit, were not the best accompaniment to swallowing a sandwich. He had read more than half the book and he had only liked one story, the one about the crippled guy without arms and legs who begged at the entrance of a cheap hotel and extorted adulterous women, asking them for sexual favours in exchange for not telling their husbands. It was a strange combination of Boccaccio and José Revueltas that had not been too bad, despite its clumsy ending – one of the husbands caught the cripple enjoying his wife so he threw him down the sewerage duct – but the rest of the tales, if they deserved the name, really were underdeveloped. Lima stood before the narrative like a bad puppeteer and overwhelmed the reader with extensive lyrical digressions impregnated with an acid social resentment. Evaristo was not reading Flaubert, that much was pretty obvious, but when he compared the landscape of Chimalistac – elegant and sober –

with the sordid, dusty streets in which Lima's stories took place, he was prepared to forgive the author's literary fumblings in favour of sentimental empathy, as if the mere fact of having written about and on behalf of those who were fucking poor had a merit that surpassed any aesthetic whim. To dedicate yourself to literature in Peñon de los Baños was like sowing flowers across a bleak plateau: what would it matter if they looked a bit colourless and sad? Compared with this, a bourgeois like Osiris, with his beautiful little house – worth probably a thousand million pesos from the old days – had everything in his favour to make it in *Belle Literature*. Or maybe it was just a bluff like Perla Tinoco's? The more he got to know the literary circle, the more he was suspicious of reputations and prestige. Who was he to believe if, in public, they were all the greatest and, in private, they tore each others entrails out?

Curious, Evaristo flickered through Fat Zepeda's poems that were on the back seat. As he imagined, they were corny and empty-worded verses, adorned with spelling mistakes:

Radiant radiance of star
that illuminates my patth
tell that girl I love the most
that I am dying for her...

Tired of reading, Evaristo turned on the radio, tuning in until he found Radio Capital. Listening to 'Angie', the old Stones' ballad, he grew melancholic and thought of Dora Elsa. It was a long time since he had loved a woman with that mixture of tenderness and lust. He had even given up the snow for her, and all to lose her in such a stupid way, just for some knickers that he didn't even take off their owner. Angrily he remembered the lecture in linguistics that Perla Tinoco had given between Fabiola's legs and imagined that Dora Elsa, as horny as she was, could have left him for any of the dancers at Sherry's, where being a dyke was daily bread. Even if she forgave him – dreaming was free – he would have to improve himself as a lover, be a man and a lesbian at the same time, because now he felt that every woman was a potential rival. He was beginning to get hot under the collar imagining how he would apply Perla Tinoco's teachings the day they made up, when, at the other side of the park, a Cavalier with darkened windows parked opposite Osiris' house. Evaristo took the Magnum, got out

Fear of Animals

of his car and quickly walked over the dried leaves, the gun concealed in his jacket pocket. The man driving the Cavalier took a while opening the gate after looking for something in the glove compartment. He had a beige mackintosh identical to that worn by whoever had attacked Evaristo the night before. When he got out of the car and was about to open his garage, Evaristo already had him at his mercy.

"Are you Osiris Cantú de la Garza?"

The man nodded. He was tall, blue-eyed, and had a Roman nose, his moustache was half-greying and, even though he was a bit overweight, he still had the poise and elegance of his university days.

"I was waiting for you, Narcopoet." Evaristo pushed the barrel of the Magnum into his ribs. "Would you grant me an interview? I want to know how you get the inspiration to write such beautiful things."

"Take my car if thee want, but don't kill me," Osiris said, using thee as a sign of respect. He shivered with fear.

"Who told you I'm a thief? We've just met and already you've started to insult me?"

"What dost thou want? I don't bother anyone. I am a man of peace, *gente de Paz*."

"Are you talking about Octavio? Well, with me, those contacts don't work. Get inside." Evaristo pushed him towards the door. "It's very cold in here and my hand is shaking. It wouldn't be my fault if a shot slipped out."

Osiris opened the two locks suddenly and, when they had entered the house, a shaven, lapping French poodle jumped up and greeted him.

"Wait, Propercio, I'm not in the mood for games." When the dog saw Evaristo, he growled at him suspiciously.

"Are you there, my darling? A woman with her hair half-done, wrapped in a bath robe, peeked from the landing. "The director of Bellas Artes called you to say he was going to leave the tickets for the Opera at the box office. I'll just finish bathing the children and will come down."

"Your husband can't go anywhere." Evaristo stepped forward to enter the lady's view. "He and I have to talk in private."

"But who are you?" The wife came down a few steps and froze when she saw the Magnum in Evaristo's hand.

"I am the law, madam." Evaristo showed her his shield.

"But this is breaking in. You can't search the house without a warrant."

"Take it easy, madam, I only want to ask your husband a few questions. You stay up there and don't let the children come down." Evaristo turned toward Osiris and his tone grew harder. "Take me where you keep the drugs."

"I don't understand." Osiris raised an eyebrow, half indignant, half surprised. "Who dost thou think I am?"

Thinking that the very same hypocrite had hit him from behind to relieve him of the notebook, Evaristo's conscience became clouded with anger, so he kneed him in the balls.

"Do you know who I think you are? A corrupted louse." He lifted the man by the mackintosh lapels and put the gun to his temple. "Are you going to get the drugs out or do you want to die right here, before your wife's eyes?"

Clenching his jaws, Osiris resisted the pain to the point of making Evaristo flinch; believing him innocent, Evaristo was about to put the gun down, when his wife squealed. "The drugs are in the safe in the study, behind the Pedro Coronel painting," she said clumsily, and burst out crying when she saw her husband's amazement and him look at her with hatred. "What did you want?" she scolded him. "That I should let him kill you?"

Without losing his cool, Osiris made a gesture for Evaristo to follow him through a narrow corridor that ended up at the door of the study, an elegant and welcoming room with a thick burgundy carpet, glass screens to protect the books from dust, and a small, used fireplace with shiny bronze pokers. Among the *objets d'art* stood a huge Baroque angel carved in wood, overlooking the desk. As Osiris keyed the combination of the safe on to an electric keypad, Evaristo remembered the dirty and depressing hovel where Lima had erected his pathetic ivory tower. It was the home of a pariah with nothing to hide. Osiris, on the other hand, was trying to dress up the inadmissible origins of his fortune with the false dignity of good taste. The Narcopoet took from the safe a polythene bag containing half a kilogram of compacted coke, a brick of marijuana and several jars of LSD and amphetamines that Evaristo received with a mocking smile.

"Where did all these come from?" Evaristo asked, pointing at the Pedro Coronel painting and Baroque angel.

"I don't do deals with the drugs, I do public relations." Osiris held his chin up in a defiant attitude. "I only supply materials to a select group of friends."

"But when you need to be paid back, you forget who your mates are, don't you?"

"Look, who knows what was said to *you* about me, but I can assure *you* I'm not a professional trafficker. To many of my friends I never seek payment. That means I do not ask for money paybacks, although all of them end up paying with favours or gifts."

"Ah, damn, I need you to explain how that works." Evaristo sat at Osiris' desk without taking his gun off him, surprised at the sudden familiarity he had adopted. He seemed to be confident of reaching an agreement because, instead of showing nervousness, he was behaving like the master of the situation. "So you are not a professional and to look good among your pals you give them drugs."

"Not so much give them: for every gram of snow and every spliff, I get triple what they are worth on the market. In this circle you are worth the contacts you hold and, to me, the drug is a way of making friends. I have a clientele of literary people who do all sorts, but they are not people who would link up with any old dealer, are you with me? I spare them the risk of being found out and arrested, and they give me their support."

"What kind of support?" Evaristo lit a cigarette, not offering one to Osiris.

"Supporting my career. In this literature thing and, most of all, in poetry, you're nobody if you are ignored by your colleagues. You need the approval of the establishment or you end up being any old poet, even if you're a genius. When I was a perfect unknown I was dying to be published in *Trasluz*, the most prestigious magazine twenty years ago, where the bigwigs in that period wrote. Naive me, I took my poems to Fidel Rivas, who was then the head of features. Years went by and he didn't publish a fucking word of mine. I'm sure he never even gave them a glance. He simply decided that I did not exist. Anyone else in my position, hurt by his disdain, would have dedicated himself to fucking writing against the *Trasluz* clique from their little marginal magazines, but I was cannier. If that arrogant shit denies that I exist, I thought, if it depends on him whether I have a name, I'm going to work on him so that he owes me. Luckily this circle is a small one, we had common friends and I started to bump into

Rivas at cocktail parties, fashionable bars and intellectuals' events where I noticed that he did coke hard. I offered him snow lines when he had cold turkey in the middle of a drinking session, or I slipped him a snow pack for the hangover next day. Pay me when you can, I would say to him. I scratch your back, you scratch mine. Later, I was his dealer of choice, but I never treated him as a client. We talked about books, we went to Tepoztlán for the weekend with our women and, to gain his trust, I gave him the coke at the price I bought it for. One day, after I got married, I invited him for lunch at my house. We had a couple of grams and I threw him the same poems. 'Wow,' he said, 'these are fucking ace. I'm going to propose them at the next features meeting.' So that's how I slipped into the pages of *Trasluz*."

"There's no doubt that, at the end of the day, quality surfaces." Evaristo puffed on his cigarette with a cheeky grin. "But there's something I'm still unclear about: where do you get the dough from, if you say your business isn't drugs?"

"It's not drugs, but prestige. In Mexico prestige means money. Thank God we have a government that spoils its intellectuals. Look at my career: when I was twenty-six years old, thanks to my friend Fidel, president of the jury, I won the López Velarde prize, and with the money I paid the deposit for this little house. Later, with the support of a very important writer whom I supplied with grass and peyote (I am not telling you his name now because he's not relevant at this moment, but he's a national treasure), I obtained a post as an assessor at the public education ministry, where I was paid like a king just for attending a monthly working breakfast with the Minister of Education. Then I had the means to float independently, so I approached the cultural chiefs, got into the Fund's mafia, appeared in various anthologies, and later came the television interviews, the Guggenheim grant, the trips abroad. Do you see this photo? This is the International Congress of Ecological Poets in San Francisco ten years ago. A junkie literary guy working at Televisa's Cultural Foundation got me the invitation. Here I am talking to Czeslaw Milosz, the Nobel prize winner. Some day, God willing, I'm going to win that one. And the most incredible thing of all is that I have only published a thirty-page *plaquette*."

"You think you're such a hot shot, don't you?" Evaristo went on the attack, sickened by his cynicism. "I congratulate you for being such a fucking pro', but I didn't come here so you could recite your

Fear of Animals

resumé to me. You'd better talk to me about the other Osiris, the thug that makes death threats to friends who owe him money."

"If I'm to confess, I'd prefer to do so to a priest. Why don't you sing clearly if you came for money?" Osiris got a wad of banknotes out of the safe. "Tell me how much the deal is and let's kill it here and now."

Smiling, without showing his indignation, Evaristo shot the Magnum towards his feet. The bullet ricocheted and ended up lodged in the picture with Czeslaw Milosz. Outside the study, Osiris' wife let out a scream.

"More respect. Put your stinking money away, because we're not of the same kind, or I'll stick the next one in your belly." Osiris obeyed rapidly with humility. "I came here because I'm investigating the death of your friend Roberto Lima. I know that you and he had some disagreements over money."

"That story was fabricated by someone who is trying to damage me. Roberto and I had stopped seeing each other a long time ago."

"You're lying again." Evaristo grabbed Osiris by the sideburns, giving him a hard tug. "Before he died, Lima left behind a note in his own writing where it says that you threatened him because he owed you money. And, as he could not pay you back, you went to see him at Peñon de los Baños and whacked him with the dictionary."

"That I threatened him is true, but I didn't kill him." Osiris fell to the carpet in pain. "I just wanted to press him. I never imagined something like that could happen."

"And don't you think it's more than a mere coincidence that someone made this threat come true for you?"

"Roberto had many enemies. Any of them could have killed him. He was a resentful man who could not stand the success of the others. A little while ago he came to blows with Claudio Vilchis."

"Yes, I know him: a pimp of the system just like you. But that dispute does not interest me. I want you to tell me about your business with him. Did Lima owe you a huge amount?"

"Five hundred thousand old pesos for an order of Colombian grass that I supplied him with about three years ago. I had written off the debt, but he did something fucking awful. He published in the *Sábado* cultural supplement a column signed under a *nom de plume* in which he wrote about my deals since the days at the faculty. He didn't call me by my name, but anyone could have guessed by the headline, 'Wanted: Egyptian Narcopoet'. Through some of my contacts I got to know that Roberto was the author. To be truthful, it hurt because I thought he was my friend, but this circle is like that: you never know where envy is going to strike. I didn't want to confront him because those kinds of people must be ignored when they pounce, and that way you can screw them better. It's the famous slap with a white glove. But some weeks later I bumped into him at El Hijo del Cuervo and, after four highballs, I couldn't pretend not to have noticed. I took him outside, I shook him on the sidewalk and, even when I had the discretion not to mention the *Sábado* story, I reminded him of our old debt and threatened to kill him if he didn't pay. It was a drunken outburst and the next day I regretted it. I must say I still can't digest the news of his murder. There is something inside me refusing to believe it. Poor Roberto: he was a bastard, but he didn't deserve to die that way."

"How sweet. Now you even feel sorry for him." Evaristo gave him an ironic pat on the shoulder. "Such a shame that all the clues point to you. Can you tell me where you were at the time of the crime?"

"I don't recall precisely. I think I was at the Academy of Language's plenary session."

"And what time did you come out of there?"

"About six o'clock."

"According to the autopsy, Lima died at seven thirty. You had plenty of time to go to his flat and avenge your exposure in *Sábado*." Evaristo pushed his face against Osiris', blowing smoke, an intimidatory tactic he copied from Humphrey Bogart. "That is how narcos operate everywhere. Why would you be the exception? Your pride was wounded because Lima had revealed you as you really are, all pretence, a stinking nit, and it was easy for you to hunt him down in his own den. You didn't count on me visiting him and drinking a few tequilas. When I had left, you entered his house and, as Lima was paralytic, he didn't fight back. You had the gun to hand that I had left for him to defend himself, but you preferred the dictionary, a refinement that a simple contract killer would not have had. Then you called *El Universal* to divert the police with the political crime version. You must be very pleased, people believed it, but you're fucked. Let's call the newspaper again, to see if the story's author identifies your voice." Evaristo dialled a number on his mobile phone. "Could you please put me though to Ignacio Carmona?... How's it going, Nacho, remember me? I'm Evaristo Reyes, the agent who questioned you at Roberto Lima's wake... No, calm down, I just want to ask you a favour. I'm going to put you through to a suspect so you can tell me if he sounds familiar to you." Evaristo gave Osiris the mobile. "Recite something nice for him."

"It was May the florid season, when the deceived stealer of Europe, half-moon, the spears his forehead and the sun every beam of his fur..."

"That's enough." Evaristo grabbed the mobile. "Is this voice similar to the one of the informant who called you the night of the crime?" There was a long pause. Evaristo's face went sombre. "Are you completely sure?... No, this is only a test... Yes, of course, I promise you the scoop will be yours." He turned the mobile off and spoke to Osiris, who had been waiting anxiously. "It's your lucky day: Carmona didn't recognise you."

"So, thou see?" Osiris went back to using thou as a sign of respect. "I swear to thee I am innocent. I have never killed anyone, I can't stand the sight of blood."

"He didn't recognise you, but he says you could have used a handkerchief. Anyway, you're going to have to accompany me to the station." Evaristo tugged him roughly by the arm.

"Wait a minute," Osiris resisted. "Thou can't just arrest me on a simple suspicion."

"And these?" Evaristo pushed Osiris' nose towards the cocaine. "You'll do between five to ten years in jail for trafficking drugs. There'll be plenty of time then to find out if you really killed Lima or just wanted to give him a fright. So go on: there in the prosecutor's office you'll have to put up with bigger bastards than me."

Evaristo frog-marched him out of the study, his Magnum out just in case Osiris tried to get away. When he went past the telephone table, he took Osiris' telephone book to investigate his literary clientele. In the lounge, her hair dishevelled and her eyelids swollen from crying, Osiris' wife gave him an imploring look.

"I'm sorry, lady. I have to detain your husband. Call a lawyer because you'll need one."

"You don't know who you're dealing with." The woman put herself between them and the door. "Attorney Tapia is our friend. He dined here last week. I'm going to tell him that you planted the drug in my house to frame my husband."

"Go ahead, but even if it costs me my job, your husband is going to appear tomorrow in the crime pages." Evaristo pushed her aside. "Can you imagine the headlines? 'Osiris Cantú de la Garza, drug baron of the literary circle, arrested'. What a shame, he won't have a street named after him anymore."

"That's what you'd love, as you clearly hate educated people, but you won't be able to do anything against us. Osiris has very powerful friends. Let's see who ends up in jail!"

Evaristo listened to Mrs Cantú's threats without even turning his head. In his place, Maytorena would have shut her up with blows, but he limited himself to smiling, amused by her air of cynical rectitude. In full moral bankruptcy, after having shown her true colours, she was still stubborn enough to demarcate class and culture, even while resorting to the same intimidation methods that made her akin to the worst of gangsters.

Before he switched on his car engine, Evaristo handcuffed Osiris to the door's armrest and put his telephone book in the glove compartment. On their way to the Attorney General's office, because of the filthy pandemonium on Avenida Insurgentes, Evaristo reflected more carefully on the wife's threats. Osiris had spent many years trafficking undisturbed, so he had to be protected by someone, even more so if he worked for a big cartel. A guy like him, encrusted in the intellectual circle and close to power, was very useful to criminal sharks because of the contacts he could establish with newly appointed public officials, well-read people, mundane and with demanding tastes that would be out of the reach of a vulgar narco. To detain him would mean exposing his clients and providers, something that could cost Evaristo his job and even his life, but despite the danger – or because of it – he felt a pleasing sensation in his veins, of plenitude and well-being, that reminded him of when he was a young man and dreamed naively of putting journalism at the service of justice. This was a thousand times better, because he was delivering justice with his own hands, without asking anyone for permission. When he arrived at Paseo de la Reforma, he turned right, making his tyres screech with a euphoria induced by the tune playing on the radio, Janis Joplin's 'Move Over'. This time he did not have any regrets for having mistreated Osiris. Sometimes violence was necessary, and he had applied it to break a swine, obeying an inner voice that ordered: hard, hard, hard, like at a student demonstration. How good it had felt when he had kneed him in the balls. Gratuitous cruelty could be sick, but beating up someone in the name of good, revelling in your own virtue, left a sensation of angelic power, as if you were the strong arm of a divine command.

Evaristo arrived with a triumphal grin at the Federal Judicial Police office at Reforma Norte and Jaime Nunó. After a brief discussion in the underground parking lot with the security guard, who did not want to let him park but whom he finally convinced with the excuse that he was taking a detainee to the office, he got out of the car with Osiris, whose hands were handcuffed behind him. On the ground floor, Evaristo remanded him before the Public Prosecutor's Office, delivering the rock of coke and the brick of marijuana as evidence, not yet mentioning his possible link to Lima's murder. In the foul-smelling and dirty lift, graffitied with obscene drawings, Evaristo bumped into Maytorena's driver, Daggers, a short guy with oriental features, a compulsive smoker of filterless Raleigh cigarettes who plastered his hair with gel and was quite a gossip.

"What's up? How's work?"

"Today it was heavy. This morning we detained a Mr Vilchis."

"So soon?" Evaristo arched his eyebrows, surprised. "How did you get him?"

"Very early in the morning we stood waiting for him outside his house in Colonia Del Valle. The fucking lazy git went to work with his suitcase at around 10, well perfumed, and we followed him all the way along Eugenia up to Patriotismo. The boss's orders were to get him where there weren't many witnesses. Luckily he turned into a road in Colonia Escandón. I pulled in front of him and Chamula went up to him with the gun. 'Get out, Vilchis, you're under arrest'. 'Where are you taking me?' he said. 'This is an outrage.' Chamula had to get him into the car with a good whacking because we were just standing there, blocking the traffic. Maytorena the boss has spent about six hours locked up with him, but Vilchis isn't singing yet."

"Take me where he's being kept."

Bewildered by the coming and goings of the day, Evaristo had completely forgotten about the man with the cigar who now occupied second place on his list of suspects. But, now that he was detained, he wanted to take advantage of the circumstances to bring him face to face with Osiris. Daggers led him through a lugubrious corridor lit by tiny lightbulbs emanating a death-like light. They went through a gate, said hello to a uniformed guard flicking through *Hello*, and went down some irregular stairs to a humid and cold basement where the whitewash had created blisters on the walls. It stank of piss, sweat and cigarette smoke. From the metallic doors, lined up to left and right, came moans muffled by the thickness of the walls. Daggers stopped at door number 17 and stuck his ear to it.

"Maybe the interrogation is finished. They had a radio at full volume so you couldn't hear the screaming, but it has been switched off."

After a few knocks on the door, Chamula decided to open it and asked for silence by putting a finger over his lips. When Evaristo entered the cell, he understood why. Collapsed on a disintegrating bunk, Maytorena was having a siesta, his belly button in the air.

"What happened to Vilchis?" Evaristo whispered in Chamula's ear.

"The arsehole didn't want to talk. He was so stubborn that the boss got angry."

"I'm bringing you another detainee so he can have a face-to-face with him."

"That's going to be difficult."

"Why?"

Chamula opened a sliding door that led to a small room equipped with an electric shock set, a thick hose and a rubbish bin full of water. In a corner, spread across a calendar exposing the large breasts of the singer Gloria Trevi, Vilchis' corpse was counting the cracks in the wall. His eyes were open and a thin thread of brown blood, close to coagulation, went down from his nose to the neck of his shirt. He had almost certainly died of an internal haemorrhage, as he had no external signs of torture that would have invalidated any confession. The look on his face did not express any fear or anxiety either, maybe because Maytorena had granted him the grace of dying with his cigar in his mouth.

Evaristo turned his face and started to cry. When he heard the cries, Maytorena got up from the bunk, opened a tin of beer and ordered him to help Chamula take the body to the dump at Santa Cruz Meyehualco.

"Just a minute, I have nothing to do with this," sobbed Evaristo. "At La Concordia I warned you that Vilchis was only a suspect. Now you've disposed of him as you wish, this is where I get off."

A subordinate had never disrespected Maytorena in such a way before, even less before a third party. Chamula got his revolver out, waiting for an order from the boss to shoot him.

Fear of Animals

"Don't shoot, we have enough on our hands with one stiff." Maytorena turned to Evaristo with a twisted grin. "Your arse shrank because you can't stand the blood, isn't that right?"

"What I can't stand is your stupidity." Evaristo held his gaze. "Today I arrested another literary person who had threatened Lima with death. He is a narco and his name is Osiris Cantú de la Garza. I wanted to give him a face-to-face with Vilchis, but you were in such a rush to look good to Tapia. See what's happened because you're such an arselicker?"

"Let me remind you that you are talking to a superior," the commander, still blind from the veil of sleep in his eyes, warned him.

"You're wrong. From now on I'm not taking anyone's orders."

Evaristo threw his metal shield at Maytorena's feet and turned to leave the cell. Chamula tried to stop him at the door, but with a gesture Maytorena ordered him to let him go.

"Fuck off if you want to, Intellectual, but you know full well: any bastard that works for me never works for anyone else." He pointed at him. "It's best if you start writing your will."

"Are you threatening me?" Evaristo smiled defiantly. "Well, you see, I have life insurance. Since I joined the Feds I've been writing a book about you, in which I tell who you are in bed with. If something happens to me, my lawyer has been instructed to publish it. Can you imagine what will happen when your children read it?"

Maytorena, blackened with rage, crushed the beer can. Evaristo went out without waiting for an answer, pushing Chamula aside. In the corridor he bumped into Fat Zepeda who, for a change, asked him if he had read *Autumn Harvest* yet. Alongside the licensed killers, who did not scare him as much as before, Fat and his question sounded repugnant.

"Yes, Fat, I read your little verses and, to be honest, they are real trash. But don't lose hope." Evaristo straightened Fat's tie gently. "Learn to write haiku and you'll see prizes falling at your feet."

When he took the lift, he was a new man: a man with a firm step and head held high who looked the most twisted of policemen straight in the eye, maybe overacting a bit in proudly displaying his status as emancipated slave, but with a gleam that inspired respect. Even the guard at the gate saluted. Like Neil Armstrong when he had stepped down from the lunar module, he felt that humanity had taken a huge step along with him and, even when he was breathing the sickening air of the dungeons, in his spirit he had risen to seventh heaven, a lunar satellite from where the Federal Judicial Police seemed like the little hell from a *pastourelle*, a syphilitic wound on this terrestrial globe.

Fear of Animals

Lying on a sun lounger, his head about to explode after three days of glugging alcohol, Evaristo looked through his dirty shades at the parachute that circled above Acapulco Bay. Even when the show provoked in him a feeling of vertigo and fear that the parachutist might crash against the rocks of Condesa beach, he could not take his eyes off him, his anxiousness being at the same time a morbid desire to smash himself alongside him. Or would a crash against the most expensive hotel of the bay, because of a sudden gust, be more cinematic? He imagined the impact on Floor 24, the explosion of his entrails, the highly alcoholic concentration of blood dripping down the façade on to those idle tourists surrounding the pool. Such a tragic and silly accident would have got him out of trouble at that moment, when the future presented itself like the mouth of an oven into which he was being dragged by an endless conveyor belt. He drank the third Bloody Mary of that morning like water and, before the waiter could lift his tray, asked for the fourth "to save him having to come round again". He did not think about eating breakfast, despite having puked blood the night before at a topless bar where he had been served adulterated whisky. Fuck being healthy. He wanted to drink to the point of saturation, to turn his death into a reproach against Dora Elsa, whom he had been calling every hour since he arrived at the port without her having the courtesy to pick up the telephone. It was now four o'clock and he had to try again. Without dreaming of success, just out of simple romantic masochism, he went up to the 18th floor and once again dialled her home number, which he now knew by heart.

"You are calling Dora Elsa Oleana's house. If you would like to leave a message, please do so after the beep."

"It's me, my love. Please answer, I know you are there. When will you understand that I never had anything to do with that bloody Fabiola? Would I be calling you every minute if I was with her? What is happening is that you don't love me anymore. Pick up and tell me straight, so I know what the score is with you, but don't leave me here talking to the bloody answering machine. I need you, me, shorty. I gave up the Feds and now I'm in big trouble. Now is when I need you the most... without you, Acapulco is like a warm beer. Come here and be with me, even if only for one night, that would be enough, Maytorena can come and kill me later. Aren't you going to pick up? I smell a rat. You may have dumped me for a lesbian and right now you are both in bed, laughing about me. Didn't you say I was your greatest love? Didn't you want to have a child with me? Answer, you bitch."

He went back defeated to his seaside bed, where on a tray waiting for him was the fourth Bloody Mary of the day. To his right, a tourist with black shades and a Hawaiian shirt was reading *Excélsior*. He turned to the other side, fearing that he would see some item about Vilchis. The newspapers would have started to kick up a stink about his mysterious disappearance, but what did he gain by reading them? He had enough reason to be anxious about his own conscience, which every second flashed back at him the image of the corpse laid out in the cell, with its inexpressive gaze like a sea bass. He could only forget the stiff under the combined effects of alcohol and cocaine, when he could attribute Vilchis' death to Maytorena's mindless violence, ignoring the fact that he had denounced him without any proof. Looking for an indulgent euphoria that would allow him to believe his own lies, he had turned into a shameful drunk, dumb and violent, and crawled through all of Acapulco's dens of iniquity and discos, from elegant clubs where he had to bribe the porter to get a table to the sordid dives of the red light zone. He remembered the night before insulting a gringo singer at the piano bar of La Cucaracha – drop the mike, you fucking arrogant blond – driving his car on the sidewalk of Costera Avenue in front of a police car, so having to bribe them, and trying to seduce his hotel receptionist, offering her money for a lay.

Thank God the vodka was starting to take effect and the most embarrassing moments of his bender, which, when he had woken up, he felt worse about than the hangover itself, began to look comical and, to a certain extent, like childish pranks. After all, Acapulco was a place for having fun and he could not lock himself up crying because, even though Vilchis' death was bearing down on him, he was also celebrating the recovery of his own freedom. He was like a horse that, having been penned up, jumps the fence and leaves, terrified, galloping through the field with the risk of falling down a ravine. His uncertain future justified his propensity towards brinkmanship, because he could not stay cool knowing that someone had put a price on his head. He was free, but not for long, and everything around him – sea, sun, women in G-strings, snow traders posing as boatsmen – invited him to spend his last hours at an orgy. Sick of tomato juice, he got up from the bed and, at the pool bar, under the shade of a thatch, he asked for a submarine of tequila and beer. The change in drink infused him with optimism. Maytorena would never forgive him for the scene at the cells, but he was satisfied about having sent him to bloody hell.

"That gringa's hot, isn't she?" the barman said, talking about an American lady, who was middle-aged but whose body was slender and youthful, and who was getting out of the swimming pool with her bikini clinging to her body.

Evaristo had not seen her, even when he was looking in the same direction. When the barman winked, he examined the woman from head to toe: she was tall and her neck was long, her face freckled, her back wide but not manly, her waist thin, breasts firm, and her butt a little turned-up and overflowing from the bikini, asking for trouble. After rubbing herself with a towel, she lay face down on a lounger opposite the aquatic bar.

"Yes, she's really hot."

He contemplated her for a period of fifteen minutes, between sips of tequila, gazing greedily between her legs, where a line of golden hairs poked from under her bikini. He would have tried to get her into his bed, but with gringas what happened to him was what happens to the Mexican football team on its trips abroad: he chickened out because of his lack of international experience. Maybe another submarine could help him conquer the language barrier, because when he was drunk he could even speak Russian, but he would not know how to handle the situation if the gringa was a fitness freak, and her gymnastic body made him fear she was. What could he do to seduce her? Buy her a celery juice and talk to her about homeopathy, aerobics or bicycles attached to machines that measured how many calories you burned? Sporty and healthy flirting was not his thing, not even in Spanish. He had decided to look elsewhere when the gringa called a waiter to ask for a margarita cocktail. Good sign: that meant her body was not a temple but a regal deposit of toxins. When the blonde finished her margarita, Evaristo asked the barman to send her another one on his behalf. From the distance, he toasted her and she acknowledged with a smile. Free from prejudices, like a football team playing at home, he walked towards her, sucking in his gut.

"Hello. Shall we eat together?," he asked in his best English.

"Please, have a seat. But don't speak to me in English, 'cause I'm Spanish."

God rewarded the audacious. Grabbing the occasion by the scruff of the neck, he bestowed on her, vivaciously and carelessly, a ton of compliments and corny, but effective, jokes that made the ritual of introduction much lighter. The lady from Spain wanted "to paint the town red", was lighthearted and celebrated his Mexican idioms – right now, bro, whassup, in a mo' – with a childish laughter that paradoxically made her forehead and dimples dance. Her name was Adela and she was an Iberia stewardess. At 40, after two marriages and a common-law relationship, she spent her time enjoying herself, seeing the world and going out with friends who would not ask for fidelity "because, let's see, man, whoever said that only men could fuck with whoever they please?" That was her problem with those bores from Madrid, who became such hard work after she came back from her trips, coming to annoy her with jealous scenes as if they didn't go out with other girls when she was away. What? Did they think she had been born yesterday? That's why she did not have a formal partner right now, just lovers who came and went, and whoever attempted to claim his right to exclusiveness she would tell to go and take a hike. Evaristo agreed with her in everything. He was also a happy deserter of monogamy and, since his divorce, had lived a lot more happily, because in variety you find pleasure and, also, the Pope should not bother us: men are promiscuous animals and women too. So Adela was a lucky woman as she had found the understanding and liberal match that she needed. Laughs, arm squeezes, another margarita and the same for me please. Do you want me to spread sun lotion over you? His hand slid downwards on her back and stopped near the bikini, hot but cautious, while Adela told him about her accidents at work – the forced landing at Tegucigalpa when the right engine had malfunctioned, the decompression at twenty thousand feet while flying from Madrid to Montreal that had made them release the air masks and had killed an asthmatic passenger ("Poor guy, he

Fear of Animals

gasped like a fish caught in a net and later the relatives sued the company") – stories that Evaristo half listened to, concentrating on her warm and olive skin, liquid nearing the belly button's equator, where his fingers traced slow circles and ellipses out of orbit from desire.

From the swimming pool, drink in hand, they went to a deserted and air-conditioned bar for "happy hour". Evaristo continued with the submarines and Adela with her margaritas so that by now they were leaving empties piled on the table like a bouquet of glasses. With drunkenness, the Spanish lady's resentments flourished. She detested the passengers, particularly those in economy class, because of their vulgarity and their tendency to believe that they were Arab sheiks, as if she didn't know that they paid for their trips in instalments.

"I am delighted to serve a first-class passenger, because people with class deserve to be well treated, that's why they pay for the seats, but those arseholes who travel like sardines and ring the bell up to eighty times per flight because they feel sick or they want a bottle for the baby, I feel like throwing them out of the hatch."

Maybe to please them with something from the good old days, the bar's DJ played Eric Burdon's 'Spill the wine', one of Evaristo's favourite songs. He took the stewardess out on to the dancefloor and, when he stood up, stumbled over one of the table legs, knocking over all the glasses. Not even this accident put him off wanting to dance. On the dancefloor he threw his whole body into the heat of the moment, jumping like a Sixties wild child, but when he came back to the table, now with the mess cleaned up and four glasses awaiting them, he felt a cold sweat and dizziness, an unequivocal sign that he was getting ill. He remembered that he had not eaten anything since the day before. It was six o'clock and his body was asking for mercy. "Hey, handsome, are you all right? You've gone as white as milk." Yes, he was burnt out, but he still had half of the snow he'd bought the morning before at Icacos beach. "I'm going to have a snort, do you want some?" Adela looked him in the eye with admiration and tenderness. "You read my mind. Are you a wizard or are you telepathic?" Each went to the toilet and, when they came out, their faces were red, their pulses fast, their nerves ready for pleasure and euphoria. Adela hung from his neck and kissed him on the lips. She was wearing a lace top over her bikini and, when he felt her breasts, he had an erection that rose like a molehill in his swimming trunks. They danced close, to some corny songs by Bread and The Carpenters, and drank until they got drunk again, petting each other without modesty among the guests who, as night fell, were beginning to fill the bar. Fearful of a setback, Evaristo invited her to his room "to recharge their batteries".

Two lines later, leaning over the balcony, Evaristo in his trunks and Adela bare-breasted, they were having fun spitting towards the hotel terrace, where there was a group of gringo tourists drinking. They wanted to be seen by some neighbour and, to call attention to themselves, had lit the balcony lamp. On the carpet were spilled crisps, crushed peanuts and empty bottles they had extracted from the minibar. Evaristo was tapping his fingers on the rail, accompanying the rap blaring from the television. "Take this you pig, and you too, cretin. I baptise you in the name of the Father, the Son and the Holy Spirit", exclaimed Adela, hacking up and spitting phlegm towards the terrace for each person in the Holy Trinity. The most comical thing about this game was that the American tourists, even when they looked up, could not locate where the baptismal water was coming from. As they looked at them wiping off the spit, Adela and Evaristo split their sides with laughter. They were like two high school kids bunking off for the first time, initiated in vandalism as they discovered freedom. Evaristo felt the gratuitous offence to others charging him with a sexual energy that would soon explode, and he believed that the stewardess was feeling the same. Sons-of-a-bitch, pygmies, ants. Whoever gave them permission to creep down there below, as they looked at them from above, like gods, horny, side by side, exerting their exterminating power as if sprinkling lemon on a plate of living clams? Hosting a violent erection, he embraced Adela from behind, rubbing the crack of her arse with the end of his penis, at the same time as he touched her clitoris, without resistance, giving a slight moan that seemed more an invitation to go further. With a quick movement of his hand, he pulled her bikini down. She pretended not to notice, still spitting on the tourists, detached from what was happening behind her, where Evaristo, kneeling and sticking out his tongue, like an altar boy receiving a host, ate her arse bravely and with dedication, plunging into the totality of his *mapa mundi*. Adela could not pretend not to know for long. Defeated by pleasure, she started to collaborate with slow pelvic movements that aroused the prisoner of her crack even more, who, feeling her humid and open, then penetrated her with a clean thrust. She grew into the punishment and facilitated Evaristo's task with a thrust of her buttocks, cautious at first, then at an outrageous speed. More, she shouted, more, despite having it all inside. Bent over the rail as if she were going to jump into the abyss, she moaned and howled, not forgetting the tourists downstairs, whom she was now not just spitting at, but cursing: bastards, sons-of-bitches, tacky shits, yes, I am talking to you, I am coming, get it, I am coming on top of you.

They came at the same time with a long, deathly rattle. Evaristo felt his knees bending and fell heavily upon a chair. It was not the sweet exhaustion following an orgasm but a comatose state, general physical collapse. He tried to light up a cigarette but the packet felt too heavy. With the little energy that he had left, he crept into the bed without turning the television off. He needed rest, the eternal peace of the grave, and, as soon as he put his head on the pillow, he turned into a blind bundle, like a piece of rotting flesh that falls from its skeleton.

He woke up six hours later, when it was still night. He extended an arm looking for Adela, not finding anything but the cold of the sheet, and when he lit the bedside lamp he discovered that she was gone. Despite the faint light, it hurt his eyes like a spotlight and he felt some kind of prickly ballbearing trapped in his cranium that bounced from ear to ear. With a titanic effort he managed to stand up, or almost, because he had just reached a vertical position when he again collapsed in bed, sweating and shivering. When he saw the sheet stained with a disgusting black liquid, he deduced that he had thrown up in his sleep. It was a miracle that he had not choked on his own puke, like Lupe Vélez and Tennessee Williams. He needed a snort urgently and to brush his teeth. But how could he look for it on the dresser if, even when he lifted his neck, he shivered with vertigo and anxiety? Instead of fighting his nausea he was defeated by the spasms and threw up again, now over the carpet. He did not have anything in his stomach, just a yellow bile with a bitter taste that must have been, he thought, the famous gastric juice from the digestive system. His head now clearer, he dared to walk towards the dresser where he had the coke sachet. It was not in the drawer. Nor was his watch or wallet, and his credit cards were spilt over the carpet. Desperate, he looked among his clothes, behind the bedboard and below the desk. When he lifted his head he discovered a note written with lipstick on the dresser mirror.

SORRY HANDSOME. NO SOUTH AMERICAN FUCKS ME FOR FREE.

He didn't even remember her surname in order to report her to the hotel. And, even if he knew it, he could not report that some bloody Spanish whore had stolen five grams of coke from him. The most probable thing was that she would be crossing the Atlantic, diligent and well-mannered, with her starched smile and her flying servant's hat. Together with his discomfort and anger that lowered his morale to rock bottom, he felt his blood numbing his wrists and ankles. He needed to eat something with lots of sugar, some hot cakes or even a fucking sweet, but that bitch Adela had even stolen the chocolates from the minibar. The paralysis was advancing through his body. Now his arms and feet were stiff, his throat closed, his mouth caught in a macabre rictus. He was suffering from hypoglycaemia, something he had experienced in his most atrocious hangovers, but not as bad as now. He needed a doctor to put him on a drip or he would die because of the sudden plunge in his blood sugar level. With difficulty, because his hand had curved inwards and did not obey him, Evaristo tried to call the receptionist, but after fifteen rings nobody answered. Bloody hotel... they charged you even for bottled water but didn't give a fuck that a guest could be dying. He would have to take the lift and ask at the reception if there was a duty doctor. With great difficulty, he dragged himself towards the door of his room, three metres from his bed – very close and at the same time so far away for an invalid with numb legs. Halfway, he stopped to take a breath and discovered a cockroach had stepped on the knuckles of his left hand. Fast, intrepid, sure of itself, it advanced towards his wrist happy and carefree, with the intuition that a wreck in Evaristo's state could not even splat it with his hand. He was right. Unable to move even a finger, he resigned himself to contemplating its ascent, feeling the goosebumps and a long shiver in the core of his bones. When it was nearing the arm, he realised that the cockroach was not common: it was a cockroach woman with hair and human features, a miniature version of Perla Tinoco.

"How vulgar of you," it said in Maytorena's deep voice. "You're going to die of a hangover without having even read Witkiewicz. But before you do, I will explore your mouth. Don't you want to see what a cockroach tastes like? Poor you, you are so common that I may make you wretch." It reached the shoulder and continued towards the clavicle, in the direction of his neck. "It's logical, finery was not made for you, you only have a very thin little smear of culture, you stayed with the *boom* and the novelists of the lost generation, read in fifth-class translations. Frankly, I don't know why people call you intellectual. It must be because, in the land of the blind, the one-eyed man is king. Intellectual, ha, ha, ha, but if you come from the gutter, it's obvious when you are drunk. Such behaviour as yesterday's with that Spanish yokel, *c'était pitoyable,* it was nasty, *comprenez vous*? But what could you understand if you've never been to Paris? Let's see, where is Proust buried? Could you name three plays by Malraux? What is a white verse? What is *Voyage au bout de la nuit* about? How was the *nouveau roman* born and who were its main writers?"

    The Maytorena-Tinoco monster was edging towards Evaristo's mouth. He tightened his lips to stop it gaining entry and, with a huge effort, as if lifting a three-hundred kilo weight, managed to bring his hand to his face and, with a delicate stroke, knock the monster to the ground. He seemed out of danger but, as soon as Evaristo resumed his journey to the door, a fat and hairy rat with Maytorena's bloated face and Perla Tinoco's ringing voice came out from behind the minibar, where it may have been nibbling crisp crumbs.

    "Are you hung over, Intellectual?" The rat climbed on to his right hand. "That's a shame, I could liven you up with a gram of coke but I like looking at you like this, on your knees, the little humble guy you always were. I'm a very good friend to my friends, you are witness to that, but when they don't do as they're told I want payback for all that is owed to me, and you owe me your life. Have you forgotten who gave you an equal share of Sherry's? Since when have you been afraid of a bloody stiff? Cunts like you never want to smear themselves with blood, ooh yucky! But, when it comes to cashing in, they are the first to stretch out their hands. Look, son, I have killed many people, I'm going to go straight to hell, but you are going to be my companion, because you always picked up the crumbs I chucked at you." Evaristo denied this, shaking his head. "Oh, you didn't? Are you going to deny that you were my secretary, the servant with good spelling who recorded my killings in clean language? Confess to me before you throw in the towel. Isn't it true that our torture killed many people before

Vilchis? Isn't it true that you gave them the *coup de grâce* with your typewriter?"

Exasperated by Evaristo's convulsive denial, the rat bared its fangs and jumped at his jugular. For a moment it remained stuck to his neck while Evaristo could not do anything to knock it away. With his last trace of energy he managed to lift one hand, the right one, and as he struggled with the disgusting rodent, even more nauseating as its fangs were covered in blood, Evaristo crept painfully towards the room's door. He was stretching his arm with the aim of twisting the doorknob when cockroach Tinoco, recovered from the blow, crept up to him through a gap in his Bermuda shorts, continuing up to his testicles in a cunning attack that made Evaristo neglect the rat for a moment. He was too disgusted to defend himself properly. His screams of panic just made the beastly duet more cocky as, seeing him defeated, they would not stop singing a repulsive tune in two voices, *mon dieu, c'est minable, even your balls aren't the right size, as well as being a pleb you must be impotent*, while Evaristo rolled on the carpet, weaker and weaker as blood gushed from his neck, *I warned you bastard, no one betrays me, because if you are not with me you are against me*, demoralised, less because of his pain than because of the internal suspicion that both the rat and the cockroach were talking on his behalf, that they were his own demons shooting at him in a crossfire, *illiterate, lumpen, fucked poor, now as it happens you are scared of blood, I used to say, as he reads so much he must be turning queer, I bet you can't even handle the cutlery, damn, if you at least knew André Malraux*, and even when he had some breath still to seek help, even when he clutched at life like the rat at his jugular, Evaristo understood that even if the fire brigade and the Red Cross, Superman, the Virgin or the Holy Child of Atocha turned up, his final defeat was unavoidable, because no external power could rescue him from himself.

Fear of Animals

"When the glucose drip is finished you will be able to get up, but I advise you not to drink for a few days, at least from now 'til Sunday, after the irritation to your stomach has passed. And if you leave the drink for good, even better. Life is not for toying with, and you were very close. You almost died of a respiratory collapse."

The doctor's gaze, compassionate and condemnatory at the same time, expressed better than his words how grave the situation had been. Evaristo accepted the reprimand silently, with the face of a child who has learned a lesson that corresponded to his moral prostration, because even though the doctor was a young man of thirty, to Evaristo, from his bed and with the drip in his arm, he looked like a father or a brother.

"Thank you, doctor. I promise you that I am going to give up drinking."

When he was left alone in the room, Evaristo filled up his lungs and exhaled with a sigh. It was three o'clock and, despite the double curtains, the inclement Acapulco sun projected a cone of light across the bed that in other circumstances would have bothered him, but now filled him with joy, because being so close to death had given him back his pleasure for life. Even the hospital sheet, rough and frayed at the edges, like his coarse cotton jail-like pyjamas, seemed to him like silk. The promise to the doctor had not been a phrase just thrown in the air: Evaristo really wanted to give up alcohol, at least until he put his life in order. He would never again experience a *delirium tremens*, nor lose consciousness in a hotel room, nor travel in an ambulance wearing an oxygen mask, with his vital signs at half mast. He'd better have his balls chopped off if he drank another glass in the next few months. Above and beyond the danger he had experienced, he regretted his hooligan behaviour, particularly the spitting bit on the balcony, such rudeness so contrary to his character. The director of the Calinda, in protest at the phlegm fest and Adela's vociferous orgasm, had banned him from staying at his hotel, or any other of the same chain, rightly so, "due to your obscene and scandalous behaviour". But what made him more anxious was not the public shame, but to discover that deep within himself there was another personality: the irascible and brutish nonentity who imposes all his frustrations upon others. He had not completely broken away from Maytorena, because deep inside he carried his double.

When Evaristo came out of the clinic to begin a more austere life, he had breakfast at a hotdog stall and went back to Mexico City using the old motorway, instead of taking the costly Autopista del Sol. From now on, no saving would be excessive. He thought about selling his car, looking for a job in a newspaper and resuming the path he had interrupted when he had joined the Feds. Maybe now he could be a better crime reporter. It had its uses, knowing the criminal underworld from backstage. But maybe it would be more convenient for him to stay away from the police environment, retreat to the countryside and set up a sandwich stall or a black market imports stall. Yes, he needed to breathe different air, the further away from the shit, the better. On the way, analysing things with serenity, he reached the conclusion that the more he stayed silent, the more Maytorena would leave him alone. Evaristo's threat of publishing a book had probably left Maytorena very worried. But, also, the Lima case was getting too complicated and it was not convenient to attract the spotlight with another stiff. Evaristo trusted that he would be able to go out into the street without fear of being shot but, nevertheless, just in case, he would try to disappear from the city for five or six years, until the beast forgot about his authority being disrespected.

When Evaristo arrived in Mexico City he felt even easier when he found his flat in order, because if Maytorena had wanted to show hostility, he would have started with a savage break-in. That night he slept without dreaming, curled up like a foetus in a placenta. The next day, strengthened by rest, he decided to face reality and nose through the most important dailies. As he supposed, Vilchis' death had shocked public opinion. Lima's murder was not now seen as an isolated incident, but as a witchhunt of intellectuals. Jiménez del Solar had ignored the District Attorney's office and handed the case to the Federal

Attorney General's office, "given its seriousness and political implications". At *El Financiero*, the political analyst Wenceslao Medina Chaires demanded justice in a shattering article entitled "Who will be next?"

We live in times of impunity in which life, literally, is worth nothing. The deaths of Roberto Lima and Claudio Vilchis, two mature writers, cunningly murdered when they were producing the best fruit of their talents, confirm that the hardest elements of the regime have the intention of sowing terror among the intellectual community of the country, with the aim of intimidating those independent voices struggling for democracy and change. Until this moment, the so-called forces of order, displaying tortoise-like speed that is believed to be deliberate, have not only taken the inquiry into a dead end, but have embarked, with methods typical of the Gestapo, on a campaign of selective repression, which includes the arbitrary arrest of Osiris Cantú de la Garza, the poet, whom the PGR intends to implicate in Lima's assassination, as his wife has publicly denounced. It seems that the excuse to detain Cantú de la Garza was his real or apparent friendship with Lima, from which it has been inferred that those responsible for the investigation have discarded the hypothesis of political motives supported by the statements of Mario Casillas, the reporter of El Matutino, *that hours before the murder he had provided Lima's address to a Federal agent. Insensitive to the demands of public opinion with regard to Lima having been assassinated because of his attacks on the President, Attorney General Tapia maintains a hermetically sealed attitude that could cast a pall over the image of Jiménez del Solar, whom* vox populi *blames for ordering the crime. Seeking a splinter in the eye of the neighbour without noticing the beam in one's own is not the best method to sanitise those institutions in charge of administering justice. If there really exists the political will to resolve these crimes – something difficult to believe in the current circumstances – the government must direct the investigation at the dungeons of power, at the security apparatus where state terrorism is harvested, even when this could mean carrying out an internal purge. Otherwise they will encourage the suspicion that the system conceals the perpetrators.*

Mario Casillas's testimony provides a clue that, until now, the authorities have not wanted to investigate in detail, as well as not follow up the denunciation of housewife Violeta Cifuentes, witness to Vilchis' kidnapping, who declared to the Public Prosecutor's Office that the writer's killers were "in a beige Phantom with the Federal Judicial Police logo". To maintain against wind and tides the official version of the assassination, according to which Vilchis was mugged and killed by blows from common delinquents, is not just an act of political arrogance but an insult to the intelligence of all Mexicans. With their press releases that oscillate from the absurd to delirious fantasy, the PGR has buried the government's credibility, already diminished after years of lies and half truths.

Disinformation is the mother of rumour. Since last week, among the political classes, a version that ties Lima's and Vilchis' deaths to the assassinations of the Archbishop of Guadalajara, the presidential candidate Luis Donaldo Colosio, and the PRI secretary-general José Francisco Ruiz Massieu has been circulating. According to that hypothesis, spread sotto voce by officers of the same government, the assassinations of intellectuals would form part of a campaign orchestrated by the dinosaurs, drug traffickers linked to the ruling PRI and the banking sharks to create a climate of insecurity that slows down the country's incipient democratic opening. By this logic, Tapia would be the missing link in the plot, the one in charge of tangling up all the findings and laying a smokescreen around the true culprits. The performance of the office in his charge indicates this, since up to this moment there has not been substantive progress in the investigation, but on the other hand the most important witnesses have been disregarded, citing legal technicalities that on other occasions are ignored by the PGR.

A modern and participatory society cannot keep its arms folded when the validity of law and order is at stake. It is now time for truth to put an end to the culture of rumour. Civil society must press the authorities, as it has been doing on all fronts, to take these investigations to their ultimate conclusion. The time to ask ourselves which is the country we want to bequeath our children has arrived. A country where the criminal underworld governs from the shadows, or a country of laws and institutions? In the current circumstances, the fight for the better implementation of justice has moved to the top spot on the country's political agenda. First was Lima, then Vilchis, who is next? It is within our hands to put a stop to the growing list of victims. It is within our hands to end the impunity.

Fear of Animals

Despite the fact that Medina Chaires was only guessing when referring to Lima and Vilchis' murders, the article excited Evaristo because of the great blow it gave Tapia. It was about time someone put that shit-eater in his place. He felt some guilt at Maytorena still being in the Feds, because he had dedicated himself to vegetating in his post without rocking the boat, leaving everything as it was, namely, rotten to the core. Evaristo checked the rest of the newspapers looking for articles against him, like a Roman circus spectator aroused by the smell of blood. In *Excélsior*, *Novedades*, *El Heraldo* and *El Sol* Tapia had spread good brown envelopes to ensure that nobody attacked him, but at *La Jornada* Palmira Jackson hit him with everything, including the kitchen sink:... *While in Chiapas the white guards kill peasants for the crime of being poor and hungry, in Mexico City the political police have declared a dirty war against the intellectual community, with the pretext of investigating the killings of Lima and Vilchis. No, Mr Attorney General, you are wrong to direct the investigation at those people who work with their imaginations and minds. In my 40 years of journalistic and literary life I have never met a writer who carries a gun. And do you know why? Because the word is our only weapon, a weapon that we use to give voice to those without a face, those without land, those left behind today and always. Roberto Lima used very coarse words to fight those in power and his defiance cost him his life. As a woman and as a Mexican, I demand punishment for the true culprits in his death. I also demand freedom for Osiris Cantú de la Garza, arrested at his house with excessive force, and a detailed investigation of the death of Claudio Vilchis who, according to trusted sources, was tortured while being held incommunicado in the holding cells by the Federal Judicial Police and interrogated about Lima's death. It is intolerable to try and involve men of literature in crimes committed by paid assassins. Or is the intention to demonise the intellectuals, like in the Argentina of Videla and Galtieri, in order to predispose public opinion against them and justify a witchhunt?*

Moved by Jackson's civic valour, Evaristo forgot for a moment his own participation in the death of Vilchis and he wished the whole issue would keep causing a reaction. After all, his performance as a detective had not been that bad, as he had put the attorney in such a tight spot that it might cost him his job; this gave Evaristo a joy similar to that of the terrorist who has placed a bomb at the headquarters of the fire brigade, detonating it from afar and then going out to admire the debris. In a certain way, he was a secret ally of Palmira Jackson, as he had prepared the ground for her to thrash the government and now, divorced from Maytorena, at peace with his own conscience, maybe he could look her in the eye without having to lower his.

At two o'clock he went out to eat at a cheap restaurant in Río Niágara where a three-course meal cost ten pesos. Among humble-looking secretaries and office workers crouching over their plates so as not to stain the less mended of their two office outfits, he felt as if he had been reintegrated as an honest person into the simple and clean world of the working class. To him, the rice with fried egg tasted like heaven, the custard reminded him of his childhood and, when he lit a cigarette for good digestion, he had a new glint in his eye: the sparkle of innocence recovered. But when he returned home and slumped on his bed to watch the telly, a feeling of loss oppressed his gut. Without Dora Elsa, his life was not worth living. It was useless and even ridiculous to wear as new a noble soul, a dignified temperament, when he had no woman, and not even a dog to keep him company. The feeling of emptiness that had remained after his fling with the air stewardess was the least similar thing to pleasure. After having tasted heaven in Dora Elsa's lips, sex without love was not enough for him. She had made him used to happiness and now she had pulled the rug out from under his feet, sentenced him to death by despising him: now he was not the same man and could not comfort himself with wham-bam lays. Fucking hell, thought Evaristo, that bitch has me wrapped around her finger. And even now, when he did not expect anything from her, he dialled her telephone number in an attempt at the impossible.

"The mistress is not here. She went shopping with her little girl," answered the cleaning girl. "Would you like to leave a message?"

"Just tell her that Evaristo called to see how she is. Do you know what time she'll be back?"

"She didn't say, but I think she'll be some time. She is really desperate to find some silver heels, because today she makes her debut with the cigarette number."

"Uh, okay. Tell her that I wish her good luck."

Fear of Animals

At least this time it had not been the answering machine, but he suspected Dora Elsa was there anyway, making signs to her maid. Her tantrum had now lasted too long. Or had she really stopped loving him? He would never know if he limited himself to seeking forgiveness by telephone. He needed to look her in the eye, speak to her face to face and even, if necessary, kneel down before her, saying sorry. To escape his predicament, he decided to see her that very night. As he knew that success would depend to a great extent on creating a good impression, he spent the rest of the afternoon improving his looks. He had his hair done at Le Parisien beauty parlour, where he was given a layered cut that took ten years off him. At Palacio de Hierro Durango he bought himself a navy blazer, an Italian tie in the latest fashion and a white silk shirt, copying the outfit displayed on the mannequin in the window. His savings could wait, love could not tolerate pennypinching. On his way out he stopped at Sanborn's tobacco shop and asked for some Middleton's cherry-flavoured mini cigars, the most expensive ones in the window. If Dora Elsa had to smoke with the most delicate region of her body to please a bunch of riffraff, she must do so like a Grand Dame, with the best quality tobacco. Back at his flat he called her again without getting a response. Never mind, he would have to take her by surprise and risk being slapped. He drenched himself in eau de cologne, took a taxi at Melchor Ocampo because the anti-pollution regulations meant his car was not allowed on the roads that day, and at ten o'clock arrived at Sherry's with a splendid bouquet of roses.

"Whassup, Efrén? Here comes your absent friend. Did you miss me? Look at the fisherman's tan I caught in Acapulco."

The maitre d' turned his face away, without answering.

"What? Aren't we friends anymore?"

Evaristo tried to pull the chain from the entrance, but Efrén prevented him forcefully.

"We have been ordered not to allow you in."

"Ordered by whom? Have you all forgotten that I have the power to close this fucking pox house?"

Efrén shrugged his shoulders.

"It was Dora Elsa, wasn't it? She told you not to let me in." The maitre d' neither affirmed nor denied it. "Give me a chance to talk to her. I promise I won't kick up a stink."

Evaristo's conciliatory tone had no effect on the maitre d'. Maybe he had heard about his argument with Maytorena and that was why he was treating him as if he had the plague. Swallowing his anger, Evaristo offered him a fifty peso bank note.

"Please, help me out. Don't be a bad sport. I just want to get in for a moment."

Without even saying thank you, Efrén pocketed the note and lowered his head. Evaristo patted his back and said ironically, "Thanks pal". Inside the club, he confirmed that he was now nobody's friend. Rosa, the cigar girl who was usually kind and flirtatious, gave him a frozen look and turned her face away when he tried to kiss her, and Juanito, his trusted waiter, warned him that, if he wanted drinks, he should pay for them in advance: these were the manager's orders and he had to obey them. Evaristo asked for a very expensive 40-peso highball that tasted like perfume. As he drank it, he swore never to go back to a brothel-bar, even if they rolled out the red carpet for him. Only a masochistic idiot could find the exploitation of horniness attractive and poetic. He looked with the eyes of a newcomer at the wallpaper, peeling from damp, the bar and its decrepit bartender, the dirty neon bulbs, the call-girls' vampire-blue skin. He had to admit it: his erotic paradise was nothing but a sad and fucked up little cave, whose regulars were the middle class of the underworld. The compère, dressed in his old pistachio green tuxedo, asked for a round of applause for Ximena, "a recently unpacked peach of a girl from Tulacingo, Hidalgo", who had just finished her naked dance at the bottydrome.

"And now, to bubble your bilirubins a bit, let me introduce to you a female so hot that she puffs smoke out of you know where. Please give a big round of applause to the greatest show of this year: the sensational *Dooraa Ellllsaaa.*"

Too sensitive to share his beloved with a crowd of yokels, Evaristo stood up when he heard the first chords of the Argentinian tango 'I wait smoking' and walked towards the back of the stage, where he had to give another fifty pesos to a made-up queen guarding the access to the dressing rooms and those used by clients to shag the variety girls. Dora Elsa had mitigated the sordidness of her miniscule dressing room by adorning it with cuddly toys, *alebrije* papier-mâché figures, artificial roses and a poster of a couple staring at a sunset in an autumn forest, with the inscription: *Love is giving everything without expecting anything.* His heart twisted when he discovered his photograph stuck with tape on the dressing table mirror. She loves me, he thought, she loves me but her pride is

Fear of Animals

stronger. He fell from his cloud when he heard the obscene shouting coming from the bar: "Puff it hard, darling"... "Shall I hold the butt for you?"... "Puff in my eye!" Every indecency hurt him as if a handful of salt was being rubbed into an open wound. Despairing, he threw the cherry-flavoured Middletons in a rubbish bin, fearing that Dora Elsa might take the present as a mocking gesture. After she had said thank you for the round of applause milked by the supplicant compère, Dora Elsa, wearing a green satin gown and a star-shaped diamanté tiara that Evaristo imagined as a Virgin's crown, pushed aside the beaded screen. Her tobacco-coloured eyes sparkled when she discovered him in the dressing room.

"What are you doing here? I told you not to come."

"I came to ask you to forgive me." He wanted to hold her by the hand, but she abruptly pulled away. "I need to talk to you, even if it is only for a minute."

"So dapper?" Dora Elsa turned her back on him to go behind a screen. "You were so scruffy when you were with me, and now you dress like a mannequin. Is it to please your old bag, the easy writer?"

"I dressed up for you. You are the only woman in the world that matters to me."

"Oh, really? Well, you fake it well. In your messages you called me a bitch and a lesbian."

"Because I'm crazy about you and crazy men are sometimes delirious."

"You shouldn't have come. It's over between us."

"So you don't love me any more?" Evaristo went pale. "Such a shame. Next week I'm moving to Guadalajara and I wanted to ask you to come with me, as man and wife."

"You're all talk. Are you really going to lumber yourself with my daughter?"

"With her and any that may come later."

"Your grandmother would believe that." Dora Elsa wanted to appear hard, but her voice gave away intense emotion. "I'm a big girl, Evaristo. If we get married now, soon you'll fuck off with another, younger woman."

While they were talking, Dora Elsa hung black suspenders and a flimsy, beaded corset on the screen. Even though he could only see her neck, Evaristo undressed her in his mind.

"I love you, my darling. I have never fallen in love like this with anyone, not even with my wife when we used to be sweethearts.

Because of you I regained my pride. You got me out of the hole I was in. Do you want me to kneel down to ask for your forgiveness?"

"No, please get up," Dora Elsa came out from behind the screen with her eyes full of tears. "I love you too, Evaristo, but this won't work. You and I are loose cannons. We like having fun, partying all night, easy money. I don't see myself raising a family with you."

"But all of this is not really our thing." Evaristo held her in his arms. "You were not born to strip and nor was I to be a policeman. We have been humiliated all our lives: you by the owners of seedy clubs, me by that bastard of a boss, who treated me like his slave. But we are not crippled, we can work on something else without anyone stamping their boot on us. With me you won't be in the money, but I'm going to break my back to make you happy."

When he kissed her lips, Evaristo lost the notion of "I": he was not a person, but a shroud tightened up around her nakedness, a sensitive piece of clothing that, from so much tightening against her beloved skin, started to lose substance, to melt in shreds of smoke. Beyond Dora Elsa there was nothing, just a blue Walt Disney night with shooting stars and rivers of light, where the wind dragged him like a happy and emancipated comet. He was enjoying a kind of spiritual orgasm, an ejaculation towards his inside more pleasant than gushing out semen, when he heard steps from the corridor and a revolver peeked through the beaded curtain.

"Break it up, bastards, or I'll throw a bucket of water on you."

Maytorena pulled the curtain back with a sinister glint in his eyes. Accompanying him, armed with huge guns, were Chamula and Fat Zepeda. By instinct, Evaristo covered Dora Elsa with his body, as she crouched under the dressing table, trembling with fear. Chamula and Fat made Evaristo let go of her by kicking him and punching him in the stomach, then forced him to face the wall, his hands above his head.

"Fucking hell, Intellectual, you get hooked by any old nail." Maytorena slid the mouth of his revolver along Dora Elsa's breasts. "Look what a fucked-up bag you were seeking: scrawny, big-mouthed and with a flat ass."

Despite his fear, Evaristo could not stand this offence in silence.

"You think she's ugly because you only fancy those girls with a bit added."

Snorting with rage, his nostrils flaring like an accordion, Maytorena smashed Evaristo's head against the wall.

Fear of Animals

"Calm down, chief, don't kill him too." Chamula took him by the shoulders. Maytorena composed himself with difficulty and it took him a couple of minutes to control his breathing. Out of the corner of his eye, among the threads of blood that trickled down his forehead, Evaristo saw Maytorena's hawkish silhouette and smiled with satisfaction: at least he had taken off Maytorena's macho mask.

"All right, I'll let him live because he'll suffer even more in jail." Maytorena leaned towards Evaristo and lifted his chin with a hand. "Did you hear me, you arsehole? You're going to be banged up from now 'til you die. And when your shag wants to bring you ciggies, the female wardens are going to stick their fingers in her."

"Neither you, nor your fucking mother can put me in jail."

"Oh, can't we? Pass me his pistol, Chamula." Maytorena took the Magnum. "We took it from your house a little while ago. It's the same one you left in Lima's house when you went to warn him about me."

Evaristo directed a disapproving look at Fat Zepeda, who was impassively chomping on a chocolate-covered doughnut.

"You guessed it," continued Maytorena. "Fat was the one who spilled the beans. He's very hurt about what you said about his poetry and yesterday came to tell me that he had found your gun at the stiff's house."

"But Lima was alive when I left his house. Someone else killed him."

"I believe you, Intellectual, I really do." Maytorena adopted a mocking tone. "I know you are very delicate and faint when you see a tampon filled up with blood, but sadly all the clues point to you. The attorney wants to shut the journalists up. They keep buggering me and buggering me, saying that the murderer was a Fed, so it's no big deal for me to sacrifice a bad agent just to please them."

"The journalists are not going to shut up when I tell them who killed Vilchis."

Maytorena punished Evaristo's defiance by kicking him in the balls.

"You're fucking wrong if you think that we're going to put microphones in your mouth. In Almoloya you'll only have the chance to talk to God."

Maytorena gave a gesture and Chamula twisted Evaristo's arm and frog-marched him out of the dressing room. When they passed through Sherry's tables, escorted by his three mastiffs, Evaristo understood in a cold sweat that there was no salvation, that his life was to end that night and, from then on, the grinding of the teeth would start. Maytorena had calculated everything very well: he was the sacrificial lamb needed by Tapia to keep his job. It would be enough for Mario Casillas to identify him at the station to convince the press about his guilt. And, if any suspicious journalist denounced this PGR manoeuvre, his protests would soon be forgotten. Mexico was a country without memory. Within a few months people would forget regicides, devaluations, slaughters and the wave of protests that occurred before each new disaster. Even more so a minor crime that had only caused outrage among a small number of intellectuals. At the seedy club's door, Efrén saluted Maytorena, who stuffed a hundred dollar note in his jacket pocket. "Thanks for the lead, bro."

On the minuscule sidewalk of Medellín, lit by a lamppost emitting an orange light, they waited for Daggers who was picking up Maytorena's van – a grey Suburban with wide tyres – from a nearby parking lot, while the passengers of a minibus stuck in the road watched the eye-catching group of agents curiously. Despite the drivers allowing him to pass, intimidated by the PGR sticker in the windscreen, Daggers took about five minutes to travel only a hundred metres because a power cut had caused a crazy traffic jam. Resigned to his fate, Evaristo looked at a baby in the minibus, as if saying: "Yes, kid, this is the country you live in". When the Suburban stopped at the entrance of the nightclub, Chamula opened the back door and, with a prod in the ribs, ordered Evaristo to get in. He had put one foot on the running board when he heard a kind of slap amid the noise of the engines. He did not realise that it was a gunshot until he saw Chamula lying on the floor. Protected behind a flowerpot adorning Sherry's entrance, Dora Elsa was shooting willy nilly with a small silver revolver. She had come out wearing her negligee and nothing underneath, and the intense orange light emphasised her nakedness. From the Suburban, Maytorena and Fat Zepeda retaliated. Dora Elsa managed to shelter behind the flowerpot, but not Efrén, who had gone to earn his tip and fell to the curbside with a shot in his neck. Without lifting his head, Evaristo crept like a worm towards Efrén and removed the .38 from his hand, ignoring the advice of Dora Elsa, who shouted, "Beat it, love, run." Indifferent to the danger, Evaristo covered her with his body and fired in the direction of the

Fear of Animals

Suburban. He could only crack the bullet-proof windows, but his reaction took Maytorena and Fat by surprise and, when they crouched to avoid the bullets, it gave him enough time to pull Dora Elsa and get away with her among the gridlock. Chamula ran after them, revolver in hand, and destroyed several windscreens while shooting and running. From the cars stuck in Medellín's huge car park came hysterical screams, prayers and choked interjections. Crawling, Evaristo and Dora Elsa crossed from lane to lane until they reached the other end of the street, their skin covered with goosebumps as the bullets sped past them. At the corner of Medellín and Campeche they hid behind a newspaper stall. From there, Evaristo responded to Chamula's fire with the few shots he had left, gaining a fraction of a second and running towards Insurgentes Avenue, the promised land where they could vanish. A VW taxi trying to avoid the gridlock turned into Campeche and Evaristo almost threw himself in front of it to stop it, carrying Dora Elsa with difficulty because she had a broken heel and was hobbling along. They got into the back seat, gasping and sweating. The driver looked at them in the rearview mirror, fearful, and tried to get out, but Evaristo put the .38 to his ear: "Put your foot down." Chamula managed to fire a last, impotent shot which ended up shattering the taxi's sidelight, but in Campeche there was little traffic and even by running he could not catch them. "Take us anywhere, but far away from here." At Insurgentes they turned right, went through a few red lights at the taxi driver's initiative and, when they reached the Metro roundabout – infested with police cars – took Chapultepec Avenue towards the forest. Nearing Sonora Avenue, when he was sure of having lost them, Evaristo put the .38 away in his inside jacket pocket.

"Fabulous job, my love," he congratulated Dora Elsa. "If it wasn't for you, they would have tortured me until I had signed a confession for them."

Dora Elsa did not say anything. Her hand was inert and cold like a glove that had been outside for many hours. Evaristo put his arm around her shoulders and his fingers became covered in blood. It seemed that they had wounded her in the back, because her satin gown was dry in the front. Fuckers. A shiver went down his spine when he shook her without getting any answer. His face lit by the front lights of the car behind, he observed her eyes without expression, the breast peeking shamelessly out of the gown, the gush of blood dripping down the seat. Desperate, he put his head on her chest making an effort to listen to her heartbeat, in vain. God was a son-of-a-bitch. Why her, fuck, why?

"Do you now know where you want to go to or do we keep driving around?"

Fear of Animals

"The ECO information network brings you the week's most relevant events in the wide world of news. As we have informed you over the past couple of days, the Federal Attorney General pledged to arrest the former Federal Judicial Police agent Evaristo Reyes Contreras, whose photo now appears on your screens, within a period of no more than ten days, as he has been singled out as a possible culprit in the murders of writers Roberto Lima and Claudio Vilchis. On Tuesday the twenty-third of this month, Reyes Contreras participated in a shooting outside Sherry's Bar nightclub, located in Medellín Street, Colonia Roma, when a group of Feds under Commander Jesús Maytorena's orders tried to detain him. There were two victims in the shooting, Mr Efrén Luna, maitre d' at the aforementioned nightclub, and a 32-year-old dancer, Dora Elsa Oleana, who fled the scene in the company of Reyes Contreras, and who appears to have died from loss of blood on the way to her house. Attorney Tapia declared this morning at a press conference: "In the face of the climate of violence that has developed in the last few days and to respond to society's demand that the cowardly homicides of Roberto Lima and Claudio Vilchis – outstanding members of the intellectual community – be resolved as soon as possible, I reiterate that we will not compromise on public security and will set up a Joint Domestic Vigilance and Prosecution Committee formed by outstanding jurists and distinguished personalities in civil society with the aim of ensuring no element linked to the criminal underworld can again gain access to the office under my charge. Under the instructions of President Jiménez del Solar, who is following the inquiry attentively, we have been ordered to speed up the search aimed at capturing Evaristo Reyes Contreras by intensifying our contacts with Interpol and the district attorneys of all our states. I have said it before and I reiterate it energetically: in Mexico the rule of law reigns, we will get to the bottom of this, whoever may be involved, the crimes against intellectuals will not go unpunished"... And now the weather forecast for the Hispanic population of the United States: in Chicago, the average temperature will be 12 degrees centigrade with strong blizzards and a high probability of rain. In Detroit it is expected to be cloudy, with scattered showers in the afternoon and a slight fall in temperature. A sunny day in Miami, where the temperature will be between 26 and 28 degrees. In Houston the good weather will continue..."

"And in your mother's arse there will be a cold snap with hurricane winds."

Sick of hearing the same news ad nauseam, Evaristo switched off the telly with a blow and stuck his head under the sheet. He needed to escape from himself, abandon his skin, be reincarnated in another living being – a tree pissed on by dogs, a worm, a rat from the sewer – or simply to fix his sights upon a vacuum, like the Buddhist monks, unfolding until reaching a point in which he lost consciousness of his pain. He was now famous, he could not complain about that. The news showed his photo front and side every half an hour in a promotional campaign that many show business stars would have envied. He had turned into a fashionable villain and now those mothers with hyperactive children could use him as a substitute for the bogeyman: go to sleep, Harry, or else Evaristo Reyes, that bad man you saw on the telly, will come and eat you up.

When he heard the howling of a police car, he jumped out of bed feeling his balls stuck in his throat. Now he was going to be nabbed. Through the window, half-covered by the hotel's advert which illuminated the room with a crimson glow, he saw two uniformed policemen dragging a young guy with porcupine hair, bleeding from the nose. This scene was more or less common in Colonia Guerrero, where he had taken refuge in a knocking shop – El Bonampak, sixty pesos per night – to hide from Maytorena and his pack of agents. The fright made him want to piss and, just because he felt like it, he did so in the sink, where it was more comfortable than the toilet. As he emptied his bladder he visualised his apartment upside down, a mess of broken furniture and clothes strewn around, like in those demolished houses in Sarajevo that he had just seen on the news. What would Maytorena have done with his books? A bonfire? Would he have ripped all the pages out to wipe his ass? Or would he have given them away to his son, the one with a BA in international relations, so he could boast of being cultured with his mates in the diplomatic corps? Better not think about that, better not think about anything. He slumped back in bed and turned on the radio that was stuck to the wall. Boleros, electric cumbias, Juan Gabriel, Luis Miguel, the Observatory hour. On Radio Joya he tuned into an old ballad by Roberto Carlos that made him hit rock bottom with depression: *This my love always sincere, without knowing what is fear, it does not seem real. It goes growing like the fire, to be truthful next to you, giving love is beautiful. And it's 'cause you, my dearest lover, give your life in just an instant without asking for payback...* Fucking hell, he was crying again. It was impossible not to remember her if all the songs seemed to have been dedicated to her, if he could still feel the smell of her hair, if she whispered in his ear while he dreamed, and if at dawn he stretched his arm out thinking they were still together. In a certain way, the news broadcasts were right: he was a criminal, not because of the deaths they were attributing to him, but for having killed Dora Elsa with his hasty visit to Sherry's. He would never forgive himself for the imprudence of having looked for her in enemy territory, knowing that Maytorena had informers everywhere and had caught him in his web. There had been plenty of danger signals, starting with Efrén's hostile attitude. Another man in his place would have smelled a rat, but his reactions were slow, stupefied by his love. His error had a romantic excuse: the only bad thing was that the dead do not accept apologies.

He was still amazed by the serenity with which he had parted from Dora Elsa when the taxi left him at the Iztacalco housing estate. Maybe the tension of that moment had left him numb. Otherwise he could not explain to himself how he could have gone up the building's stairs carrying her in his arms, like a newly wed taking his bride to the nuptial chamber. Distant, serene, locked in an ambiguous silence, Dora Elsa wore her death like an elegant dress or a title of nobility, but her expression of satisfied martyr did not move him, because he knew first hand that she had sacrificed herself for a brute. That was what hurt him the most when he called the Green Cross to ask for an ambulance to collect her body. And it still hurt him a week later, when he remembered how he had seen her for the last time, her yellow eyelids and mouth half open, with her bloodstained gown that gave a macabre touch to her childlike rococo bedroom.

Enrique Serna

The moment he had abandoned her he felt sorry for himself as he had killed what he loved the most, like the prisoner in Wilde's Reading Gaol. After eight days locked in the Bonampak, he saw things in a different light. His main mistake had been to believe that, after having crept for more than fifteen years in the Feds' sewer, he could return to the surface smelling of roses and fall in love with a woman without harming her. No: abjection had to be paid for sooner or later, in one's own flesh or someone else's. Dora Elsa's death had returned him dramatically to the underworld that he was trying to escape, but now as a victim. He wiped his tears with the blanket and lit a cigarette to amuse himself with the smoke rings. Half a bottle of Sauza Hornitos tequila was left on the bedside table. He gave it a long swig, kept the tequila in his mouth to get used to the flavour and, when he swallowed it, felt a slight burning in his throat. But, if the sorrow and the feelings of guilt were not enough, he was beginning to turn crazy with claustrophobia. More than a precaution, his confinement seemed like training for jail. Each morning he woke up with great angst when he heard the maid knocking at the door, believing that she was the police. The hotel's manager, a bald, pot-bellied and sweaty man who spent all day watching soaps in the reception, could identify him any minute and tell the PGR. Maybe he even suspected Evaristo by now, because it must have appeared strange to him that he always wore the same clothes and went into the street just once a day to buy sandwiches in nearby cafes without even bringing a woman to his room.

The second slug of Sauza Hornitos cleared his mind. Even when he had the noose around his neck, he could still defend himself against public opinion, which in Mexico reflexively distrusted the government. Proof of this could be found in the newspapers of the last few days. The political writers had grown tired of formulating hypotheses over Lima's and Vilchis' deaths. Some of them thought that behind the crimes there was a conspiracy by the *drug traffickers linked to the PRI*, others denounced a terrorist campaign put together and sponsored by the financial oligarchy in an effort to encourage a new fall in the peso. What they all agreed on was in pointing out that he was a hired assassin paid by people at the very top: *the investigations must reach their ultimate conclusion* – demanded *Reforma*'s editorial – *not stopping with Evaristo Reyes, the presumed material author of the crime, who at this point may well be sleeping underground, as has happened with other paid killers of his kind.*

It was not the fault of the press that they published absurdities, as they had all based their reports on the PGR's press release, and it was impossible to elucidate the truth when you start with a lie. But the journalists' conjectures, even while absurd, sometimes had real repercussions, as had happened with the accusations that linked the PGR to the deaths of Lima and Vilchis. To defend himself from their attacks, Attorney Tapia had taken the safe route: so you want the culprit to be a Fed? Well, there you have him, you arseholes, and now let's see if you stop kicking up a fuss. Luckily, the fuss had not stopped. By opening a small cave, Tapia had only ensured that the press would see a gigantic sewer. This gave Evaristo a great opportunity as, now, with the scandal at boiling point, the table was set for him to get out of the catacombs, accuse Maytorena of Vilchis' death and Tapia of having used him as a sacrificial lamb. Later, they could hunt him with tanks and mortars: he would bare his chest to the bullets to get back on Dora Elsa's side as soon as possible.

Excited by his plan, he went out to buy a bunch of papers and a pen at the stationery shop on the corner, covering his face as he went past the reception. Back in his room he wrote an extensive chronicle of his participation in the Lima case at flying speed, referring to the circumstance of his first and only encounter with the victim, his progress in his investigations of the literary circle that had led him to suspect some of the intellectuals with enmity towards the deceased, and the brutal assassination of Vilchis by Maytorena – the reason for his resignation from the Feds. *It was not the first time the commander had overdone it when torturing –* he clarified *– as a member of his team I witnessed many other deadly beatings, about which I would be willing to make a statement before the Public Prosecutor's Office.* As an extra, he hit out at Osiris Cantú de la Garza, denouncing *the client-trader relationship he maintains with his colleagues in the literary circle, to whom he supplies drugs in exchange for recognition*, and pointed to him as the main suspect in Lima's assassination, as he had threatened him with death weeks before the murder. To conclude, in an emotive style that broke with the brief objectivity of the letter, he begged forgiveness from the people of Mexico for his long complicity with the dregs of the police and volunteered to collaborate in resolving the crimes: *If there is any worth in the* *word of a man like myself, with only the moral solvency of regretting what he has done, I declare my will to surrender before the authorities, as long as I am granted a legal process supervised by non-governmental human rights organisations. My life is far from exemplary in every way and I am willing to accept any punishment that society imposes on me. What I do not and will never accept is being branded a criminal because, despite all my errors, my hands are free from blood.*

His idea was to photocopy the declaration and post it by mail to all the capital's newspapers, but that same night, when the euphoria of writing had faded, as he twisted and turned in bed unable to sleep, he discovered a weak point in his plot: what would happen if no newspaper in the country published the letter? The sell-out newspapers in the pocket of the government would never give it space, but even the independent press could suspect something dirty. Many of the journalists considered him dead already. Suspicious by nature, the editors would think some opportunist was using his name to divert public opinion. It would be imprudent to drop a bomb like this at a moment of general uncertainty, when rumours of unknown origin only contributed to hindering the investigation of these crimes. And he couldn't just go to the newsdesks to show them that the letter was authentic, and so risk arrest. Dawn found him with his eyes open and his neck stiff from being neurotic, so that he was unable to turn his head to the side. Bloody insomnia, it had demoralised him without even giving him an idea of how to escape the situation he was in. After a cold shower he went back to bed a bit more relaxed and turned on the telly to soothe himself: he needed to sleep for at least two hours in order not to spend the whole day like a zombie. During the cultural section of "Good Morning" a green-eyed presenter with a maternal voice handed an invitation to the kind viewers.

"This evening at seven o'clock at the Justo Sierra Auditorium of the National University there will be a homage to Palmira Jackson for her 35 years as a writer, journalist and social activist. The political commentator Wenceslao Medina Chaires, the novelist Javier Loperena and Doctor Efraín Pulido, head of the faculty of philosophy and literature, will also participate. After the presentation at this great house of study, there will be a series of round tables dedicated to analysing the author's works with the participation of outstanding intellectuals from Mexico and abroad."

Fear of Animals

He felt it dawning on him again in his troubled head: why hadn't he thought of Palmira Jackson? She could be his bridge to get to the media, as long as he could convince her that his cause was fair. If the letter was preceded by a commentary by her, it would have a greater impact than if published simply under his own name. A murder suspect might inspire suspicion in her but, if it was true that she had a sixth sense to distinguish the honest among people, as he himself believed from her books, at the end of the day she would lend him a hand, as she had done with the striking seamstresses, the political prisoners, the striking teachers and the victims of floods and earthquakes. After all, he was also someone who was persecuted, an innocent with the noose around his neck, like the Mexicans whom Jackson had always defended. He would intercept her as she was coming down from the stage at the end of the presentation. He risked frightening or angering her with the letter, but if he managed to move her or at least to awaken her curiosity, she would probably receive him in private. It would not be easy for Palmira to forgive him his previous life as a Fed, but he preferred the risk of failure to waiting with his arms folded for Maytorena.

Drugged with hope, he fell asleep like a newborn baby until three o'clock, when he was awoken by the knocking of the chambermaid asking him for permission to clean the room. Under the shower he sang and danced like a teenager. The mere fact of going through the city was now a reason to be happy, after a week of watching television. He showered with hot water and, when he came out, wrote a message addressed to Palmira Jackson, which he attached to the front of the letter with a paperclip, in which he apologised for approaching her through deceit and left her the telephone number of the Hotel Bonampak for future contact. When he put the pen down, he looked at himself in the mirror: his beard had grown enough for him not to be recognised at first glance. He was not another guy, but people would need to scrutinise him carefully to realise he was the malefactor in the news. His clothes, however, were a serious problem: the navy blazer he had bought at Palacio de Hierro was stained with Dora Elsa's blood. He had hidden it under the bed and didn't even think of getting it out, as a precaution and for his mental health. So how was he going to hide Efrén's .38, then? He had to leave just wearing his shirt and walk up to Avenida Guerrero, two blocks from the hotel, to buy himself a corduroy jacket and a pair of dark shades. Back at the Bonampak, he hid the pistol in the inside jacket pocket and stuffed the letter in a manila envelope. His car was in the hotel car park – he had managed to transfer it from the car park he used to keep it in, at the corner of Río Niágara and Río Mississippi, the day after the shooting – but he could not risk some policeman identifying the number plate. He preferred to walk towards Metro Hidalgo, mingling with a thick and downcast mob in which it was easy to walk unnoticed because nobody raised their eyes to look around. He had not had any food the whole day and his guts were beginning to riot. When he arrived at the entrance of the station, he stopped to eat at a *quesadilla* stall. Two chorizo *quesadillas* and an orange Gatorade were enough to fill the gap and he went down the stairs amid a thousand others, invaded by feelings of belonging with that mob that diminished him as a human being, but feeling at the same time that the mob made his sins lighter, returning him to a state of pleasant insignificance. Amid the collective frustration, his personal tragedy did not mean anything: he was yet another ghost in the underground circle of tormented souls where the only signs of life came from the *chavos banda*, the gang of youngsters pushing each other as they entered the station, cackling as they made dirty jokes. Twenty years later, when everyday reality had kicked the shit out of them, they would go down the same stairs looking like battered cows, with the inexpressive grimace of those adults who now moved aside to let them in.

On the long journey to University City he took his turn at balancing between an almost dwarfed, but incredibly fat lady and a man wearing a grey suit who was reading *Latest News*. "AS USUAL: DEFEATED" moaned the headline, referring to the most recent international failure of the national soccer team. He tried to draw in upon himself and not to think about anything in order to stand the stink and physical strain of the trip, but the defeatist headline and the sepulchral atmosphere of the carriage, where nobody talked to each other despite it being so crowded, inspired in him a bitter anti-Mexican reflection. To those people and to him, love of the homeland was not a feeling of extolment, but an unconscious burden, a perennial source of self-deprecation. "It would be better to come from nowhere. We're fucked, but who fucked us? The PRI, the Spaniards, God, History?"

Evaristo disembarked at Copilco and, from there, walked to the faculty of philosophy and literature, avidly reading the graffiti supporting the Zapatista Army on the volcanic-stone walls surrounding the university. *Long live the Sub, death to the PRI, self-government for the indigenous communities of Chiapas. Down with the Supreme Government.* Well done. It was a relief to verify that those kids were not the living dead, like the lobotomised ghosts in the Metro. Their fanatical devotion for Marcos could be naive, but at least they raised their voice and fought for their ideas. Inside the Justo Sierra Auditorium he found a very similar environment to the one in his dream, where he had achieved his ephemeral literary consecration: the same overcrowding, the same student audience and the same TV cameramen with their lights pointing at the top table. He was not surprised: Palmira Jackson was a superstar and she had followers everywhere, even more so at the university, where she had practically displaced the Virgin of Guadalupe. The event had already started and he had to sit on the stairs because there was not a single chair available. The presenter, some guy called Arturo Pineda, a technical secretary at the faculty, was reading a brief biographical sketch of *La* Jackson, highlighting her humanitarian vocation and dedication to the popular causes that had allowed her to turn the writer's trade – usually a lonely pursuit – into a mutually binding and participatory profession. After listing her national and international prizes, he passed the microphone to the head of the faculty, a thin and arrogant academic dressed in a checked jacket, who blinked a lot and had the profile of a Spanish cavalier.

"Fellow ladies and gentlemen, friends: I feel very honoured to chair such a well-deserved homage as the one we pay today to Palmira Jackson. I met Palmira many years ago, when she first began in the profession of journalism and, ever since, I have admired her for her talent, for her nobility, for her civic courage in facing those in power and giving voice to the weak. When the bayonets have drowned the fair demands of civil society in blood, Palmira has been the spokeswoman of our outrage. When those marginalised from the countryside and cities have gone into the streets to demand a dignified life, Palmira has remonstrated with them to leave us a testimony of her courage. When repression or fear have silenced independent voices, Palmira has broken the sordid monologue of power with her cry for freedom. Palmira dearest: our debt to you is enormous because, thanks to you, the written word keeps maintaining among us the power to shake consciences. Our admiration for you keeps growing year after year and, alongside it, our brotherly love. Your books are not yours anymore, because they belong to everyone. Thank you, Palmira, for your winged heart, for your love that floods like a swollen river, for your infectious youth, for your smile that returns to us our faith in men..."

Evaristo did not take his eyes off Jackson, who had blushed after the head's words and drummed her fingers. Without doubt she was suffering because of her proverbial modesty, which had led her to the extreme of not giving interviews. She was attractive, even though she was in her sixties and her sand-colour hair had started to grey. She had a pearl necklace and an elegant blue dress that exposed her bourgeois rank, but, to the eyes of the public, her being well off did not take away her merits. On the contrary, her fans loved her even more because she revealed herself just as she was, and Evaristo agreed with them because, even while she could be an idle, high society lady, she had turned into the critical conscience of her class. A woman from the people fighting against social injustice would not be strange: what was admirable was that such a distinguished lady, educated in the best boarding schools in Europe, would identify with the poor and those being politically persecuted, out of loyalty to a moral commitment that went beyond mere philanthropy. Excited to have her so near, Evaristo vibrated in unison with the kids packing the auditorium, feeling himself part of a great fellowship. That was something those exquisite intellectuals like Perla Tinoco and Claudio Vilchis would never achieve, even by adorning themselves with quotations in twenty languages. The explanation was easy: they lacked the human qualities that Jackson exuded from every pore. He had been right to come and see her, he was sure, because, when she'd get to know his situation, she would not leave him to die alone.

"Now it is the turn of Javier Loperena, who has recently been awarded the National Literature Prize and who practically does not require an introduction as he is an unrivalled personality within Mexican narrative. Professor Loperena is promoting his most recent historical novel about General Santa Anna's life and agreed to cut short his tour around the United States to be with us as a gesture of friendship to Palmira for which we are very grateful."

"On the contrary, thank you for inviting me," said Loperena, a white-haired, dark man with deep circles around his eyes and the appearance of a retired fisherman, who must have had a lot of practice in public speaking as he did not have a written speech. "I belong to the large club of those eternally in love with Palmira Jackson who, through different ages, have admired her as a woman, as a rebel and as a writer. We met in the turbulent '50s in Paris when she was a philosophy student at the Sorbonne and I worked at a bookshop in the Latin Quarter. At that time Sartre was our Supreme Pontiff and the youths had thrown themselves into the streets to support the independence of Algeria, the last bastion of French colonialism, where General De Gaulle was suffering a moral defeat. I remember Palmira at demonstrations in the Boulevard Raspail, bursting with youth, wearing black sunglasses and with her hair in a scarf, risking being expelled from the country as a foreigner. Since then she has known that the cause of an oppressed people is the cause of all peoples. Since then she has had in her eyes that light of the *aurora borealis* that she has given us in so many moments of darkness..."

Suddenly Evaristo felt the hairs rise on the back of his neck, suspecting someone was looking at him with an insolent insistence from behind, and, when he turned his head, he discovered his squashing companion from the Metro carriage, the man with the grey suit reading *Latest News*. He was sitting on the same stairs, ten steps higher, and when Evaristo turned to look at him, the man covered his face with the newspaper. The imbecile did not want to attract attention but was achieving exactly the opposite. What was he doing in the auditorium if he couldn't give a fuck about the tribute to Palmira Jackson? The libraries and the toilets were available if he wanted to read. Maybe he was a novice Fed, anxious to get to the big money, who had identified Evaristo at the Metro and followed him to the auditorium. Evaristo reproached himself for his stupidity at having gone out into the streets with his little week-old beard that, apparently, had fooled no one.

Luckily, he was carrying the .38 in his jacket pocket. He would have to use it if the bastard had already asked for backup to arrest him at the end of the tribute. Or maybe he was an interior ministry agent who had infiltrated the event to note down what was said. They were typically sent to meetings and gatherings of the left. In that case, it would be more convenient to pretend to be blind and behave naturally, even though his heart was pounding and his legs trembling. Making an effort to control himself, he tried to pay attention to Loperena.

Enrique Serna

"In her columns, Palmira achieves the spirit and expressive weight of José Martí in the memorable *Letters from New York*, although she imprints upon them a feminine touch that reveals the more human aspect of social struggles: the festive cheer, the quiet self-respect, the furious tenderness of the men and women who demand freedom, democracy, and a just remuneration for their work. Palmira has fought with them shoulder to shoulder without making concessions under the pressures of a repressive apparatus that, many times, has tried to intimidate or censor her. I remember that in the 70s, when the government had militarily besieged Lucio Cabañas' guerrillas, Palmira managed to get to the heart of the sierra to pen the best reports ever written about that movement, which has been reborn today in the Lacandón jungle. When her reports appeared, Palmira called me one night, most alarmed, because she had received telephone threats that put her life and the lives of her children in danger. I advised her to leave the country for a time, but, with impulsive courage, she decided not just to remain in Mexico to deal with the tempest but also to denounce the intimidation publicly. The relative freedom of expression that we have enjoyed for some years now is not a gift from the government: it has been won by independent writers such as Palmira, who have never buckled under princely pressures. My very admired comrade: we love you because of your velvet and fiery prose, because of your merciless war against those executioners of hope, and because we know how much you have done to free us from their chains. Your pen is a flaming sword when it comes to raising a voice against injustice, but it is also a source of clear water when you paint with it the spirit of your people – a noble and generous people weathered by adversity, who face pain with a smile. How many times, in moments of sadness and desperation, has a book of yours reconciled me to the human race? Gorgeous Palmira, orchid of the Americas, keep forever your smile as a womanly fountain, womanly rainbow, womanly mountain. I hope that with this tribute we begin to pay you back the great deal that we owe you."

Evaristo again felt the spy's gaze like a stiletto sinking into his cervical vertebrae and, even though he tried to suppress his curiosity, he ended up suddenly turning to catch him unawares, but the guy had already got up and, reacting quickly at that moment, turned away so that Evaristo could not see his face. Had

Fear of Animals

he frightened him, or was he going to bring more agents? To a certain extent Evaristo was protected in the middle of the crowd, but with the Feds you could never tell: they were capable of starting a shooting in the middle of the ceremony, even though they could take out fifteen students with it. In the middle of the central aisle, where a red curtain separated the foyer from the auditorium, the man with the grey suit met another man of the same size and gave him the *Latest News*. Fuck, the backup had arrived. The Channel 11 cameramen blocked his view, but he managed to see that the first agent was standing next to the curtain, to cut Evaristo's exit in case he intended to flee, while the other was coming down the stairs, approaching him dangerously. He was wearing jeans, white trainers, dark shades, a peaked cap and an olive-green war veteran's jacket. He remained leaning against the wall about five steps away from Evaristo, concealed by the students filling the stairs, in an ideal position to observe without being observed himself. At least something was for sure: they would not dare detain him while the homage was taking place, otherwise they would have acted by now. Clutching the butt of his .38, moist with sweat, he strained to look at the guy with the cap out of the corner of his eye, while pretending to concentrate on the top table, where Wenceslao Medina Chaires, a heavily built, middle-aged man with greasy hair, wearing a black jacket covered in dandruff, was now speaking.

"To love Palmira Jackson is a destiny, almost a vocation for those of us who have had the luck of knowing her since the start of her career, when she was a little blonde with pigtails, happy and uninhibited, who marvelled the newsdesk chiefs with the spontaneity of her reports. We became friends more than 25 years ago, when I had just come out of Lecumberri jail, where I was a prisoner because of my participation in the movement of '68. Recently freed from jail, I was living with my first wife in a very cold hut at Desierto de los Leones and Palmira came to see me with a pile of wood. Grateful for her gesture of friendship, I nicknamed her "wood girl" and I suspect that nickname was prophetic, as since then she has not stopped in her pledge to maintain and stoke the fire of civic protest. From '68 until now, the wood girl has lit many chimneys and will keep lighting them, even when she burns her eyelashes or chokes with so much monstrous reality. The warmth and light are for all who read you and admire you. Your books, Palmira, are alight in us, stuck to our souls like a needed and comfortable coat. Like a little blue flame. Like your burning eyes..."

Even though the tribute was about to finish, people kept arriving at the auditorium and crowding the stairs, something that made the second agent's spying difficult. "He thinks I'm going to beat it by taking advantage of the tumult," thought Evaristo, looking at the guy stretching his neck in the middle of the tight circle of students. He had forgotten that his objective was to give the letter to Palmira and now he only cared about escaping from there. But, in the event that he got out of the auditorium unscathed, who could tell whether there were more Feds outside? Knowing Maytorena, it was to be expected that he would violate the university's autonomy for the sake of his beautiful balls and besiege the faculty with a police regiment. Medina Chaires received the warmest round of applause of the evening and the chair passed the microphone to Palmira Jackson. There would be only a few minutes for the inevitable encounter with Evaristo's two hunters and his guts were in a knot. The shooting at Sherry's had caught him by surprise, not giving him time to gauge the danger; this was a thousand times worse, because the little courage that he had was fading and he was on the verge of panic. Looking for a better view, the man with a cap went down a few steps and took off his dark shades. Before he could cover himself with the newspaper, Evaristo recognised Chamula's haggard face.

"García Márquez says that he writes for his friends to love him. I write to have a great family and, on occasions like this, I can prove that my luck has not been that bad. Among all of you, I feel at home, and I am not just referring to my companions at this table, who have said so many beautiful things about me, but to all the precious people who accompany me. I give thanks to the university for this tribute, and thank the university students for the affection they have always shown me. I cannot accept the praises I have received because, really, I do not write, I just try to polish everybody else's words and my only merit, if I have one, is to put love into what I do. For me writing a book is not an effort, not at all, it is an enjoyable rite, like watering the geraniums on my balcony or making a meal for my children..."

Both men exchanged a defiant gaze across the row of students. Chamula's eyes were bloodshot and the spots on his forehead had swollen more than usual. It was not the face of a paid assassin. He looked more like a furious madman, or maybe he had been given

Fear of Animals

a coke overdose. Poor simpleton: he shared Maytorena's hatred as if he were his own father. Deep down, he was a victim of poverty, like the millions of fucked-up people who voted PRI in exchange for a sandwich. Since he was a kid he had been taught not to complain, not to pretend to be equal, to be happy with the crumbs that were thrown at him under the table. How could you explain to him that his great benefactor had robbed him of his dignity and his soul? If it was about friendship, Evaristo loved Chamula even more than Maytorena. And, nonetheless, Chamula was hunting him from only a few metres away on the instructions of a swine who despised them both. The situation reminded him of some verses by José Emilio Pacheco: "We go in blindness through darkness, in the fire we walk in darkness". Such was life: a grotesque misunderstanding. In the midst of confusion, people would side with their enemies and fight against their true allies. Evaristo was beginning to calm down a little when he saw the barrel of Chamula's revolver peeking out from under the newspaper he was holding.

"This is why I do not consider myself a writer. I would say that, better still, I am a professional of hope. When I write I think about the elderly ladies who go to the park to feed crumbs to the pigeons. I do the same thing, but, instead of bread, I use words, words that are crumbs of tenderness. But at other times, when I see that everything is dark around me, instead of words, poisoned darts come out. With them I would like to inspire courage in my male and female readers, to summon them to follow the example of the indigenous people of Chiapas, who are the most dignified citizens of Mexico."

There was no escape at the back. Evaristo had to go down the stairs pushing to open his way, and run striding through the narrow aisle that separated the seats in the theatre, to the protests of students telling him to fuck his mother, watch out, bastard, look where you are standing that he heard as an accompaniment beyond the only sound that mattered to him – the steps of Chamula, who was about two metres behind him and who, maybe, was giving him a few seconds of grace because he did not have a clear shot. When they saw him cross, running towards the top table, the student audience noted that something odd was happening and there was a condemnatory murmur, but when Chamula crossed exactly the same place carrying a gun, the murmur turned into a collective scream and Palmira Jackson went mute with terror. It was the most dangerous moment because now there were no people between the two men and Chamula had him in full view. Evaristo got out his .38 to impose some respect and shot wildly into the air as he ran to the emergency exit. The students cleared away from it in a jiffy when they saw him flying at them like an arrow. Everyone at the event had fallen to the ground, including the intellectuals on stage, who in their rush to hide under the table had left Palmira Jackson unprotected. Evaristo dodged through the emergency exit in one jump but, as he descended a ramp that in theory would get him out of the auditorium, he tripped over a cameraman's cable. It was a providential fall, because thanks to it he managed to dodge a shot from Chamula that would have perforated his temple. From the ground, Evaristo fired three times towards the bulk approaching him, closing his eyes as he pulled the trigger. One of his bullets ended up in Chamula's stomach, another in his neck and one more in a lamp on the ceiling. By an irrational impulse, he went closer to watch Chamula slump to the floor and make sure he was fatally injured: a fading tremor convulsed Chamula's right leg, his chest was drenched in blood and, as his shroud, he clutched the newspaper with the phrase: "AS USUAL: DEFEATED".

Evaristo could not stay to see him close his eyes, because the man in the grey suit would appear at any minute. With a surreal feeling, he went down the ramp until he came to an avenue on the university circuit. So it was that easy to kill a man? He crossed the auditorium's car park with the intention of getting to Insurgentes, where he hoped to take a taxi or minibus. He still had the warm revolver in his hand and the students walking towards him moved aside fearfully or dropped their books on the floor. In order not to attract attention, he put the gun in his jacket pocket and continued, quickening his pace. An old and battered Volkswagen coming out of its space charged against him with its back bumper, throwing him face first against a stone wall. The driver got out and, surprised, Evaristo recognised him: it was Rubén Estrella.

"Did I hurt you?"

Evaristo shook his head, but his groaning contradicted him.

"Get in, mate. I'll give you a lift."

"I'm going to barrio Guerrero."

"It's on my way. I live in Colonia San Rafael."

Holding on to his shoulder, Evaristo got into the front seat.

Fear of Animals

"Did you come for the tribute to Palmira Jackson?" Evaristo asked Estrella.

"No. I've just come out of a conference given by Fernando Savater in the main hall."

When he made sure that Estrella had not seen the shooting at the auditorium, Evaristo felt more at ease, but not totally confident, because he knew Rubén was a moralist wedded to the ideals of his youth. He had been scandalised when he had learned Evaristo was a Fed. What would he think now that he was accused of murder?

"Aren't you afraid of having a man on the run in your car?" Evaristo asked him, half joking, half serious, when they stopped at traffic lights in Copilco.

"Well, the real truth is that now I trust you more. Since I saw you on the telly, I said, nope, this bastard didn't kill Roberto. They want to lumber him with the stiff to protect the real culprits."

"You don't even know me. How do you know it wasn't me?"

"Because, in this country, the killers roam free and have mega posts in government."

"In your place I'd be more careful. If they catch you with me you'll end up in fucking hell."

"Do you want to get out or what?" Estrella stopped the car and looked at him impatiently. "I told you that, to me, you're innocent. Even more, you need only a little to become the good guy of the movie, but if you're so paranoid you'd better walk."

His nobility moved Evaristo, who for a long time had not received moral support from anyone: he was not alone against the world, at least someone trusted him. They exchanged smiles and Rubén put his foot down. Softened by his unusual sign of affection, Evaristo played back in his head the cheap thriller scene he had just performed in the auditorium, feeling that he had committed an atrocious crime. Now he was a Fed through and through. He now knew what it was like to kill with impunity. He remembered his piss-ups with Chamula, the christening of his first-born – who was now an orphan – at the little house in San Juan de Aragón, where he let in all the neighbours in the barrio, as at all village parties. He did not deserve to die like that, he was a good beast after all. Rubén's friendly words, compared with the horrible vision of Chamula at death's threshold, seemed an ironic condemnation: *You need only a little to become the good guy of the movie...* He wished he could think the same.

Fear of Animals

As a result of the shooting at Palmira Jackson's tribute, which public opinion attributed to a group of "plants", the protests by intellectuals and journalists at "the fascist escalation that threatens to suppress freedom of expression" grew so much that it provoked Attorney Tapia's resignation. President Jiménez del Solar appointed in his place Doctor Jaime Cisneros Topete, a Yale graduate, who committed himself before the TV cameras to ending the impunity and corruption of the police and announced the Comprehensive Citizen Protection Programme under Commander Jesús Maytorena, "a policeman of proven honesty, with wide experience in combatting delinquency, and who can count on my full support in accomplishing his difficult task". This promotion made Maytorena change his tracksuits for suits and get his tooth decay treated in order to appear on television as a model cop. Exonerated for lack of evidence, Osiris Cantú de la Garza was freed the day after Cisneros assumed his post and the newspapers did not even mention the reason for his detention, despite it being on the record. Evaristo saw the hairy hand of drug trafficking behind Cantú's freedom, but the cultural community, who believed in Osiris' innocence and had now turned him into some kind of martyr, congratulated the new attorney in a letter signed by more than a hundred writers and artists.

From the outset, political analysts connected the shooting at the Justo Sierra Auditorium with the killings of Lima and Vilchis, despite the fact that none of those attending the homage had identified Evaristo because the incident had occurred so quickly. A commentator at *Reforma* risked the hypothesis that Palmira Jackson was really the target of the attempt, but Chamula at the last minute had had second thoughts, and the gunman looking after his back had killed him to prevent him making a statement that could compromise the author of the plot – presumably politicians from the PRI old guard who risked losing their privileges and power because of the incipient Mexican *glasnost*. Again, the confusion came from the cryptic PGR press release in which there was no mention of Chamula being an agent of the Federal Judicial Police. Used to writing press releases of the same sort, Evaristo guessed the reason for the omission: with the spotlight on him because of his recent promotion, Maytorena did not want to admit that one of his men had let the most wanted criminal in Mexico get away. If in life he had not ceased to humiliate Chamula, in his death he portrayed him as a "trigger-happy paid killer at the service of dark forces", without even conceding to him the modest glory of an honourable epitaph.

Given the uncertainty of not knowing if the agent in the grey suit had recognised him in the Metro or had seen him walking towards Hidalgo station, in which case the police would be combing Colonia Guerrero, Evaristo chose to move to a safer hotel, the Oslo, at the corner of Viaducto and the Eje Central highway. To get his car out of Bonampak's car park without attracting the attention of the police, he stole the number plates of another car, as there was no security guard, and placed them on his own, thereby managing to go unnoticed by the police cars he encountered on the way. Rubén Estrella had offered his home as a refuge but, if he had taken the offer up, Evaristo would have exposed him to a sentence of up to ten years for complicity and he was not prepared to drag more innocents into this affair. However, because of his support, Rubén had given him something more important than a place to hide: he now believed in people again. He had been wrong to consider him a ridiculous fossil from the Sixties – there was nothing wrong with being loyal to a universal fraternity that had transformed the world. He himself, under the layers of dung accumulated over years with the Feds, had the soul of a Sixties kid. If corruption and his own lack of character had not caused him to buckle when he had begun to make his way in life, he would have continued on friendly terms with the human race, without accepting the stinking hierarchies of society based on power, riches and merit. Maybe Rubén had seen the human side of his temperament when he stopped looking at him as a Fed and began to see him as a victim. And if Rubén Estrella had exonerated him so easily, Palmira Jackson, who was also a gal with a heart and belonged to the same tribe of rebels, would understand at first sight that a man like him – romantic, leftish and repentant about his past – could not in any way be a paid assassin.

Fear of Animals

Confident of making a good impression, Evaristo began a new campaign from his room at the Oslo hotel to get close to Palmira, this time via telephone. It was not difficult to get in touch with her because her number was in the telephone book of the Narcopoet, Osiris Cantú de la Garza, which he had saved in his Spirit's glove compartment after he had detained him. What was difficult was getting Palmira to answer the telephone. Like any celebrity, she had a system to fend off the journalists and admirers. During the day the calls were answered by a French secretary with the airs of a Grande Dame and, in the evenings, by Jackson's son, a teenager with a nasal voice and rude manners who seemed to be fed up being his mother's messenger. Because he did not want to frighten Palmira, Evaristo preferred to give a false name, but his strategy was counterproductive. Both subjected him to a preventative form of questioning (Who are you? Where are you calling from? Do you want to ask her for an article or an interview?) so that he could not win them over as some unknown calling about a "personal matter", which naturally made them distrust him.

"Aye'm sohrry. Missees Jackson is vehrry beesy, but tell me what you want and I weel pass your message."

"I can't, I must speak to her directly."

"Den aye don't theenk she can take jourh coll."

By the third day, sick of hearing the same answer, he had a bedside piss-up and, with the heat of the alcohol, warned the secretary that his call was a matter of life and death. That was the only way that he managed to get Palmira to take the call, but not exactly to chat in a friendly way.

"Listen, you arsehole, when are you going to stop bothering me?"

"Forgive my insistence, madam. I just wanted to ask for an appointment..."

"An appointment? What for? You and I have nothing to talk about."

"I have some information for you about Roberto Lima's murder." Evaristo's voice was mellow and he had difficulty articulating his words. "I was with him on the day he died..."

"And why are you ringing me? Who told you that I'm a reporter in the crime section?"

"I thought you would be interested in knowing that the presumed murderer is a sacrificial lamb."

"I am not interested in the imaginings of a drunkard. If you really know something, go to the police. And don't dare call me again, because I'm going to ask the new attorney to trace your call."

The abrupt end to the conversation demoralised Evaristo to the point where he did not touch food for two days. He needed Palmira's support to refute the PGR and prove his innocence but, above all, to get rid of the guilt that tormented him because of the deaths of Dora Elsa and Chamula. He believed in *La* Jackson as others believe in the Bible and felt spiritually abandoned, like an assassin to whom the confessor denies absolution. Without doubt, Palmira had not thought him a trustworthy person. And maybe she was right: a long process of degradation like that which he had undergone with the Feds left scars that were not easy to conceal, even over the telephone.

Devalued, he felt an insurmountable impulse to get back his previous life – that of the decadent wastrel who saw the light of dawn covered in his own vomit – so he went out at night to pick up a whore by Viaducto. He used her speedily and brutally, hating her and hating himself, with his sight nailed to the satellite porno channel. The next day, with a hangover from hell, he had another attack of hypoglycaemia that curled his fingers inwards. Thank God he had left a Pepsi on the bedside table and the sugar brought back the flexibility of his muscles. When he felt better, he saw the crossroads he had reached more clearly. Any moment now the Feds would come to arrest him and, except for Rubén Estrella, who had neither moral leadership nor any weight in public opinion, no ex-friend of Lima would raise his voice to defend him. His arrest would mean the definitive triumph of the insolent and conceited assassin who had branded him an animal and later taken away the only proof against him, as if to support his insult with facts. Waiting for him was like a long torture session directed by Maytorena, the hose bath in the holding cells, the invented declaration in front of the news cameras and a secure jail cell where he would surely end up turning mad. It was not fair: it was better to end the little life he had left. He walked to the dressing table mirror and put the .38 to his temple with a determination that surprised him. He imagined that killing himself would be as easy as switching off a television using the remote. That was death: surfing from a distressing and brainless show into the warm prenatal darkness. Without a tremor in his pulse or cold sweat, he pulled the trigger, but instead of the explosion heard a stupid click. He had run out of bullets at the shooting with Chamula. Was God protecting him or taking the mickey?

When Evaristo realised what an atrocity he had just committed, he slumped over in bed, crying. He now understood the value of living and even his own suffering seemed to him a treasure that could not be refused, a burning nail that, regardless, he must clutch with fingernails and teeth. Nothing was worse than nothing, not even the most inhospitable jail on earth. He wished like never before to reach old age, even if in a wheelchair and with a pacemaker. His other life was a lie: he had got close enough to the edge of the precipice to feel that, at the other side, there was only a black hole. Purified after crying, he discovered inside an unknown fortitude. He was safe because it was not yet his turn to die, because he still had a mission to accomplish. Maybe he had put his gun to his temple because he did not have the guts to face adversity. Yes, deep down he was a coward horrified by the idea of failure. He would not have taken Palmira Jackson's predictable answer so seriously otherwise. How did he want her to react if he had called while drunk and given a false name, presenting his affairs to her like a thriller? In the midst of a full crisis, with the country falling apart and political crimes every day, a call like that had to annoy her. But all was not lost. If he managed to see Palmira and personally lay out his case with absolute sincerity, as she liked to treat people, maybe he could convince her of his innocence or, at least, sow some doubt about the actions of the authorities in Lima's case.

"I am not coming to ask for your support," he would tell her by way of introduction, "I just want you to judge for yourself who is telling the truth and who is inventing a culprit."

In Osiris Cantú de la Garza's book was her address: Monte Líbano 237, Lomas de Chapultepec. Without wasting any more time on calls that got him nowhere, he went there by taxi, leaving the Spirit in the hotel car park, because he feared that by now the true owner of his number plates would have told the police about them. Among the surrounding mansions, Palmira Jackson's was more or less modest, but with a touch of distinction from the splendidly carved wooden door that adorned the entrance, probably a relic of an ancient nunnery. It was two o'clock and the sun shone fully upon the ivy-covered wall that at times looked like a fountain of light. Maybe Palmira would arrive for lunch in a few minutes, maybe she was working at home, but at any moment she would come or go and then, putting his pride to one side, he would kneel down asking her to listen to him. He regretted not bringing a book, or at least a newspaper, because the wait was going to be long. The street was deserted, a few cars would pass every now and then, but no one would walk along the spotless sidewalks and his presence would appear suspicious to the neighbours. To avoid being mistaken for a burglar, he went to the corner of Monte Líbano and Palmas Avenue where there was a telephone booth. From there, about forty metres from the house, he waited anxiously for Palmira to show up, pretending to be talking on the telephone. An hour went by. Residential areas were insufferably monotonous. Even the maids used the car to go shopping, escorted by the house chauffeur, like important ladies. A football match would be unthinkable. Why, if the kids from this area had gardens the size of football pitches? At about a quarter past three, a burgundy Tsuru stopped at Jackson's house and a lanky, long-haired youth got out, probably her son coming back from school. Maybe Palmira was giving a conference outside Mexico City and would not be back until Monday. He began to lose hope when, from his observation place, he saw three cars full of people turning to the right at Monte Líbano and parking behind the Tsuru. He ran towards them for a closer check on their passengers and felt a hollow in his stomach when he saw Palmira getting out of the car linking arms with two gentlemen, Javier Loperena and Medina Chaires, who joked with her merrily. In the other cars came a large contingent of intellectuals, some with their wives, most by themselves, dressed in elegant *sport* clothing, like in the Chivas Regal adverts. Among them a small, scruffy and malnourished man stood out. He must have been a journalist, as he had a tape recorder in his hand. He felt embarrassed to approach Palmira in the midst of so many people, so he hid behind a tree, paralysed with shyness.

When Jackson entered her house accompanied by her group of friends, Evaristo realised that it would be impossible to mingle with them. He admired them with all his heart, but a cultural or class barrier prevented him from considering them as equals. They belonged to another world, the world of generous utopias, where he would never fit in because he represented the darkest reality. He had become accustomed to dealing with the intellectual elite and had even lost respect for them, but they were something

Fear of Animals

apart, a challenging and critical, morally irreproachable minority who had put their prestige and intelligence at the service of the people. Maybe he would dare to talk to Palmira alone, but not in front of that tribunal of purity, where his guilty voice would echo like the shrieks of a pig infiltrating a choir of nightingales. Maybe he knew his country better than they did, maybe he could open their eyes about some naivetés and show them they had been mistaken when they idealised the people, but his lack of moral solvency discredited him in advance. The best thing he could do, therefore, was leave, take a taxi to Palmas and get drunk again in his room at the Oslo.

He was walking along the sidewalk with his hands in his pockets, morally defeated, when an inner voice ordered him to go back and fight. It was his freedom that was at stake and, because he was already there, he had to see things through. Or was he going to chicken out like some queen? After hesitating for a long time, during which he listed all the lows of his life and contrasted them with Palmira's exemplary life, he plucked up the courage to ring the bell.

"Who is it?" responded the French secretary.

"I am Evaristo Reyes. I would like to speak for a moment with Mrs Jackson."

"Where are you coming from?"

"It is a personal matter."

"Zwaite a moment."

The secretary went to consult with Palmira and took some minutes to get back to the intercom.

"Ze lady says she can't rhecieve you rhight now."

"And when will she have the time?"

"Aye don't know. Ask hehr fohr an appointement by telefon and she will tell you."

Unbelievable: after such a long wait and such an inner struggle, he was back to square one. Maybe Palmira had not remembered his name, or the telephone calls had left her shaky. Now who was going to help him? He walked towards Palmas, when an orange van parked behind the Tsuru. On the side of it he read the advertisement *Lion House, everything for your parties and banquets*, so he deduced that Jackson had contracted caterers to serve her guests. This was confirmed when he saw a waiter wearing a white jacket and bowtie get out of the van, taking from it a pile of white tablecloths and serviettes. When he had made sure he was alone, Evaristo had a crazy idea: he followed the waiter discreetly up to the house entrance, walking on the grass verge of the sidewalk so as not to make noise, took the .38 from his jacket and, before the waiter could knock at the door, hit him on the back of the head with the butt of the gun. When he fell, the waiter dropped the pile of tablecloths and serviettes. For a moment Evaristo thought he had killed him, but, after making sure that he was still breathing, he controlled his desire to run away and proceeded with the second part of his plan. Taking him by the arms, Evaristo dragged the waiter to the van, the veins in his neck bulging with the effort. He took the van's keys from the waiter's pocket, opened the sliding door and put him inside in stages, first his head and torso, then the waist and finally the legs, which he had to bend as if they were a ragdoll's. Exhausted, he lay next to his victim inside. When he had regained his breath, he stripped the waiter and put on his clothes, which were slightly too small for him, particularly the trousers, good for skipping in puddles. Pleased with his disguise, he quickly picked up the tablecloths and serviettes spread on the road and rang the bell.

"Who is it?"

"I am the waiter from *Lion House*," Evaristo lied, covering his mouth with the serviette.

"U wehr teiking youhr time, come in."

A maid in uniform took him into the kitchen where he was met by the *madame*, a fifty-something ash-blonde, nice looking for her age, wearing a *Tehuana* dress and with her hair plaited with colourful ribbons, like a European Frida Kahlo.

"Heer are ze whisky bottles, heer de rhhum ones and heer de wine ones," she said in a nagging voice, annoyed by his late arrival. "Aye haf counted dem, so be veggy cahreful, if dere is one meesing aye will discount it fom youhr pay. Sehrve the thray with highballs and cubas, and rhhum to the sitting goom, but hurrhy, please, that evehryone is dying of thihrst. Den you come back fohr the canapé thray... Eef yoo need me, aye am going to be upstairs working at the studio. My name is Giselle."

He obeyed her instructions fully, trying not to serve the drinks too full so the bottles would last. From the kitchen he could listen to the animated chatter of the guests.

"There were more than a hundred thousand peasants. I saw the meeting from the restaurant, the Hotel Majestic and Zócalo was chock-a-block. After this, the President will have to give in."

"I doubt it. Jiménez del Solar would die rather than give in. He is capable of sending in the army to break the picket."

Fear of Animals

"Well, now it's difficult for him because if he does not resolve anything, tomorrow they will grab their machetes and join the guerrillas."

"Maybe that's what Jiménez wants, for them to give him an excuse to unleash the repression."

"And where is Valtierra, the demo's co-ordinator? Didn't you invite him, Palmira?"

"He must be on his way. He said, very formally, that he'd come. We have to organise the solidarity days. He wants to organise a meeting of intellectuals to get wider coverage for the movement."

"Truly, I was fearing that today there would be another massacre like that of 1968 in the Tlatelolco plaza. That's why I didn't want to get down in Zócalo square. At my age I'm not game for the bazooka."

When Evaristo appeared in the sitting room carrying the drinks tray, the chatter was interrupted and the guests turned to look at him with an expression of excitement.

"Bravo, I was dying of thirst," exclaimed Javier Loperena, standing up to take a glass. "I thought you were applying the Dry Laws to us, Palmira."

"Knowing how much of a drunkard you are? I would risk you never coming back to my house again. And you, don't you want some?" she said to the rest of the guests. "If you leave the tray to Javier, he is likely to drink it all."

Palmira occupied a magnificent Regency-style chair at the centre of the room, under an oil painting by Rodolfo Morales, representing two women dog-sellers in a hallway. Flanking her on either side were two youths who could not get a chair and had sat on the floor, hanging on her words, like the pageboys of a queen. Immediately, the drinks walked. Following Giselle's instructions to the letter, Evaristo went back to the kitchen to get the baby eels, caviar and smoked salmon canapés. His beard had grown in the last couple of days and he was relatively sure his face could not be recognised, although he feared that his trousers would give him away because they stopped at his ankles. Fortunately, Palmira and her friends were so engrossed in their chat that nobody paid him any attention. The luxury of the sitting room intimidated him and he had to manoeuvre with extreme care not to knock over the pots shaped like Egyptian amphoras, the Chinese porcelain figures, the little ivory elephants and hand-cut crystal ashtrays. When he had finished passing the canapé tray, the doorbell rang.

"It must be Valtierra." Palmira turned to Evaristo. "Would you be so kind as to open the door?"

Startled by her piercing gaze, Evaristo lowered his head in a gesture of submission. He had entered the lion's den: Palmira had looked at him in a strange manner and it would not take her long to identify him, as soon as the penny dropped. It was one thing for her not to remember his name, but quite another not to remember his face, after so much exposure in the news. Or was this the way she looked at everyone, with that intensity that pierced your skin? On his way to the door, in the wide entrance hall with polished terracotta floors, he stopped for an instant to contemplate the glass cabinet adorned with Palmira's portraits next to great celebrities: María Félix, Siqueiros, Fidel Castro, Buñuel, Günter Grass, Mother Teresa of Calcutta. That's why she looked at him in that way: rubbing shoulders with those higher up had taught her to impose herself upon the rest from the first gaze. Recovered from the fright, he opened the door for Valtierra, a stocky ranger with a bushy moustache, denim jacket and a bandanna tied around his neck. Palmira and her guests received him with great shows of affection.

"Congratulations, pal." Medina Chaires hugged him. "The march was a great success, and the meeting was one of the most emotive I have ever seen. That speech by Rosario Ibarra made many people cry. You'll see how much coverage you get in the papers tomorrow."

"Thanks, professor, but the credit is not mine, it belongs to all the comrades who came on foot from Oaxaca and Guerrero."

"How was the long walk?" asked Palmira. "Were there any provocations?"

"Just a few, but we didn't rise to the bait. The bad thing was that many people got sick and we even had to bury a newborn. But we have now accomplished our objective to get to the Zócalo. We are not budging from it until we get our lands."

"And have you not thought of the possibility that the government may violently evict you all?" asked the scrawny reporter, who had turned his tape recorder on.

"That will be even worse for them. If they want violence, a hundred thousand more peasants will come to the capital. They will have to resolve the problem or else kill us all."

"That's the way to speak." Palmira patted him on the back. "Don't you want something to drink, to cool you down from the morning sun?"

Fear of Animals

"A little beer, please."

With a wink from Palmira, Evaristo rushed to the kitchen, where he prepared a new round of drinks, to which he added a Corona in a glass for the peasant leader. He was earning his interview with Jackson, but he would have to wait until the end of the gathering to talk to her in private. When he came out with the new round, he noted a change in the position of the guests: in a corner of the sitting room, under a lithograph by Velasco depicting marine flora, Palmira, Javier Loperena and Medina Chaires had formed a circle around Valtierra, while the rest of the guests – people of little importance, he thought, which is why they must be excluded – were commenting on the country's political situation in alarmed voices.

Thirsty, Javier Loperena called him with a gesture and took two whiskies from the tray, "So I don't keep bothering you, bro". Valtierra spoke in a low voice, as if fearful of being heard by a spy from the interior ministry.

"As part of the strategy to spread our cause, the movement's directorate commissioned me to invite you to participate in an act of support that we are thinking about celebrating on Thursday at the Ho Chi Minh auditorium. The press advertisements will carry our motto: 'The land belongs to those who work it: all united with the Sierra Madre Peasant Front'."

"Good title. And, apart from us, who else are you inviting?" asked Palmira.

"The idea is to gather a group of well-known, prestigious writers, intellectuals and artists committed to popular causes, to create a mosaic representing civil society. There will be eight of them in total and they will have slots of fifteen minutes each, so as not to tire the audience."

"But who are they?" insisted Palmira.

Evaristo had to leave the select group to serve the guests calling him from the other end of the sitting room. Curious, he would have loved to have kept on discreetly listening to the conversation of the famous, but he had to perform his role as a waiter with due diligence. He was serving the second-division guests when Palmira gave out an angry yell.

"Rita Bolaños? But where do you get the idea that that clown is an intellectual of any prestige?"

Guests from sections one and two turned to look at her in amazement. She was breathing fast, upset, and a severe frown had disfigured her face.

"Don't get upset, *Doña* Palmira, I did not compile the list," apologised Valtierra. "The executive committee thought that comrade Bolaños deserved to be invited."

"Well, the committee is going to have to decide whether they invite her or me, because I do not mingle with that rat-eating snake. Do you support me in this?"

Medina Chaires and Javier Loperena nodded. Valtierra gulped, nervously.

"Well, we can still reconsider, but Comrade Bolaños has been very supportive of our movement. She came with the march from Iguala, she interviewed lots of peasant farmers, she was at the baby's burial and then she published a report in the whole of the middle section of *Siempre* magazine for us."

"And do you think she did that out of the goodness of her heart? Don't be naive, Mr Valtierra. She always has to copy everything I do. She has been like that since she started her career. If I wrote a column about the San Juanico tragedy, she wrote a similar one the following week. If I interviewed the striking seamstresses, she followed me asking the same questions, with her little hypocrite's face and her crocodile tears. She even copied my style. Now she has learned that I am preparing a book about you lot and logically she wants to get there first."

"With all due respect, I don't think Mrs Bolaños can be such a bad person," insisted Valtierra.

"That's because you don't really know her." Palmira raised her voice even more. "Look, I have been in this game for years and I know how to distinguish between people who are authentic, the writers who really are committed, and those opportunists just seeking notoriety. Rita has used you to create prestige for herself that she does not have. That's the way she has made her little name, profiting from the suffering of others. Why do you think she gloated over the child's death? Vile sensationalism! But she is mad if she thinks that I will let her sit next to me at an intellectual's table. I'd rather be dead. Fancy a sandal-wearer wanting to tread all over me."

Evaristo forgot to serve the guests for a moment, staring at her with his mouth wide open. Palmira Jackson, the patron saint of the Mexican left, the flag-bearer of all noble causes, turned into a velociraptor foaming at the mouth!

"Then, should we cross her off?" capitulated Valtierra.

"With a double cross," ordered Palmira. "Who else is on the list?"

Fear of Animals

Giselle came down the stairs alarmed by Palmira's shouting, and, when she saw Evaristo waiting expectantly with the tray resting on an eighteenth-century Viennese sideboard, scolded him and ordered him to go to the kitchen for a tablecloth to put on the dining room table where the buffet would be served. Evaristo obeyed her as best he could in his confusion. So Palmira was also a monster of vanity, an arrogant snob obsessed with hierarchies? What made her different from Perla Tinoco or Claudio Vilchis then? How could you believe in her human qualities if she threw those infatuated *vedette* tantrums? Did she really love the poor, the victims of natural disasters or political repression, or had she used them as a springboard to celebrity status? The dining room table was not far from the corner where Jackson held her unofficial meeting and, when he placed the tablecloth, he did so very slowly so as to keep listening.

"Another one of the writers that we thought of inviting is Joaquín Peniche," commented Valtierra.

"Does anyone know who he is?" asked Palmira, twisting her mouth in a sign of annoyance.

"Newly arrived to culture," pronounced Javier Loperena. "He has published two or three cheap articles and has created some fame as a belligerent because he insults half the world in his little column in *El Financiero*."

"We need recognised people, not upstarts. Cross him off too," Valtierra obeyed instantly, transformed into a secretary without a voice or vote. "Who's next?"

"Pedro Filisola, the historian."

Palmira clicked her tongue, shaking her head.

"Don't you think he's a bit of a lightweight?"

"Frankly, yes," Javier Loperena supported her again. "He has not even been translated into French."

Foreseeing Palmira's orders, Valtierra crossed him off. In the distance, Evaristo had a look at Valtierra's guest list, which now looked like a graveyard.

"Now we have eliminated four writers," Valtierra informed them. "There is only one left on the list: the crime novelist Patricio Menchaca."

"Well, we have to recognise that Menchaca has been translated into various languages, although in my opinion he is shit," defended Medina Chaires.

"I agree, and also his breath stinks," complained Palmira. "He sat next to me at the railway workers' solidarity event and I will not put up with him again for anything in the world."

"If we cross off Menchaca, there will only be you three," Valtierra warned them.

"So what? Like that, we can talk for longer. After all, the people are going to be attending because of us, don't you think?" Palmira smiled with malice. "Why do we need a whole heap of second bests?"

When Giselle saw Evaristo smoothing the tablecloth for a tenth time, she threatened to call *Lion House* asking for another waiter if he kept pretending not to know what to do in order to avoid working. His contract was for the time worked and he had to *worhk* his pay minute by minute. *What was he waiting fog, go to ze kitchen and bhring ze dishes with ze food.* It was going to get cold if he didn't bring it to the table soon. In the kitchen, because of his nerves, he nearly dropped a splendid Tonalá salad bowl, which Giselle would surely have asked him to pay for. He made four trips from the kitchen to the dining room, bringing pots with green *mole*, *rajas* with cheese and *huitlacoche* crépes. He was hot, the bow tie restricting his circulation at the jugular, and his shirt was tight over his ribs. But far greater than the physical discomfort was the certainty that he would not be able to move Palmira. Her business was virtue preached with loudspeakers, open letters abundant with the message of "Love thy neighbour". The defence of a murder suspect, an ex-Fed, to make matters worse, would not make him any cleaner before a public that expected an inflexible rectitude from her. So he was risking himself in vain, because, if any of the guests present discovered his identity, he would be accused of breaking into Palmira's home with the intention of killing her.

In one of his multiple trips from the kitchen to the dining room he bumped into Javier Loperena, who was a bit tipsy. When they hugged in order not to fall, there was a moment in which they ended up face to face and, because of the writer's expression of amazement, Evaristo thought he had been found out.

"Excuse me, young man, my reflexes failed me," smiled Loperena, who left, stumbling towards the visitor's toilet.

Evaristo recovered his composure, but at that moment Palmira called him with a gesture and he now feared that fate had finally caught up with him.

"One sparkling water, please, and for the men give them the same as they've been drinking..."

Fear of Animals

"I'm happy that everything is now to your entire satisfaction," concluded Valtierra. "I'm going to tell the comrades on the committee that only Mr Loperena and you two will participate in the event. We still have time to change the paid insertions in the press."

"Wait, don't leave so quickly." Palmira returned him to his seat and lowered her voice in a confidential tone. "Look, I really love Javier, we have been friends all our lives, but lately he has been doing really badly. Isn't that true Wenceslao?" Medina Chaires nodded, with a severe expression. "Because everyone says he is the Mexican Faulkner, the poor guy believed it and now he drinks a bottle of whisky a day. His alcoholism is now uncontrollable and I wouldn't be surprised if he turns up drunk at the auditorium."

"Well, on the day of your tribute he looked very lucid," Valtierra dared to comment.

"Lucid? But he was in a shameful state. The poor guy was slurring like a little drunkard from a circus."

Feverish and beginning to feel nauseous, Evaristo had to go to the kitchen for the drinks. When he returned, *La* Jackson had already crucified the Mexican Faulkner.

"Say no more." Valtierra wiped his sweaty brow with the bandanna. "If that's what you want, we shall have to uninvite Mr Loperena."

"But don't tell him I asked you to," Palmira coached him. "Call him on the phone in the middle of the week and tell him that the committee decided to reduce the number of invitations. He will understand that a movement such as yours, attacked from every side, cannot compromise its good image just because of a little drunkard. Who knows, maybe we're doing him a favour and the disappointment will serve as a deterrent to drop drinking?"

Palmira suddenly went mute when she saw Javier Loperena approaching them.

"I was telling them how much I loved your latest novel. I got it one night and, when I put it down, the sun was coming up."

"Thank you, Palmira, darling." Javier kissed her on the cheek. "You're so generous with me that I even feel I might have been your husband. Could you bring me another highball, bro?"

As Evaristo went to the kitchen to serve the drink, Palmira's son came down the stairs with a racquet and dressed for the tennis court. He was a lanky, long-legged teenager with a spotty forehead and red gnome's nose. He went past like an arrow, without even saying good afternoon, and continued towards the door.

"Where are you going, Guillermo? Come here and say hello like a decent person."

In the kitchen, Evaristo stopped to reflect. *La* Jackson had deceived him. Among the coterie of literates, the tournaments between vanities could be forgiven to a certain extent, but she was not a simple writer: she was dissidence canonised. In a champion of good deeds, protagonism and the urge for supremacy were doubly grotesque because of their implicit deceit. By backing up social struggle with altruistic displays, Palmira was betraying herself, but also betraying literature. Would she know it or was she so convinced of her goodness that she could not see anything negative in it? He remembered Baudelaire's opinion about George Sand: "She is a great idiot, but she is possessed. The Devil has persuaded her to trust in her good heart." When Evaristo came out of the kitchen, with Javier Lopenera's highball, Palmira's son was talking to the sad-looking reporter, who had turned on his tape recorder again.

"I learned that you will be distributing the video of the Zapatista Army in the United States."

"Yes, my mother put me in touch with the producers." Guillermo lit a cigarette and exchanged looks with his mother, who was watching him closely. "Tomorrow I'm going to Los Angeles to meet the distributor who is going to promote it on television."

"I hope it's a success. It's very important to spread the Zapatista struggle abroad. Do you think it will sell a lot?"

"I hope so, because I will have a percentage of the sales and, with what I earn, I'm thinking about buying a Ferrari."

"Don't take any notice of him. That money is for a shelter in the Lacandón jungle. Guillermo has the habit of pretending to be funny in front of my friends."

"Tell them the truth, Mummy." Guillermo smiled cheekily. "There's nothing bad about doing business."

"Shut up, imbecile. You said hello now, didn't you? Why are you waiting to clear off to the club?"

Evaristo took the highball to Loperena with his hand trembling. His blood pressure was low, he needed to loosen his tie and rest for a moment. Defying Giselle, he went into the visitor's toilet, which was exquisitely decorated with Talavera tiles and hand-crafted Hindu figures. Wetting his head in the sink calmed his nausea, but not his anger. How stupid he had been to blindly believe in Palmira's nobility and sincerity. Deep down, she was identical to

Fear of Animals

the posh Jockey Club ladies who did charity work with twenty reporters around them so as to appear the following day in the Society section. She had deceived everybody else, but not her son, who knew her too well and, logically, detested her. In his cynicism, Guillermo was more congruent: what was so bad about exploiting the misfortunes of other people if his mother had done so all her life, turning the redeeming embrace for the poor into a resource for self-promotion?

"Get owt! Ze peeople is starting to eet and yoo haf to sehrve ze wine. Fohr zis aye will discount yoo twenty pesos."

Giselle's knocks shook the bathroom door and returned him abruptly to reality. He filled all the guests' glasses in an exhausting round through the sitting and dining rooms, pouring from a bottle of wine in a clumsy wicker basket. Halfway through the dessert, the doorbell rang again. Giselle ordered Evaristo to open the door, but warned him not to let any other journalists in. When he passed by Palmira, who had stayed behind with Valtierra, he caught another snippet of their conversation.

"... and please be very careful with the press advertisement. Wenceslao is my best friend, but I always appear first."

Moved by her high concept of friendship, Evaristo decided to spit in the coffee pot, if he could dodge Giselle's scrutiny for a moment. This idea put him in good humour and he even whistled a merry tune anticipatedly celebrating his revenge, but when he opened the door he stood there frozen: it was the *Lion House* waiter, barefoot and furious, wearing a tablecloth as a makeshift tunic. Instinctively, he threw him a punch on the chin and slammed the door shut again. He had to do something before the man knocked again and Palmira realised that Evaristo had taken the waiter's place. He strode across the sitting room, ignoring the French warden who fulminated at him from the dining room with a disapproving gaze. In the kitchen he took off the jacket and bow tie and fled through the door into the back garden, where there was a reproduction of Chac Mool and a colonial-style fountain. Without looking back, he ran towards a wall with barbed wire guarded by an Alsatian that charged towards him, thinking he wanted to play. *Where are you going? I ohrded yoo to open ze doohr*, shouted Giselle from the kitchen. Excited by the danger, Evaristo shook the dog away with a single push and speedily climbed the ivy-covered wall, grasping a rusty nail that tore his skin, and then he fell face down into an abandoned plot of land. From the other side of the wall, Giselle was asking the guests for help: "Ze waitehr is leaving, stop 'im, 'es a zief." Among old tyres and metal rods, Evaristo stumbled to the wire mesh, which he didn't need to climb over because there was a hole in it of suitable proportions to crawl through.

The *Lion House* waiter must have been telling the whole world how Evaristo had impersonated him by now, and Palmira's friends would not be long in coming after him with sticks and stones. The effort of jumping the wall had left him breathless, but he found reserves at the bottom of his lungs to run towards Palmas and round the block. At the corner with the phone booth, he stopped for air and took a little look. The waiter had entered Palmira's house, but he could hear voices at the other side of the block, in the street with the abandoned plot. He was in a dead end, the hounds were near and he neither had anywhere to run nor the energy to continue fleeing. He was resigned to being caught when he remembered that he had the van's keys in his trouser pocket. With a roll of drums in his chest, he opened the car door and turned the engine on, feeling around to find the gears. When he pulled out, he saw the semi-naked waiter in the rearview mirror, running behind him, leading the contingent of hunters, venting their anger by shouting at Evaristo to go fuck his mother. He put his foot down and, with the horn, sent back the insults to his mother: *hasta la vista, baby.*

Driving at the old van's full power – less than ninety kilometres per hour on a flat road – he took a leafy street that led him to the second section of Chapultepec. He followed a series of arrows to get on to the Periférico, where the traffic was at a standstill and the ice-pop sellers were offering their wares in the fast lanes. Trapped in the gridlock, he looked at his hurt, bleeding and swollen left hand. The nail had left him looking like *ecce homo* and in half an hour he would start to scream in pain. Bloody Palmira. All he needed now was to lose his hand just for having got into her house. But the state of his hands was of secondary importance. What was really heavy and painful in his soul was that, from then onwards, he would not have anyone to believe in. He had lost his faith in the rest and knew himself too well to trust himself. Others turned their rage against the world into inner fortitude. He was weak and inclined to self-pity. Whoever peeked into his soul would only find a swamp of guilt and the enormous hole left by Dora Elsa. In these conditions he could not face reality. Condemned to inaction, to anguish without hope, he had to be content with being just a spectator in his own nightmare, and to hope it ended quickly.

Fear of Animals

In his lugubrious and sterile room at the Hotel Oslo, with the curtains shut because he feared being seen by someone from nearby buildings, Evaristo resorted to an old weakness that was now an important part of his personality: going from depression to drunkenness. From one whisky to the next, after clumsily bandaging his wounded hand, he exaggerated the incidents of that afternoon until he saw in Palmira the symbol of the humanity that had betrayed him. The whole world had sunken into corruption, including those who should be fighting against it. People invented masks to conceal how vile they were, and the most dangerous of these was the mask of the righteous, because it gave idiots an idealised reflection of their own character. He himself had fallen into that snare, thinking some noble soul would help him to demonstrate his innocence. Poor imbecile. Which noble souls? Where were they?

He felt a lump in his throat, a lump of impotence created by the truths that only he knew and nobody wanted to hear. Condemned to silence, he would die with his truth, shot by the police or rotting in jail, with the slanderous label of a career criminal.

But, before arriving at the date with his fucking fate, his final wish would be to vent his anger on someone, preferably Palmira herself or, if she did not answer the telephone, on her French poodle or even Little Guillermo. He would insult her with speed and accuracy, employing a brief telegram language to hurt her in the maximum way with minimum words. He looked for her number in Osiris Cantú de la Garza's book and, when he flicked through the pages, suddenly found a name that rang a bell: Ignacio Carmona, tel: 654 21 22. Who was he and why did it attract Evaristo's attention that Osiris had him in his phonebook? He lay in bed, intrigued and annoyed by his mental gaps. He took a long sip of his whisky, waiting for the alcohol to refresh his memory. His intuition told him that it must have been an important fact, but he could not remember why. To rid his doubts he dialled Carmona's number.

"*El Universal*. Who would you like to speak to?"

That was why the name rang a bell! Carmona had done a great favour for Lima's killer when he broadcast the version that the government had killed him because of his attacks on the President. Carmona's friendship with Osiris Cantú de la Garza explained why he had given so much weight to a mysterious anonymous call, presenting a baseless rumour as a leak "coming from well-informed sources". Maybe he owed Osiris a favour or was in debt to him in every sense of the word and, under threat of blackmail, had to conceal his identity without suspecting that his hoax would turn into an official truth. That is why he was so nervous at Lima's wake, when Evaristo had told him off for trusting an anonymous source, and why he had stammered like an idiot when Evaristo rang him from Osiris' house to identify the voice of his source. He rang the newspaper again and this time asked for the newsdesk.

"Excuse me, miss, could you put me through to Mr Ignacio Carmona?"

"He has left for the day. On Saturdays he only comes here to deliver his stories."

"And do you know where I can find him? I have to give him some important news."

"If you want, I can give you his home number, but he'll be back very late. It is easier for you to find him at La Vencedora, a cantina in Izazaga, near Salto del Agua. That's where I always pass his messages on."

"Would you be so kind as to give me that number?"

Evaristo scribbled the cantina's number on a cigarette packet, but stopped before he dialled. He wanted to catch Carmona unawares. He emptied his glass in the sink, picked up his corduroy jacket, hurriedly combed his hair in front of the dressing table mirror and left the room with the firm intent of making the journalist speak, whether he wanted to or not. The thrill of discovery had sobered him up and the fresh night air had the effect of strong coffee. After finding himself down a dead end, he had once again found the right path: the one that would take him towards resolving Lima's killing.

At Eje Central he took an environmentally friendly green taxi that, in less than ten minutes, left him at Izazaga. La Vencedora had a fetching neon sign of orange letters that could be seen from fifty metres away. It was a cantina from the old days, with a floor covered in sawdust, brass coat hangers, spittoons, and an antique wooden bar, with high chairs, in which no women or uniformed men were allowed. The only new thing was the jukebox at the end, a brightly coloured monstrosity adorned with posters of singers, which was playing a sad cumbia by the group Bronco. In the middle of the week the office workers of the area would fill up the place, but it was Saturday – a bad day for cantinas – and there were only a few tables occupied by domino players. Evaristo did not see Carmona among them, which produced in him a deep anxiety. He sat at the bar, tended by a muscular barman whose chest was covered in hair. Evaristo asked for an Old Parr with soda and a packet of Marlboros.

"Has Ignacio Carmona been here? I was told I could find him here."

"There he is, at the table at the end." The barman pointed to a cubicle.

Reanimated, Evaristo walked in his direction with glass in hand. Carmona was drinking on his own, looking through a magazine that half obscured his face. Despite the warm night, he was wearing a thick, woollen umber jumper under his jacket. His sparse beard, discoloured by nicotine, gave him a sickly air. Under the neon light, which accentuated the bloatedness of his face, he looked like a cartoon bohemian, half intellectual, half amphibian.

"How's it going, Nachito? Can I sit with you for a moment?"

When Carmona recognised him, he was startled and dropped the magazine. Evaristo picked it up off the floor.

"*Der Spiegel*? Uh, yikes. I thought you were more stupid. Are you going to tell me that you understand German?"

"What do you want?"

"To talk with you." Evaristo sat opposite him. "I need to know why you covered up Lima's killer."

"I didn't cover up for any assassin, I have told you. I just published confidential information."

"Look, Nachito, I didn't come here to play games. Look under the table."

Carmona went pale when he saw the .38 pointing towards his stomach. It did not have bullets, but Evaristo maintained his bluff.

"The police are lumbering me with two stiffs and I wouldn't care about adding a third to my list. Are you going to help me or not?" Evaristo cocked the gun.

"What do you want to know?"

"That's better. Now we're talking." Evaristo lit a cigarette and took a drink from his glass, leaving the revolver under the table. "Explain to me why you published that story. Did you owe anything to the killer or did you have something against Lima?"

"Well, the truth is that Lima was a bastard to me. He hated me because I published a negative critique of his book of short stories."

"How long ago was that?"

"About fifteen years, at the beginning of the Eighties."

"And how did he get back at you?"

"To explain that I would have to explain the history of my life. It's a long story and I don't think you'll be interested."

"Anything to do with Lima matters to me." Evaristo flicked his ash on Carmona's hand. "I want the full story."

"All right, but put the gun away because you are making me nervous." Evaristo acceded to the request and Carmona calmed down. "I am from Tlaxcala and, at the end of the Seventies, I went to Germany on a scholarship from the government of my state. The grant was given to me by my Uncle Genaro, may he rest in peace, when he was the culture minister in the administration of Servio Tulio Hernández. I was supposed to go and study philosophy at Göttingen University, but I could never really learn the language. I read it more or less but I don't understand a fuck when people talk to me fast. In the lessons I ended up dizzy listening to the teachers, and I never dared ask any questions because I was afraid of looking ridiculous. Halfway through the first term I abandoned it. I spent all day drinking beer in taverns in the Turkish district among whores and hash dealers, not even touching my Kant and Schelling books, or I would sit in the parks lazing about, listening to rock on my Walkman..."

"But what does that have to do with Lima?" Evaristo asked impatiently.

"I'm getting there, just wait. You want the full story, don't you?"

"Yes, but quick." Evaristo snapped his fingers.

"When I was expelled from the university I did not tell my uncle anything and I kept cashing the grant for a year. It wasn't much money, but it was enough to buy a train ticket and travel the whole of Europe with my bag on my shoulder. I was in Florence, in Paris, in Vienna. I saw all the museums and all the cathedrals. I used to buy bread, a hundred grams of ham or

Fear of Animals

cheese and a bottle of wine, and with that I had enough for the day. I could even afford weed. In Amsterdam I got together with a bunch of hardcore Argentinians who I'd met at a youth hostel. I went with them to a Queen concert, and then to London with a Bolivian girl who clung on to me, really quite gorgeous, but then left me for a Nigerian..."

"I didn't come to hear about your luck with girls. Can you get to the point, please?"

"While I strutted about like a prince in Europe, I wrote to my uncle every month telling him that I was getting spectacular marks. I even invented a story that the head of my university had congratulated me. The second year I went to Spain and from there I went to Tangiers, where the hash was super cheap. Then I went to Copenhagen, where I lived in a commune. In Tlaxcala they thought I had a masters degree and I asked my uncle to extend the help so I could get a doctorate, but suddenly they sacked him from the government and I had to come back fucking quick to Mexico, because they cut my grant from one day to the next. Bastards. What if I had really been studying? When I came back, the first thing I was asked for at the ministry of culture of my state was my master's certificate. I got out the contract for the room I rented in Göttingen that had numbers that looked like grade marks and a very flash logo. 'There it is,' I said. 'Passed with honours'. I was lucky, at the ministry nobody knew a word of German so they offered me a job at the University of Tlaxcala co-ordinating the department of humanities, with a mega salary and latest-model car. That's what Lima could never forgive me for. He was fucked with his little proofreading jobs and he was furious because I earned ten times more, with a sabbatical and all the perks."

"But where did you two meet? Was Lima also from Tlaxcala?"

"No, he was from Mexico City. I met him in the capital before I travelled to Germany, when I took Silverio Lanza's literary workshop."

"Yes, I've heard of him. An Ecuadorian writer. Very witty, wasn't he?"

"Exactly. He taught us the A-B-C of literature, from where to put the full stops and the commas to how to write an inner monologue. Then we all believed we were fucking marvels and nobody had any qualms about destroying everyone else's texts. Lima was the cruellest of all because he was being published in supplements by then, and he thought he was the king of the castle.

With me he took pleasure in doing so, because he thought I was some provincial arsehole who only made everyone else waste their time. He could not read more than half the page without pointing out the errors."

"So that's why you took revenge when he published his book of short stories."

"It was such a silly thing to do, I recognise that, revenge from the guts and stupid. With my job at the university and my academic prestige, I did not have to lower myself by shouting out his defects, but I really wanted to make him suffer. The article appeared in *La Semana de Bellas Artes*, a very well-read supplement that the arts institute distributed in all the newspapers in Mexico, and Lima probably got diarrhoea after that, because I wrote with very bad blood. I said it was a dreadful imitation of Revueltas, full of garble, arrogant, and that he had the syntax of a secretary. It was a very hurtful article, even more so for a big-headed guy like him who was famous in the circle. His revenge took more than a year, but he was such a bastard."

"Did he shit on one of your books too?"

"I wish that had been enough for him." Carmona combed his moustache, his gaze sobered by a bitter memory. "I don't know how he got to know that I had deceived the people of Tlaxcala with my fake master's degree. The fact is that he published a letter in *Unomásuno* in which he denounced me as an imposter, put in question my knowledge of German and suggested that they should write to Berlin to verify my presumed academic grade. By then I had been promoted several tiers at the University of Tlaxcala, I was director of extension studies and was one of three candidates to replace the rector. I intended to discredit Lima in the local newspapers by branding him as resentful, but the rest of the candidates sent for a German translator to whom they gave my documents. I experienced the worst shame of my life when the minister of culture came in person with two policemen to evict me from my office, which was adorned with statues of Kant and Schelling that I smashed with a hammer the following day. There are wounds that never heal. After that blow, I have never been able to walk with my head high."

"I understand." Evaristo squashed the cigarette end in the ashtray. "With Lima's murder, you felt avenged."

"I'd be lying to you if I said his death hurt me. Thanks to that bastard I have seen very hard times. In order not to starve I had to sweat my socks off in the lower depths of journalism, first as a cultural reporter and now in a thousand trades, doing night shifts on the newsdesks or writing unsigned editorials. Nobody respects me in the circle. I earn a pittance because the section chiefs always keep the brown envelopes, and because sometimes I get pissed and don't deliver on time. I get the sack everywhere without even the right to compensation." Carmona paused to wipe away his tears. "Roberto Lima fucked my life. Don't you think I had reason to hate him?"

"The same reasons you have to hate yourself." Evaristo looked into his eyes with disgust. "I see that you enjoy the role of victim, but you aren't going to move me with your tears. Lima is dead and you are an accomplice to the killer. This is the story that you still have to tell me. How did you and Osiris Cantú de la Garza come to an agreement?"

"Osiris Cantú de la Garza?" Carmona frowned. "He's not my friend. I barely know him."

"We agreed that you were going to tell me the truth." Evaristo stood up and grabbed him by the neck, bringing the .38 to his temple. "When I asked you to identify his voice on the mobile, I didn't know that Osiris and you were accomplices. But I have proof that you knew each other from before. Your telephone number is in his phonebook."

"So what? He asked me to interview him a few months ago, when he was granted the Belisario Domínguez medal. That's why he had my number."

"Did you owe him a lot of money?" Stretching over the table, Evaristo tightened his grip on his neck. "Admit it: the Narcopoet had you by the balls."

"Osiris didn't kill Lima," Carmona whispered with a thread of voice.

"Then who killed him? Speak or you'll die."

"I'm going to tell you, but let go of me. You're suffocating me."

Evaristo reduced the pressure, and Carmona's purple face went back to its normal colour, yellow bordering on green. He took a sip of mineral water, exhaled and looked intensely at Evaristo, who awaited his answer anxiously, when a shower of bullets swept the drinks off the table. Evaristo threw himself to the floor, holding Carmona. There was a second heavier spray, that put the neon lights out, silenced the Rock-Ola and smashed a mirror on the wall. It seemed like it was a Kalashnikov. Without doubt

Maytorena had found him and, at any moment, would flash a torch in his face. But the minutes went by and nobody entered the cantina to give them the coup de grâce. When the domino players began to show signs of life, Evaristo stood up and gave Carmona a hand, but he was still crouched under the table. When Evaristo realised there was no reaction, he held a cigarette lighter near Carmona's face: his eyes were turned off, his face white and there was a discreet hole in his forehead from which trails of blood flowed. Infuriated, Evaristo smashed his fist on the table. He had been so close! Indifferent to the danger, he ran towards the window from where the bullets had come. It faced on to a dark and narrow street: not a soul, not a car, just a peeling wall and a dog pissing in the moonlight. It seemed that the aggressor or aggressors had fled in a car after emptying their magazine – a clumsy action that Maytorena would never have committed. No, the author of this crime could only be the killer whom Carmona was about to snitch on, that cigar smoker hiding at Lima's building, that escaping shadow who always got away after his attack before one could defend oneself. His attempts were the best barometer of how near or far from the truth he was. The killer had left Evaristo alone while he approached Palmira Jackson, because it was convenient to have Evaristo fail to shed light on Lima's death. But now, when Carmona had been ready to sing, the killer had got in the way once again, taking away the only witness who could have incriminated him.

Evaristo left La Vencedora before the police cars arrived and ran along the Izazaga sidewalk towards the Eje Central, blending in with the pedestrians going into and coming out of the Metro. In the window of a Viana store, to his horror, he discovered that his jacket was bloodstained. He took it off and threw it in some bushes, but when he did so he noticed that the stain reached down to his trousers. Even though people were going by without even looking at him, he felt scrutinised and threatened. He needed to change his clothes, but he could not go back to the Hotel Oslo because his hunter already knew where he was staying. He must have been following him from the hotel to the cantina and undoubtedly would try to kill him once he realised that he had only killed Carmona. Carried forward by the inertia of the crowd, Evaristo entered Salto del Agua station and took the Metro without noticing in which direction he was going. The main thing was to get far away from there. Later he could sleep in any cheap hotel and make plans calmly. Would they also lumber him with Carmona's death? The barman at La Vencedora would identify him immediately when he saw his photo. And, even though he could say that the gunshots had come from the street, the PGR would modify his statement to make Evaristo appear the author of the crime. The paradoxes of justice Mexican-style: he was turning into a multiple killer, but no one attributed to him the death of the only man he had really killed, maybe because in the eyes of the law Chamula was a second-grade victim.

When he neared Pino Suárez, Evaristo realised that he had made a tragic error: to sleep in a room he needed money and his credit cards had been in the jacket he had thrown away in Salto del Agua. He would have to go back for it, risking arrest, or sleep on a park bench like any old street drunk. He did not fancy the alternative. Looking for a banknote he might have forgotten in his pockets, he searched in his trousers and shirt. He did not find money, but a piece of paper with Rubén Estrella's address (Manuel María Contreras 49, interior 6, Colonia San Rafael) that reminded him of his generous offer of asylum. This was the moment to take Rubén at his word, even if only for one night. He stopped at La Merced to change platforms and took the Metro that went in the opposite direction. Pushing his way forward through the crowd at the Pino Suárez catacombs, he changed trains to Línea 2, direction Cuatro Caminos. Luckily everyone was so wrapped up in their thoughts that nobody noticed the blood spots tinting his fly. If they ask me why, I can say that it's because it's my period, he thought, amazed that he could still see the funny side of things. And, if looked at objectively, why shouldn't he laugh about his bad luck, if that helped him to endure it? The more besieged he felt, the greater the clarity with which he began to see that his situation was bordering on farce. It was impossible to take some louse like Carmona seriously, even after his death. And what could one say about the Narcopoet or the ineffable Palmira Jackson? Faced with the most grotesque examples of intellectual fauna, as the main character in a nightmare governed by the logic of the absurd, Evaristo's field of action was reduced dramatically, leaving him no choice but to let out an agonised cackle.

When he left the Metro next to the old Mascarones building, he walked towards Circuito Interior through Ribera de San Cosme, among the racket of the street vendors who had begun to clear up their stalls. At Manuel María Contreras he turned left, refreshed by a current of air that gave him goosebumps. He was wearing a short-sleeved shirt and, in contrast to the heat in the Metro, the cool air gave him a feeling of freedom. But all freedom has a price and he paid for his with a sneeze. Just what he needed: pneumonia to close the day with a golden padlock. He pulled up his collar and hurried his step, trying to get to Rubén Estrella's house before the virus reached his throat. The cul-de-sac where Rubén lived was a shapeless mess with no colour, grey façades with a rustic finish and brick-coloured metal doors. When he crossed the hallway, Evaristo stepped on a loose floor tile and almost fell. A great water tank occupied the centre of the patio. He felt sorry for his friend when he saw the peeling walls and the wires sticking out: why do the noblest of people always have to be the most fucked up? There were four flats on the ground floor and another four on the first floor, where he could hear Nina Hagen's rock-and-roll version of 'My Way', together with voices. It looked as if Rubén was having a party: a bad moment to seek asylum. He went up the metal stairs and knocked determinedly at the door to make himself heard over the racket. A sleepy hook-nosed girl with bags under her eyes, but a very tasty body, opened the door.

"Can I find Rubén here?"

The girl invited him in without answering, thinking that he was another guest. The smell of ganja hit him as he came through the door. In the little sitting room, decorated with masks and film posters, Rubén was conversing with Pablo Segura and Daniel Nieto, who were accompanied by their wives, sitting in the lotus position on the carpet. He was angry to find them there, because he had distrusted them since his chat at the Trocadero bar. Rubén looked at him amazed, blinking as if he was trying to erase an optical illusion.

"What's up broder? Why the miracle?"

"I need to talk to you," Evaristo whispered in his ear. "I had a problem and need you to do me a favour."

Rubén took him to the only bedroom in the flat, which was narrow, lined with books, badly ventilated and stank of sex.

"What's the problem?" he asked, closing the door.

Evaristo told him briefly about his interview with Ignacio Carmona and the way it had ended when the reporter was about to tell him who Lima's killer was.

"I ended up with my clothes all bloodstained. Look at my trousers. So, when I left, I threw my jacket in the street, without realising that my wallet was inside it. I need to hide, but I have no money for the hotel. I wanted to ask you to let me spend the night here."

"What bad luck, broder, I'd have you here with pleasure, but my house is full today. My partner is going to stay with me for the whole weekend and the day before yesterday a cousin from Torreón landed and is now sleeping on the couch."

Evaristo understood that Rubén was having second thoughts. Of course, it was one thing to offer help without meaning it and another to take the risk of having him in his house when the whole of the Federal Judicial Police was on the lookout for him.

"Then lend me some dough," Evaristo begged. "If I have fifty pesos, I'll be okay."

Rubén shook his head, worried.

"Don't think I'm being mean, but I'm broke. This afternoon I went to Chopo to buy a bundle of grass. I was left with twenty pesos and that's all I've got 'til Monday."

"Well, I'll have to see what I can do. Thanks anyway, mate."

Evaristo shook his hand and made to leave, with a funereal grin. But then Rubén snapped his fingers and stopped him at the door.

"Wait. I know where you can hide! Do you know the Institute of Arts and Literature's warehouse?" Evaristo shook his head. "It's in Atzcapotzalco, fifteen minutes away from here. I have the key, because sometimes I go there to get old issues of the magazine. It's an enormous shed with mountains of books. You can spend the night there and, if you want, you can stay there until Sunday, because at the weekend it stays empty. What do you think?"

Rubén completed the favour by taking him to the warehouse in his battered Volkswagen, telling his friends he would be back in an hour. On the way, Evaristo asked him if Daniel Nieto and Pablo Segura were trustworthy people.

"Don't worry about them. We have talked about you a lot and we think the government wants to use you as a fall guy. Do they think we are a bunch of idiots or what? They haven't even said what your motive was."

When they had passed the Monumento a la Raza they entered an industrial zone that Evaristo thought as alien as a suburb of Calcutta or Moscow. He had never been to Atzcapotzalco, not even when he was a crime reporter, and felt a foreigner in his own city. After a long trip around lower-middle-class suburbs and immense roads that he had never even heard of before, they arrived in a cul-de-sac protected by a fence.

"Crouch down," ordered Rubén.

The guard at the entrance shone a torch at the car and Rubén showed him his institute ID.

"I need to get some magazines that I forgot to pick up on Friday."

"Go on, young man," yawned the guard, lifting the barrier.

"Leave it open, I won't be very long," asked Rubén.

The warehouse door could be seen from the guard's booth. To avoid being seen, Evaristo had to wait in the car while Rubén lifted the metal shutter. When Rubén made a signal, Evaristo got out of the Volkswagen and walked barefoot across the pebbled floor to the interior of the great warehouse. Rubén closed the curtain and turned on the light. Boxes of books formed very high towers that reached to the beams in the ceiling. When they went in among the rows of boxes covered with thick cobwebs, they tripped and some broken books spilled on the ground. It smelt of mildewed paper and rat droppings, but the worst thing about the place was the dust, an old and undisturbed dust that made the eyes itch.

"Welcome to the graveyard of national culture," joked Rubén. "Can you see the millions of books piled up here? Well, nobody is ever going to read them because the same government that makes a big song and dance about promoting culture also needs to keep the people ignorant to stay in power." Rubén took a book at random and blew the dust from its cover. "*Selected Works* of wee Mr Adolfo Reyes. Wow, what a relic. This book has been in the warehouse for forty years and there are others even older that were published at the time of Miguel Alemán. This is where all our classics end up."

"Where do you think I could sleep?"

"On the book boxes. Choose your favourite author and lie down on top of him."

"Thanks, Rubén." Evaristo embraced him, moved. "I'll never forget what you've done for me."

"It's nothing, man. That's what friends are for." Rubén withdrew. "I have to go because I don't want Daniel and Pablo smoking all the grass. I'm going to switch the light off, but I'll leave the door open so you can leave tomorrow. I recommend that you leave at half-six, when they change guards."

By himself, in the darkness, Evaristo felt his childhood terrors

Fear of Animals

being reborn, like when he wet the bed because he was scared of God. The stench intensified or his nose perceived it more acutely, and the screeching of rats made his skin prickle. There were hundreds, thousands, and they crawled wherever they pleased among the mountains of books, undoubtedly choosing the most nutritious for dinner. He had to sleep on top of the boxes otherwise the rats would eat him alive. Evaristo climbed a tower of books with difficulty, raising a cloud of dust that made him sneeze. When he reached the top, after having climbed more than six metres, he lay face up on top of the boxes. Curious, he opened one of them, took out a book contained within and, to the light of a match, read the title: *The Georgics by Virgil*, Latin Classics collection. He tried to read the first verses when a huge tarantula came out of the bottom of the box, with a page between its legs. He let out a howl of horror and another of pain, because on top of the fright he had burned himself. A short distance away there was another mountain of books, not quite as high, but, if he failed the jump, he would smash the fuck out of himself. When he felt the tarantula, slimy and hairy, on his left ankle, he forgot about his fears and jumped the abyss. The mountain shook for a few moments, but Evaristo recovered his balance, clutching on to the cardboard boxes like a professional rock climber.

Fearful of finding more creatures, he lit a cigarette to scare them away, just as hunters light a bonfire when they camp in the middle of the jungle. The boxes were damp, which he attributed to leaks in the ceiling, but even so he lay down, feeling shivers along his spine. He had to control his nerves and accept the idea of spending the entire night in that foul cave, otherwise he would suffer twice as much. He needed to think about something pleasant and imagined that he was in Rubén's house, warm and happy, talking about literature while holding a whisky. That was the life he would have wanted to live: of a penniless bohemian dedicated to his vocation. And that was the life he would lead from now on, if he managed to prove his innocence. Despite what had happened at La Vencedora, his morale was high, because he now had a group of allies – Rubén and his gang – who could testify in his favour as friends of the victim, when the trial took place. Carmona was dead, but he had provided a definite clue to get to Lima's killer. After Evaristo handed over the culprit, with the support of those who trusted him, he would come out of the judicial proceedings clean and even maybe manage to get Maytorena jailed. Trusting his lucky stars, little by little Evaristo began to recover his peace of mind until he fell asleep.

He dreamt about Dora Elsa: she was in heaven and had turned into an angel, but was wearing the same thong she had used in her Sherry's act. Kneeling on a pink candyfloss cloud, she begged God to let her come down to earth. "My man is alone, he needs me, don't be mean, let me spend the night with him." God was not the bearded and venerable elder of the religious prints, but a fat guy with oily hair who managed a brothel. "All right, mummy, but you have to pay if you want me to let you out." After she had given him two hundred pesos, Dora Elsa went to her wardrobe to get her satin gown and went flying out through a gate in heaven adorned with a purple neon sign, like a table-dancing dive. During her trip to earth she crossed the black clouds of Mexico City and came out with her wings covered in soot. She had also not been to Atzcapotzalco and flew from one side of the city to the other until a human dove, the Holy Spirit acting as a boy scout, guided her to the national cultural graveyard. On his mountain of books, Evaristo awaited her with a hard on and cried with joy when he saw her filtering through a wall. "It's me, my darling. I felt you calling me and I came to spend this night with you." Standing on top of Dora Elsa's shoulder, the Holy Spirit shook its wings impatiently. Evaristo gave it five pesos for a drink and the white-feathered dove went flying off with the coin in its beak. Slowly, with an otherworldly horniness, Dora Elsa took off her wings, her bra, her thong and her silver heels. She looked fitter than ever, but when he tried to hold her, Evaristo discovered that her body was a mirage: "Lord, have mercy on me, I want her to be flesh and blood," he shouted, and the Eternal Father answered in a baritone voice: "All right, sonny, I will resuscitate her, but you'll have to give me five hundred pesos, plus extra if you want to get her tits." Through the Holy Spirit, now in its role as cashier, Evaristo sent the money to God, who, after greedily counting the notes, gave Dora Elsa back her carnal self. But when Evaristo held her in his arms again, he discovered that his beloved's chest was bloodstained and the bullet wounds were fresh, as if on the night of the shooting when they were escaping in the VW taxi. Suddenly he was not in the warehouse anymore, but at Sherry's. With her last breath Dora Elsa smoked a cherry-flavoured Middleton with her vagina in front of a helpless Evaristo, who was looking at her bleeding slowly while the public ridiculed her by whistling and shouting obscenities.

Fear of Animals

He was awoken by a metallic sound, similar to that of a cart being dragged over asphalt: someone wanted to enter the warehouse and had lifted the metal curtain. He heard footsteps growing closer, the clinking of some keys, and someone clearing his throat. Stupor cut short his inspiration. Maytorena had found out his hiding place and was looking for him among the book towers, carrying a Kalashnikov.

"Give yourself up, Intellectual, or you'll die like these fucking rats!"

Maytorena shot a shower of machine-gun fire at the floor, provoking a stampede of rodents. He was wearing a blue tracksuit with yellow trim, his voice was mellow and he swayed as he walked. Maybe he had interrupted a party halfway through for this lead. He thought immediately of Pablo Segura and Daniel Nieto. It seemed that they were not as trustworthy as Rubén may have thought.

Undoubtedly they had betrayed him, as they had with Perla Tinoco, calling the Feds as soon as they had come out. Or the shadow had followed him to the warehouse to complete the job from La Vencedora, delivering him up to Maytorena.

"I ordered you to come out, did you hear me?" Maytorena fired again, making holes in a row of boxes. "I know why you came to hide in here, among so many books. Even though you are wanted by the law you can't stop your craving for reading books. If I were in your place, I'd be reading the Bible to offer my soul to the Lord."

Up in his watchtower, Evaristo felt relatively safe, as he could see Maytorena without being seen. The .38 was heavy on his waist, as useless and decorative as the flaccid penis of an impotent man. He spat with anger: a loaded gun would have helped him get out of there.

"It smells of intellectual's shit." Maytorena continued shooting here and there, lost in the labyrinth of boxes. "Aren't you shitting with fear?"

The commander was clearly taking Evaristo's capture as something personal, otherwise he would have asked for reinforcements. In his mighty post as chief of chiefs he could mobilise the whole of the Federal Judicial Police with the snap of his fingers, but it seemed that he wanted to punish with his own hands the only man on earth to have branded him as gay. Evaristo had a cold sweat thinking about the torture that awaited him if he were arrested. Would Maytorena be happy just with raping him or would he shove a pole smeared with toothpaste up his arse? The cold sweat made him want to sneeze. Damn cold: it had to happen now, just now, when the slightest noise would result in a death sentence. He managed to get out of danger by pinching his nose, but his resistance provoked a second sneeze.

"Poor you, you have a cold. That's what happens when you sleep in such cold places." Maytorena came closer to Evaristo's mountain of books, looking up. "Get down from there, or I'll bring you down like a pigeon." He shot a burst towards the top that smashed against the beams of the ceiling. To distract him, Evaristo flung a book as far as he could but, when Maytorena was walking in the direction of the noise a few metres away, another sneeze pulled him back.

"I can see where you are. Get down or I'll come for you!"

This time Maytorena was right and he started to climb the mountain, with the Kalashnikov on his shoulder. From above, Evaristo could see him climbing up, with growing anxiety. A shudder of cowardice went down his spine: he still had time to wave a white flag. Maybe he should respect the law of the strongest and give himself up with hands held high. Standing on a pile that was sticking out, Maytorena placed his foot on a box containing Heidegger's *Being and Time*. In a moment of inspiration, Evaristo pulled away Maytorena's point of support, causing a spectacular collapse of the boxes. He heard a yell, the dry crash of his body against the floor and the impact of the boxes crushing him. When Maytorena stopped moaning, Evaristo dared to look down. Buried by an avalanche of philosophy, with his nose smashed to a pulp and his neck twisted, the commander exhaled his last breath with a perplexed expression.

Evaristo climbed down fast as he feared that the guard would come at any minute or would seek reinforcements, alarmed by the burst of machine-gun fire. The warehouse was not a safe place to sleep anymore and he preferred to wait for dawn before walking the streets. When he walked beside the commander's body, he saw with disgust a grey rat the size of a beaver nibbling the crushed man's ear. When he went closer to take away the Kalashnikov, he almost died with fright as Maytorena returned to life and put his weapon against Evaristo's chest. They wrestled on the floor for a moment, fighting over the machine gun, which gave out a shot that just missed Evaristo. Maytorena was in agony, but found the strength to strangle Evaristo with his wrestler's arms. Evaristo

Fear of Animals

managed to knee him in the genitals but, instead of losing grip, Maytorena grabbed him by the hair and smashed his head against the floor three times, leaving him concussed. Maytorena had him at his mercy, but had lost so much blood that he could barely lift the machine gun and fell to the ground.

When Evaristo woke up, he saw, with sick pleasure, the rats gorging on Maytorena's corpse. He rested for a moment, leaning on the boxes to recover. His skull throbbed at the tiniest movement, like the cymbals in a drum kit. He breathed in and exhaled slowly, little by little coming back to life. What a night: two assassination attempts in less than four hours. All he needed was to be bitten by a dog or crapped on by a bird. He lit a cigarette but put it out after two puffs, remembering the guard. He had to get out of there as soon as possible. He picked up the Kalashnikov and turned off the light. Still reeling from the blows to his head, he lifted the metal shutter through which he had entered with Rubén. When he came out of the warehouse, he was frozen by a loudspeaker.

"Stop! One more step and you're dead. Throw the weapon down and put your hands against the wall!"

Ten or fifteen police cars and a truck of riot police parked in a semi-circle were aiming their lights at him. Ready behind doors and anti-riot shields, a hundred policemen, uniformed and Feds, pointed at him with high-calibre rifles. The one using the loud speaker was Fat Zepeda, whom Evaristo recognised from his unmistakable pig-like outline. Two agents from the elite Zorro group, bank robbery specialists, frog-marched him into a Suburban with wire mesh on the windows. To a certain extent he was happy the nightmare was ending, because he wouldn't have to be running from here to there and hiding away like a leper. He was at peace with his conscience and in jail he would recover the tranquillity of spirit that he had lost in the last few days, which had been a mess of tensions and anxieties. He had been a loser from birth. What other destiny could await him? On his way to the holding cells, flanked by two gorillas who beat his genitals, liver and kidneys, Evaristo understood that the nightmare was just beginning.

Fear of Animals

After a brief and arbitrary trial in which he was found guilty of multiple homicides, criminal association and carrying illegal weapons, Evaristo was handed a 50-year jail sentence, subject to reduction for good behaviour. He had no trouble being a model prisoner, since in Almoloya de Juárez jail it was impossible to misbehave. Designed to house highly dangerous criminals – killers, corrupt public officials, drug barons – the jail had been built in the shape of different islands so the prisoners could not communicate with each other. Even in the workshops there were CCTV cameras and in the recreation area the guards did not allow more than three prisoners to talk together. There were no plants or green areas, not even bright colours: just impenetrable walls, remote-controlled iron doors and cold, damp-smelling corridors. In the first months of his confinement, his books were his talisman against madness. The jail library was not well stocked, but he voraciously devoured the *History of the Second World War* edited by the Readers Digest and *The Manual of Car Mechanics*. He read with the devotion of a monk from 7am to 10pm, when the bell announced lights out. Even asleep, he continued his reading, projecting on a black screen a text without beginning or end that flowed from his subconscious, as if dictating the script of a dream that he could not quite set into images.

Among his multiple and abundant readings he stumbled across Dostoevsky's jail memoirs. Almoloya and Siberia were two of hell's antipodes where inmates were tortured in diametrically opposite ways. For Dostoevsky, the worst thing about life in prison was the lack of privacy, the torture of having to share a room with twenty other inmates, without having a minute to oneself. Evaristo, instead, would have wished to have been locked up in a dungeon jam-packed with criminals because his loneliness was heavier to bear than his confinement. Reading was his lifeline, but, after seven hours diving into books, he needed to escape from himself,

211

even when it could mean talking a lot of crap with a warden. And in Almoloya the wardens did not talk unless it was necessary. Their conversation consisted of a series of grunts that ceased abruptly when the inmate adopted a friendly tone. Condemned to a monologue, Evaristo began to develop an autistic mentality that isolated him even more from reality and, when he was taken to appear before the Public Prosecutor's Office, the warden had to repeat the same question two or three times because he only heard the voice inside himself.

Because he lacked the means to pay the cost of an expert in criminal law, Evaristo had been assigned a trainee defence counsel who visited him once a week, made him sign incomprehensible papers and tried to fill him with enthusiasm about the seductive promise of cutting a bit off his sentence, so he could start a new life when he was 80. A few weeks after he had been sentenced, he received a visit from Gladys, his ex-wife. She had aged and was now plump, her face bloated, with a riverine net of varicose veins on her legs and her hair tangled like a piece of burlap. She had not come to pity him, she warned him, and even less for a conjugal visit, but to demand the maintenance payments that had been cut since he had gone to jail. In vain, Evaristo tried to explain to her that he had neither property nor money in the bank. She thought he had become rich during his years as a Fed and must have a little stash. Or what? Was he thinking of leaving Chabela in the streets? The poor kid had suffered enough from the trauma of having a father who was a murderer. At her stinky school, many of her friends had stopped talking to her. The school fees were more expensive every day and her mother did not want to put her into a state high school because the child was now used to the good life. Anyway, if he did not want to help them, he could keep his damned money. Sooner or later he would call her to ask forgiveness, regretting all the damage he had done to her, and then she would leave him to die alone like a dog... To end the litany of insults and moans, Evaristo called the guard before the visit was finished and went back to his cell with shattered nerves.

From then onwards he withdrew even more. If Gladys was the best thing on offer from reality, it was no use going back to it. In answer to his need to escape, his literary vocation was reborn. There was only one step from the unconscious monologue to writing: it would be enough to put everything he had told and retold himself on to paper without caring too much about the style or syntax. As he wrote without the intention of publishing, he easily conquered the fear of failure that had paralysed him when he had intended to open the Federal Judicial Police sewer from the inside. Now he did not aspire to becoming a great figure of critical journalism, but to revealing his truth plainly and simply, the truth that the judges had not wanted to hear. After he had filled the first notebook with small, tightly packed letters, an autobiographical tale began to take shape, half confessional novel and half thriller, in which Evaristo bared his soul and admitted his complicity with Maytorena in certain crimes and abuses without shame, but defended with detailed arguments any implication in Lima's death and the rest of the crimes attributed to him: *Corrupted by easy money, I participated in the grave crime of covering up a killer who had infiltrated the judicial apparatus, but when I tried to mend my ways, I was turned into the victim of a vendetta characteristic of our police force, which does not tolerate desertion for reasons of conscience and, when it comes to difficult cases, when exposed to the scrutiny of public opinion, uses its own agents as bait.* Even when he tried to maintain his objectivity, he could not avoid involving himself emotionally in the story. Without neglecting his anecdotal material, he compiled whole pages describing the transformations in his temperament since the day Maytorena had shown him the newspaper clipping in which Lima had insulted Jiménez del Solar. The leap from introspection to writing produced a healthy catharsis. For the first time in his life he was managing to express himself, something he had wished for since his days as a reporter, when he had struggled to put his personal imprint on his articles. He even became a poet in the chapters in which he spoke about Dora Elsa. He wanted to erect a monument to her memory and could not resist the temptation of idealising her, using delicate and euphemistic language to conceal her trade.

When he was about to complete two years in Almoloya, a twist of fortune allowed him to appeal before a qualifying judge to review his case. Juan Nepomuceno Herrera, the drug trafficker arrested in San Diego by agents of the Drug Enforcement Agency, had denounced Jesús Maytorena as the Tijuana cartel's main police plant and some of his crimes were exposed. *Proceso* published a long report about it in which Maytorena was accused of complicity with the now deceased former attorney Cisneros Topete, because he had been promoted to head the Comprehensive Citizen Protection

Programme. The new administration was at war with supporters of Jiménez del Solar, who had left the country bankrupt, and the new Attorney General, from the National Action Party, had ordered an investigation into the links between Maytorena and Cisneros Topete. The newspapers mentioned Evaristo once more, making new conjectures about Maytorena's death. He was not now treated as a killer who had betrayed his boss, but as a possible victim of the commander. The columnist Granados Chapa defended him in *Reforma* with a hint of irony: *Despite any motive that Evaristo Reyes, currently serving a prison sentence in Almoloya de Juárez, may have had, society is indebted to him for having ridden us of his boss, Commander Jesús Maytorena, whose long list of crimes has begun to surface.* Evaristo's lawyer took advantage of the outrage to appeal to the Supreme Court, handing over new evidence, and managed to have him exonerated of the deaths of Vilchis and Carmona, which had been attributed to him with feeble evidence. Public opinion attributed the two crimes to Maytorena and, even though Evaristo knew the commander was innocent of the second, he kept back the truth to expose in his book. Half vindicated, he was still guilty of Lima's homicide in the eyes of the law, because the testimony of Mario Casillas, the *El Matutino* reporter who had given him Roberto Lima's address, was still bearing down on him. Nonetheless, his lawyer managed to get his sentence reduced to 22 years and have him transferred to the Reclusorio Oriente, a less inhospitable jail where he was able to re-establish contact with the human species.

In his new, jam-packed home Evaristo shared a cell with two other convicts who treated him with respect and even fear, impressed by his reputation as a multiple killer, whose victims included a hated commander of the Feds. He took some time to understand the inmates' moral compass and their peculiar sense of justice. They impaled rapists, beat to a pulp parricides and child kidnappers, but admired those fucking aces like him who had the merit of thrashing the police. Thanks to his good reputation, he obtained the position of librarian, which allowed him to dedicate himself to writing in his spare time. There was a lot of this, because almost nobody asked for books. He went ahead with his novel, increasingly conscious of his style and with a greater preoccupation with the language, which he now handled easily, writing several sheets in one sitting. The library was stocked with the complete works of the greatest masters of the 19th century

Fear of Animals

(Stendhal, Flaubert, Balzac, Maupassant, Dostoevsky, Dickens, Pérez Galdós), which he now read with the eyes of a writer, paying attention to the construction of the plot and the introduction of characters. Studying the classics allowed him to enrich the meaning of his own story. In particular, a novel by Balzac, *Lost Illusions*, that looked like his in terms of its subject, caught his attention. The main character, the young poet Lucien de Rubempré, travels to Paris with the dream of forging a literary career without betraying his ideals, but when he becomes involved in the petty literary world of the time, a dunghill in which no critic says what he thinks and gangster-like shady deals decide the success or failure of a book, he ends up turned into a Pharisee, selling out his dignity to writers' cliques that hold the literary power. When Evaristo had finished reading it, he identified with Lucien de Rubempré. Without thinking about it, because of the ups and downs of an eventful police inquiry, his destiny had been to come to know the petty literary world of his own country from the inside, a world even more pestilent than that of the Paris of Balzac's times, and, while he had gone from suspect to suspect following misleading clues, he had suffered a long chain of deceptions until he had lost his faith in writers. In particular, he detested those champions of civil society in a permanent struggle for cameras and microphones. Dealing with them had made him look at his life from another perspective. What was he looking for when he had entered the Feds with the idea of reporting his experiences? To denounce corruption or to enrol in that circle of humanitarian vultures headed by Palmira Jackson? Before, he had ached at not having fulfilled his dreams. Now, he was horrified at having dreamt of something so vile. Victim of an impure ambition, like the main character in *Lost Illusions*, he called his novel *Decapitated Dreams,* adding as an epigraph a quotation from Balzac: *"Don't imagine that the political world is much cleaner than the literary world: in both bribery is the rule; every man bribes or is bribed..."* To achieve better correspondence between content and form, he framed the narrative within two dreams: that of his literary consecration and the no less frightening dream of the warehouse, both interrupted by Maytorena, the evil spirit acting as an agent of disillusion.

When Evaristo wrote the book's final chapter, the idea of publishing it began to tempt him but, alongside this, a doubt emerged: what right had he to ridicule such writers in his novel if he was identical to them? The more he invented noble justifications to publish, deep down he knew that he was seeking fame, recognition and prestige. Demoralised, he felt stranded in a depressive lake that exiled him from his notebooks for several days. After a rigorous examination of his conscience, he admitted that vanity was one of his reasons, but not the main or only one. In reality, he was still acting like a detective, only before, he was investigating the truth about a crime and now he was after another truth, the truth hidden in the hearts of men. That was the most important search within his novel, over and above the police investigation. He had already embarked on this with absolute sincerity, treating himself with the same harshness as the other characters.

Free from guilt and sanctimonious scruples, Evaristo wrote the ending, which consisted of a series of conjectures about an unresolved killing, as in the novels of Leonardo Sciascia. He did not want to make up facts to invent a culprit, because, despite having changed the names of the real-life characters to avoid legal problems, he had the certainty that his novel would be read like a testimony, if anyone ever published it. The roll call of presumed culprits included, of course, Claudio Vilchis and Fabiola Nava, whose probable complicity Evaristo never ruled out, but also Daniel Nieto and Pablo Segura, who may have bickered with him, and Perla Tinoco, who could have disputed Fabiola's love for Vilchis. But Evaristo had not been able to investigate the complex history of the victim deeply and allowed himself to think that the assassin could have been any other literary enemy of Lima – exquisite or lumpen, consecrated or unknown – with whom the victim may have had difficulties in his last years. He even contemplated the not impossible hypothesis that Maytorena himself could have executed Lima behind Evaristo's back to encourage the fall of Attorney Tapia and end up better off at the Federal Judicial Police. Maybe Carmona was his accomplice – there was still the mystery of the anonymous source – as he was sure that even Lima's best chums didn't read his articles in *El Matutino*. To complete the deception, Maytorena would have ordered him to investigate the crime, knowing Evaristo would not discover anything. *Too many suppositions* – he admitted in his epilogue – *but I wonder who can have certainty in a country like ours, where the perfect crime has turned into a tradition.*

After typing more than three hundred pages on an old Olivetti

Fear of Animals

with a stiff roller, he tapped in the final full stop of the book and, for a while, felt empty, like a mother who has just given birth. With the sentence Evaristo had stretching out before him, he had enough time to write twenty more novels, but when was he going to live? Searching for an escape other than writing, he befriended The Doll, an old prisoner from Coatzacoalcos who controlled the trade of alcohol and drugs in the jail. Interested in reading, The Doll frequented the library and discussed with Evaristo the books he liked best. In his magnificent cell, equipped with a satellite dish, velvet sofas and a Jacuzzi, the best parties in the prison took place in the face of the wardens' complacency. The Doll gave Evaristo rum and joints on credit and, from time to time, allowed him to get laid with one of the whores he had brought in from the street. Too desperate to make love to them serenely, Evaristo ejaculated when he began foreplay and then went into a depression for whole weeks, tortured by the memories of Dora Elsa. In his trips on dope and alcohol he did not know how to tell if jail was reality or if reality was a jail. Far from the walls and turrets perhaps a wider prison began, from which he would only escape when his insides exploded.

A fortunate discovery gave him back his will to live when he was beginning to turn anaemic from his lack of appetite. Flicking through an old issue of *Unomásuno,* he found a notice regarding the Eureka novel prize, organised by the publisher Quinto Sol. This was the opportunity he had been waiting for to make himself heard outside the prison. He feared they might put his original aside, without even browsing it, but the dream of winning was stronger than his lack of trust, so he sent the novel under a *nom de plume* to the suggested address with childish excitement. Hope kept him intensely active for more than six months. He stopped visiting The Doll and relapsed into his literary task, now with the idea of writing fiction to put the realism to rest. When the day arrived for the jury's verdict, Evaristo checked the main newspapers for several weeks. Nothing: not even a word about the Eureka prize. He supposed that the decision had been delayed and called the publishing house to ask for information, but the telephone numbers on the notice belonged to another business, a meat-packing factory, where they hung up rudely. For some months, he avidly read the cultural sections of all the dailies that fell into his hands. He did not find anything about the prize, but updated himself about news within the literary circle. By working her arse off, Fabiola Nava had at last managed to publish *Below the Belt* in Conafoc's Final Period collection. At the cocktail party launch, Doctor Perla Tinoco, recently awarded the Academic Palm by the French government, had praised "the narrative courage and purified language" of the promising young woman. By presidential appointment, Osiris Cantú de la Garza was appointed the new director of the Fund for the Promotion of Reading. Pablo Segura had achieved a grant for life from the National Talent Scheme and even Fat Zepeda had slipped through the service door into the Parnaso, when he won first prize at the Floral Games in Tláhuac. The excess of information demoralised Evaristo, as it hurt him to prove to himself that the swines went forward triumphant while he rotted in jail. As a matter of mental health and to avoid attacks of nausea, he stopped reading the cultural section of any daily, convinced that the Eureka prize was a hoax.

Filled with indignation at the world, he adopted an air of moral superiority in his dealings with The Doll, whom he had now branded as corrupt. Halfway through the domino game he reproached him for his shady businesses in the prison. Don't you feel ashamed making yourself rich by exploiting the others? How many prisoners have died from drinking your bloody adulterated rum? One afternoon, tired of his scolding, The Doll smashed a family sized Coca-Cola bottle on his head and kicked him until he was unconscious. Evaristo spent a month in the sick room, planning his revenge, which consisted of sticking a fork in his intestines. When he was given the all-clear, the prison doctor told him that he had a visitor. It must be Gladys again, he thought, and, annoyed, went to the recreation patio, a walled rectangle where the inmates spent Sundays with their families. Rubén Estrella was swaying on a swing. He was wearing a black leather jacket and a tie-dye T-shirt with an image of the Virgin of Guadalupe. When he got closer to hug him, Evaristo noticed that Rubén's breath smelt of alcohol.

"What a miracle. I thought you'd forgotten about me or were afraid to see me." Estrella let Evaristo embrace him halfheartedly. "My lawyer said you had been accused of concealing evidence."

"The night guard at the warehouse gave a statement against me, but they could never prove that I hid you there," explained Rubén.

"I'm happy for you. I wouldn't have liked to drag you into this."

Fear of Animals

"I found out that your sentence was reduced." Estrella lit a cigarette while his hand trembled. "Congratulations. You only have twenty years left."

"Did you come to make fun of me?" Evaristo was offended.

"I came to talk about literature." A child playing with a ball crossed between them. "Is there a place where we can talk in peace?"

Evaristo pointed him to the concrete tables at the end of the garden, where a couple of families were having a picnic. They walked silently towards the nearest one, watched attentively by the turret guard. Rubén had a baguette in a bag and a newspaper rolled up under his right arm. By the way he gesticulated, he looked as if he was on the verge of a nervous breakdown. They sat down opposite each other.

"Why didn't you tell me that you wrote too?"

"I started to write here in jail. With all the spare time I have, I had to find a pastime. But you, how did you get to know that?"

"I know a lot more than you can imagine." Rubén raised his voice. "I know you wrote a little thriller and now think you're fucking ace, as if all the inmates were a bunch of idiots next to you."

"What's your problem, imbecile?" Evaristo moved away from the table. "How dare you come here to have a go at me?"

"If you want, I'll leave, but you're going to regret having told me to. I have some information that could be of use in your novel."

Evaristo did not answer, hesitating between beating him up or calling a guard. Slowly, Rubén took a cigar from his jacket, lit it with the burning end of his cigarette and gave it a long puff.

"Was it you?" Evaristo went pale with anger.

"First correct guess you have made in your life." Rubén clapped mockingly. "I don't understand how you can write a thriller if you are such a stupid detective."

"I dedicated myself to studying Lima's enemies. I thought you were his friend."

"I thought so too. One goes through life thinking one has friends, but suddenly one sees their fangs dripping with blood. Roberto was my bro, almost my flesh and blood, but he was conning me."

"Did you kill him because of Fabiola Nava? Did you also have the hots for her?"

"You're wrong again in your deductions. We never had trouble over any woman, and even less over a slut like her." Rubén paused, took a flask with tequila out of his jacket and gave it a long swig. "The problem was that Roberto couldn't stand the success of others. It hurt him to be any old writer and, even when he made an effort to conceal it, I discovered that he envied me with all his soul."

"Envy you?" Evaristo smiled. "Don't you think you are being too self-important?"

"Roberto was incapable of admiring any of his friends. In that, he was really mean. He didn't attack me because we were friends, but I could never squeeze praise out of him. He became annoyed about what I published, my prizes, my interviews. He simply ignored me in his articles, as if I didn't exist."

"And haven't you thought that maybe he just didn't like your books?" scolded Evaristo. "If he had commented on them, he would have fucking trashed them and that would have hurt you even more. Lima was a bastard, but very honest."

"Do you think it's honest talking badly of a friend of yours behind his back?" cried Rubén, his eyes bloodshot with anger. "You didn't know Roberto. That is why you have idealised him. He was a bastard who used people and then kicked them in the arse. I was his best friend, the only one who stayed partying with him until midday, drinking beer at Santa Cecilia market, and how did he repay me? Excluding me from the last writers' encounter in Villahermosa. I got to know this from a very trusted source: at the University Cultural Trust he was called to a meeting to choose who should be invited, and do you know what he said when they asked him his opinion of me? 'I love him very much, but cross him off: he's a dreadful writer'."

"So now we know." Evaristo looked him in the eye. "Lima didn't want to fall into cronyism and you were so pissed off that you went to his house to kill him..."

"First I went to La Vencedora, to have a few drinks with the now deceased Ignacio Carmona, an old friend who I had met at Silverio Lanza's workshop."

"Another wrong guess. I believed him to be an accomplice of Osiris Cantú de la Garza."

"It was your most fortunate error. A little more and you would have discovered me by fluke."

"And how much did you pay Carmona for the story in *El Universal*?"

"Didn't have to. He hated Roberto even more than me. When

Fear of Animals

I told him about his betrayal, he suggested we go smash his face. 'That bastard doesn't respect even his friends,' he said. 'Lots of people have been murdered for less than that.' At about nine o'clock he began to nod off and fell asleep on the table, but he had already heated up my blood. I went to Roberto's house with no intention of killing him. It was not a premeditated crime. I only wanted to vent my anger somehow, but Roberto had a visitor."

"I know the rest. You waited on the stairs smoking a cigar. As you were pissed, you didn't see me coming out and then we bumped into each other on the stairs." Evaristo lowered his head, repentant. "That event cost poor Claudio Vilchis his life."

"Who told him to smoke the same brand of cigars as I smoke?" Rubén smiled mischievously. "You didn't see me when we bumped on the stairs, but I saw you, because I had spent half an hour hiding and I had become accustomed to darkness. That's why I recognised you at the wake when you started to interview people."

"What I don't understand is why you didn't kill Lima with my gun, if it was at hand? Or did he threaten you with it?"

"No, Roberto didn't even see it coming. When I got into his flat we gave each other the hug of hypocrites, I poured myself a tequila and we talked nonsense for a while. Suddenly I asked him, as if I didn't know, why I hadn't been invited to the encounter in Villahermosa. 'It was the politics of the committee,' he said, very serious. 'I defended you till the very end but those bureaucrats from Tabasco imposed another writer on us.' I stood up as if blind, dazzled by an orange-coloured flame. Roberto had turned his back to change a record and I saw the synonyms and antonyms dictionary on a chair. I didn't think – hatred doesn't allow you to think – I just allowed myself to be carried away with rage. The flame didn't go out until I saw him on the floor, blood coming out of his mouth and nose. Then I got scared and left the house, running."

"But, beforehand, you stole Lima's ticket to Villahermosa in order to slip into the writers' encounter."

"No, that was a lucky strike. When they got to know that Lima was dead, the organisers invited me in his place. Finally, justice had been served."

"What about Carmona's story? You say it was not a premeditated crime, but that bastard had already made a deal with you."

"I called his house an hour later, when my mind was clearer. I needed to divert the police's attention and I thought of taking advantage of Roberto's insults about the President. I was the only one of his friends who had read them, because he showed them to me. Say that they killed him over that, I suggested. Make it up as if you had had an anonymous call."

"And you repaid the favour with a burst of bullets when he was going to squeal on you at La Vencedora."

"My plan was to kill you both, but the Kalashnikov failed me."

"Where did you get it from? Those assault rifles are only used by drug dealers and the police."

"I bought it in Tepito from someone who sells illegal imported goods. As you were an outlaw, I wanted the Feds lumbered with the stiff. But then you came to my house and I realised that I had failed. I was reeling from the fright, I'm telling you. I couldn't kill you after my friends had seen you there, but I took you to the institute's warehouse and gave the tip to Maytorena."

"Why so much beating about the bush? If you had wanted to kill me, you could have done so beforehand, when we met in University City and you gave me a lift to my hotel."

"You weren't really a danger then. You were very busy following Palmira Jackson. But I wanted to set a trap for you anyway. I was a little scared that you might discover me in the year 2016. Don't you remember that I invited you to my apartment? If you had taken me up, I would have handed you over to the police."

"Since when were you following me? Were you the one who left me the notes on the windscreen?"

"Now you are getting it. Shame it's too late." Rubén blew his smoke into Evaristo's face. "Did you like my little message about fear of animals? It was an insult, to disarm you. I thought you were a beast, like all the Feds. Who was going to know that you were a real intellectual?"

"Even intellectuals have their savage side," responded Evaristo. "Among yourselves you bare your teeth in order to rise above the rest."

"And what's so bad about that? That's how humanity has progressed. Haven't you read Nietzsche? The superior man's actions are not ruled by the moral of the crowd: he rules himself through animal instinct. He is free like a beast and can even employ crime to get what he wants."

Fear of Animals

"Give me a break. Now, as it happens, you are Superman."
"At least I'm more of a fucking ace than you. You can't deny that." Estrella had another swig of tequila. "First I made you nervous, then I gave you the clue about Fabiola Nava so you would trust me. But I didn't appreciate seeing you coming out of her house with Roberto's diary. I thought he had written something about the Villahermosa encounter and didn't want you to know anything about it. Sorry about the blow. Really, it was pointless, because the notebook only contained little poems and nonsense."

"Congratulations." Evaristo raised his eyes looking for a guard. "You fooled me from the start with your heavy rocker image. I even felt ashamed of being a Fed when speaking to you. What I don't understand is why you came to make fun of me?"

"I wanted to tell you for your novel, so you don't make a fool of yourself when you publish it." Rubén clutched the baguette with his fist. "Be grateful that I'm helping you, arsehole. Thanks to me the crap you wrote is going to have a decent ending."

"Now, as it happens, you seem to be the angry one." Evaristo raised his voice to catch the guards' attention. "You've got me rotting in jail and you still want to kick up a stink."

"For me, literature is the most important thing in the world." Rubén banged the table with the newspaper. "I detest upstarts like you who feel they are the greatest shits for having written a crap novel."

Rubén had lost his cool and his voice was breaking. He looked capable of anything, even of confessing his crimes in front of witnesses, but the guards were at the other end of the patio, where the wall was not as high. To exasperate him even more, Evaristo adopted a conciliatory tone.

"Calm down, bro, you're going to have a heart attack. I can't compete with a writer of your kind."

"Son of a fucking bitch. You made a deal with the jury, didn't you?"

"Which jury, what are you talking about?"

"Don't pretend you don't know. There was a deal under the table. If the contest had been fair, I would have won."

"Did you lose in a contest? And what's that got to do with me?"

"Don't you know the result?" Rubén threw the newspaper at his face. "Look what a big deal you are."

Evaristo read a headline with the news: "Convict wins Eureka novel prize". Under it was his name and the mugshot with the number on his chest that was taken the day he was locked up.

"Congratulations. You planned everything so well." Rubén stood up and pointed an accusing finger at him. "You knew that a sensationalist book like yours would have to be liked by the publisher. How much did they pay you to write it?"

"It was a clean win," Evaristo defended himself. "I didn't do a deal with anyone."

"Let your fucking mother believe that. It's all part of a marketing strategy. With those prizes it's known beforehand who's going to win."

"Then why did you enter?"

"Because I'm an idiot. I thought that good literature could impose itself upon the commercial crap, and look what I got: a bloody honourable mention!" Rubén tore at his hair.

A guard was approaching and Evaristo changed the subject to get a confession out of him.

"Learn to be a good loser," he said in a persuasive tone. "Look at me. I'm taking up your place in jail and I'm not complaining about anything."

"Thinking about it, I should have killed you at the warehouse." Rubén wiped the sweat on his forehead. "People like you don't deserve to live."

"Envy is such an ugly thing, Rubén. You hate me because I won a literary prize, but you won the biggest prize of the lottery. You're free after having killed a couple of bastards. What else do you want?"

"Revenge against you. Revenge against the whole mediocre brotherhood that has joined forces against me. Do you know why I didn't win the contest? Do you know why all doors are closed to me? Because my talent hurts them!"

"Praise in your mouth is condemnation. If I were you, I'd be more discreet."

"Fuck your discretion! Now you feel superior to me, like bloody Roberto, but this pleasure is not going to last long."

Rubén opened the cheese and ham baguette that he had brought for lunch and took a small revolver from inside.

"Such a shame, bro. You won't get to collect your prize."

There was a detonation and Evaristo fell backwards. On the

Fear of Animals

ground, he felt his arms and chest: he was unscathed. The guard was the one who had shot, hitting Rubén in the neck before he could pull the trigger. The women visitors screamed in panic. The child with the ball approached the corpse and touched the blood on its head.

"Is he dead, Mum? Is he dead?"

Fear of Animals

After publishing his novel, Evaristo achieved fame and became renowned in literary circles, despite the many who criticised his lack of skill. For a few months he lived from one cocktail party to the next, made friends with important writers who praised him in public, and granted interviews to the radio, press and television, avoiding the direct questions of reporters who tried to identify the characters in his book. He enjoyed success but kept a cool head. The government, now seeking to ingratiate itself with him, offered him writing grants and jobs within the state's cultural apparatus, but he knew that his path would be different. He missed the action. He missed the police underworld. He missed reality. He could not write idly at home knowing that, out there, an army of assassins dispensed justice. As the new Attorney General was seeking to surround himself with honest people, Evaristo asked to be interviewed and re-admitted to the Federal Judicial Police as a team leader. Bewildered by his decision, but satisfied at having such a good recruit, the Attorney General allowed Evaristo to choose where he wanted to be posted. He chose Culiacán, the scorched earth of drug trafficking, where the cartels had bought up half the police already. On the day of his departure, a Channel 11 reporter stopped him at the airport. He wanted to know why Evaristo had gone back to the police force, if he now had an important place as a writer.

"For that very reason," he answered. "I needed to breathe clean air."

In cultural circles, his answer was taken as a joke in bad taste.